Jasper's Nemesis

Frances Parker-Smith

rowanvale books

First published 2022
by Rowanvale Books Ltd
The Gate
Keppoch Street
Roath
Cardiff
CF24 3JW
www.rowanvalebooks.com

A CIP catalogue record for this book is available from the British Library.
Paperback ISBN: 978-1-913662-87-5

Smiles may hide the sadness,
but love lingers in the heart

Contents

Prologue

Jasper Carmichael's heavy footsteps sank into the soft sand. His heart was breaking, his mind overflowing with the sound of her words.

"Fuck me, Bruce. I'm dying inside. I need you to fuck me."

Jasper wouldn't have hesitated. He knew what Kate needed. He had soothed her emotional turmoil many times. She needed him and he needed her. How could they survive apart?

He didn't know. But survive they must.

The sudden splashing of water caught Jasper's attention. Someone was wading into the sea. It was Kate.

He ripped off his jacket and sprinted towards the sea, kicking off his trainers. He shouted her name, but his words were lost to the waves. He panicked when a wave crashed over her head and she didn't surface. He dived under the water, but his fingertips only brushed her arm. Jasper surfaced and gulped air before he ducked under again. With renewed energy, he caught Kate's arm and pulled her towards him. She struggled, but he wrapped her in his arms.

Bruce was wading out towards them. He suddenly stopped. Anger welled through him when he saw Kate clinging to Jasper's neck, staring into his eyes.

"Kiss me," she murmured.

"I'll never love another, Kate."

She threaded her fingers through Jasper's wet hair as their kiss deepened.

"Take me with you," she mumbled.

A jealous rage consumed Bruce as he watched the woman he loved kissing Jasper. Kate had never kissed him in such a way.

Breaking the kiss, Jasper turned and reluctantly put Kate in Bruce's arms. The sea sloshed around them, and Kate's outstretched hand caressed Jasper's face.

He looked into Bruce's angry eyes.

"Look after her. Hurt her and you're a dead man." Jasper planted hurried kisses on her eyes, cheeks, lips, his index finger gently following her hairline. "Goodbye, my love."

Kate was sobbing, her arms outstretched, reaching for the love of her life.

Tears dripped off Jasper's chin as he waded back to the beach. His Carmichael demons were stirring. He would have his revenge on the man who had taken his beloved from him. He swore it. Jasper was a Carmichael, and no one blackmailed and threatened Jasper Carmichael.

Chapter One

The late winter sun bathed the narrow tarmac roads that circled the cemetery, with its neat rows of graves that cast long shadows. Kate stopped the Evoque and turned and stared at a small headstone.

My beloved Bruce.
Smiles hid the sadness.
Your love lingers in my heart.

After a long moment, she lifted her small folding stool from the back of the Evoque and carried it to his graveside.

"Hello, my love. I'm sorry I haven't been to visit, but the snow has been deep and my old Evoque struggles so in the bad weather. Also, I've had a touch of flu. I shivered for days, and my body ached terribly.

"A lot has happened since your passing. Harry and Oliver are nagging me to sponsor them in their business ventures. Harry wants to open a jewellery outlet—what he means is a diamond jewellery outlet—and Oliver wants to open a pub to rival The George.

"My reluctance to invest in their schemes has annoyed them so much that they're trying to find Jasper.

"Harry knows how I feel about diamonds, and Oliver hasn't the staying power for a business. You know Oliver, he will lose interest.

"They look more like Jasper each day, particularly Harry, dressed in designer clothes. If it wasn't for his blond hair, he'd be mistaken for his dad. And of course, there's that Carmichael smile."

Tears dripped from Kate's eyes.

"There are no words to describe how I miss you. I know you wouldn't want to see me like this.

"But I'm trying to pull myself together. Only you know the turmoil I'm in. I'll never be the same again.

"I've returned to the office and my studio at Isaacs House. I spend most of my time sketching in pencil. I try hard to concentrate on you, but Jasper floats in and out of my mind. I think I'm being followed. I can feel their eyes on me. They've been outside Isaacs all winter. It's something to do with Jasper—I just know it. Trouble is brewing, and you're not here to protect me."

Cold, piercing sleet began to fall.

"I shall have to leave you, my love. I'm shivering again."

Kate stood, folded her stool, touched the headstone and walked back to her faithful Evoque.

She didn't notice two men hiding behind a row of bushes. She didn't hear the raspy voice whisper, "*You make a sound and she's dead meat.*"

***

It had been six months since Bruce's fatal heart attack. Kate had put on a brave face that hid the dull, empty feeling that lay heavy inside her. Only when she was alone did the mask slip, and the tears that were never far away would trickle down her cheeks.

She still lay naked on their bed, imaging Bruce caressing her body, his gentle touch igniting her sexual need. She couldn't imagine life without his loving smile and his wise counsel. He had been her rock when Jasper left. When she had slipped into the abyss of despair, Bruce had pulled her out.

But she had never given herself to him like she had with Jasper. She had promised herself she would never do that with another man. And now Bruce was no longer with her, she felt guilty. Bruce had deserved all of her, but only one man had ever peeled her layers away and entered her inner soul.

Bruce's love had been so different from Jasper's. Bruce was gentle, tender. He was a giver. He had given her love by the bucket-load.

Jasper's sexual desire, though, had excited her. His blue piercing eyes, the way he moved and smiled. With just a flick of her hair, she would have his attention. When they argued she was aware that her flushed cheeks and fiery eyes would excite him. He would claim her mouth and fuck her because that was what they desired, and during Jasper's darkest hours she would love him until he was free of his demons.

She had been his strength, and his love had recharged her strength.

But Jasper had left her for diamonds, and her Bruce never would. Kate was all Bruce had ever wanted: a woman to love.

She felt herself slipping into the abyss. She had lost them both.

***

A cold sweat covered Jasper. He was naked, lying on a single bed with just a sheet for cover. Behind his eyelids, he searched for Kate's smiling face, her sparkling green eyes and flushed cheeks. But he would never see her smile again or nuzzle her breasts, never feel her legs wrapped around his waist, or the warmth that lay deep inside her.

Kate filled both his waking and sleeping hours. His mind would recall that time when they were diamond-free and happy. He never should have left her. Not for any number of diamonds. She was worth much more.

However, he had come to accept his fate. He was dying, and death had opened its door. He hadn't the strength to fight. His captors were starving him, and what little food he had was drugged. But early that morning when the food delivery man had been fucking his captors, he had helped himself to fresh milk and a pack of sandwiches, and imagined Kate sitting beside him, sharing his stolen food.

He didn't want to open his eyes to be greeted by the cold, unwelcoming darkness, but nature called, and he didn't want to sleep on a wet bed.

His heart missed a beat when he heard voices.

"Is he asleep?" asked a male voice—food delivery man.

"I've increased his dose. He'll be asleep until next week," said a woman's voice that Jasper had come to recognise as Captor Number One. Laughter bounced off the walls of his bedroom. "He's a good boy; he eats all his meals."

Jasper's captors didn't know that, this time, most of his food had been flushed down the toilet. Every mouthful of their drugged food brought him a step closer to death, and he wasn't ready to leave his Kate.

"The boss says if he finds out about Kate, he'll be trouble."

Jasper's heart suddenly raced. What had happened to her?

"I'll just have to increase his dose then."

More laughter.

"Let's do it tonight," said the woman's voice Jasper had dubbed Captor Number Two.

"Later! I want him to be awake and feel the pain his old man dished out." Jasper froze as he recognised Sebastian Manning's voice. There was bad blood between him and Sebastian after Sebastian had tried to seduce Kate. "His old man shot six men, and my old man was one of them. I want him to feel fear as I shoot him in the head, just like his father did to mine. I want revenge."

"What about Kate?" said the delivery driver.

"She's gone to pieces since Bruce's heart attack. She'll be easy pickings. I can't wait to fuck her. She refused me, and no one gets away with that." Sebastian's venomous tongue drifted into the night air as the group walked away.

Jasper continued to lie perfectly still while his thoughts played ping pong. *Bruce is dead. Kate will be heartbroken. She's alone.*

Suddenly, his stomach retched. He hurried into the bathroom as fast as his legs would carry him.

When he was satisfied that his stomach had settled, he stood under the shower's cold-water spray. Naked and dripping wet, he stared at his reflection in the cracked wall mirror. He was in no fit state to rescue Kate. Black circles surrounded his once piercing blue eyes; a long beard covered his face.

He needed fresh, unadulterated food and clothes.

His captors had left the door to his bedroom unlocked. He stepped outside, leaving his dirty T-shirt and shorts on the bed. The keen night wind made him shiver as he stared straight ahead to the edge of the patio, where a sheer cliff dropped to the valley below. He looked to his right to the

7

twelve-foot-high steel gates that his women jailers normally kept locked. They had become careless. The gates were open, with a truck parked between them. It would have been easy for the old Jasper to take advantage of this and escape, but he was too weak. He was no use to his beloved like this.

He had only ever been allowed to walk to the gates once, but that had been sufficient for him to notice a door that he assumed led into a house. A quick glance above the house showed a reinforced structure. A helipad flashed into his mind.

Shivering, he slowly walked towards a dim light that shone from an open door. He gingerly crept through into a warm kitchen. He waited and listened. Raucous laughter filtered into the kitchen from the upstairs bedroom. Nerves swirled in his stomach as he edged further into the kitchen to the American-style fridge. He wrenched the fridge door open and his eyes feasted on the fresh food. He ripped the leg off a cooked chicken.

While he ate, he found a plastic container and filled it with chicken, cheese and tomatoes to take back to his room. He held on to the work surface as his stomach tried to reject the chicken he had just eaten. He lifted a jug of milk from the fridge door and sat on a stool, gulping the milk.

A pair of swing doors led from the kitchen. Out of curiosity, he pushed them open. To his surprise, they opened to the office. He ventured inside and stared at the white powder and empty wine bottles littering a desktop. Keys, mobile phones and a gun had been left where they could be easily picked up. Jasper turned his attention away from the desk to a work surface that stretched along the side wall. It held a short-wave radio, computers and a box with 'Carmichael' written on the side. He leaned against a filing cabinet and opened the box. His eyes widened—he couldn't believe his luck. Inside the box were his clothes, wallet, cash, passport, mobile phone, watch and diamonds: everything he'd had with him the night he was captured.

Suddenly the hairs on his neck twitched. Jasper turned. Sebastian Manning was staring at him. Sebastian's eyes quickly moved to the gun on the desk. Jasper was slow to react, and Sebastian reached it first. Jasper stopped by the desk, using his hand to steady himself while he glared down the gun barrel. Sebastian sniggered as he waved the gun at Jasper. The snigger dropped when the naked Jasper took a step closer. Sebastian's gun hand started to tremble. He momentarily took his eyes off Jasper to steady the gun.

A moment was all Jasper needed. He lunged and tried to snatch the gun. But he was no match for Sebastian. He lost his balance and stumbled into a chair.

An evil smile spread across Sebastian's face as he realised he had the upper hand.

"Thinking of her?" Sebastian taunted as he pointed the gun at Jasper's head. "Tomorrow I'll be fucking her over and over."

Jasper was winded, and at Sebastian's mercy. All he could do was wait for Sebastian to make a mistake.

"Not such a great man now," Sebastian gloated, holding the gun to Jasper's forehead.

Beads of sweat dripped against the barrel. Sebastian began to laugh, and he lost his concentration.

Jasper summoned all his strength and kneed Sebastian between the legs. Sebastian fell backwards, dropping the gun and holding his crotch.

"You fuckin' bastard!" he yelled.

Jasper's eyes followed the gun. He fell to the floor and gripped it. Without hesitation, he pointed it at Sebastian's head and pulled the trigger.

You won't fuck her now, you bastard.

Jasper sat staring at Sebastian's lifeless body and listened. A deadly silence hovered. He stepped over the body and slowly and silently climbed the stairs to the bedroom. The smell of sex and alcohol filled his nose as he pushed the bedroom door open.

Empty wine bottles and clothes littered the floor. Jasper stopped and stared at the three naked people that were huddled together in the bed. Their faces were masks of shock and confusion.

"Expecting Manning?" he said as he pointed the gun first at Number One, then Number Two and finally the delivery man. Without flinching, he pulled the trigger.

One shot in the head of each of his female jailers and delivery man.

Without so much as a glance at the dead bodies, he returned to the office. He now had time to eat, drink, shower, shave and cut his hair, but above all, he could plan how he would return to his beloved.

He found a downstairs bathroom with a small shower. Warm water and soap revived his emaciated body. He felt like a new man when he cut his hair and shaved.

He gazed at himself in the full-length mirror on the back of the bathroom door. His designer clothes and handmade loafers were too big for him, but he had to make do.

He staggered back into the kitchen. His head and stomach had decided to join forces as waves of nausea made him sit and rest. He waited until his stomach quietened before warming a bowl of milk in the microwave and crumbling a plain biscuit into it.

When his head and stomach had settled, he wandered into the office. The laptops immediately caught his eye and he slipped them into a small canvas holdall that he had found lying next to the desk. He flicked through the drawers of the metal filing cabinet and found an empty file labelled 'Carmichael'.

He cursed as he put two and two together. The man who'd put him in this hellhole now held information on him and his diamond network. In a fit of temper, Jasper destroyed the two-way radio and threw the mobile phones in the microwave.

He stared at his few possessions he'd had with him when he was kidnapped: mobile, wallet and Cartier watch. He slipped his mobile and wallet into his into his jacket pockets, along with any cash he could find. Before securing his Cartier watch on to his wrist he took a moment to read the inscription on the back.

All my love, Kate.

He recalled his beloved smiling at him. He remembered her passionate kisses as he'd carried her to their bedroom.

"I'm coming, my love. I'm coming," he swore as he dropped the gun into the holdall.

***

Jasper felt like a new man as he sat in the delivery truck, familiarising himself with the controls while sipping water and nibbling biscuits.

The keys had been left dangling in the ignition. He pressed down the clutch and turned the key. The truck fired, first turn.

He lifted a newspaper that had been left on the dash and dropped it in the passenger footwell. The loose pages fell open. A small photograph caught Jasper's eye, with 'Carmichael' written above it. It was of Kate at a graveside. Jasper's Spanish was rusty, but he understood enough to know Kate was standing at Bruce's grave. The words of the truck driver flashed into his mind: *"If he finds out about Kate, he'll be trouble."*

They have no idea, Jasper thought as he selected a gear and the truck moved out of the gate.

Chapter Two

Lord Wellsbury, aka W, stood in an empty hangar waiting for his private jet to land. For his age he was an attractive man, with high cheekbones and piercing blue eyes hidden behind a pair of rimless spectacles, complemented by a well-trimmed head of silver hair. When with company, he rarely lost his temper and he never smiled. He was noted for his immaculate dress sense. His Saville Row suit fitted like a glove.

Back straight, he stared at the sky, his impassive features hiding the turmoil that racked his body. W was angry.

He had been in control of the special intelligence unit from its conception. The unit had a reputation of always getting its man, but their impeccable conviction record now hung by a thread, and all because of one man. Jasper Carmichael. W should have had him killed instead of recruiting him into the unit. But Carmichael was the Teflon man. He was a murderer, money launderer and a diamond dealer that had evaded prison. His only weakness was his wife, Kate. He had murdered before, just because she had been roughed up.

He waited till his jet had taxied towards the hangar before striding towards it. He settled in one of the plush leather seats and closed his eyes and reflected on his involvement with his nemesis.

W had needed Jasper to join his team. Jasper had left Kate and his sons for the riches of diamonds. When W had heard that Jasper was using the alias Mason Clarke to visit Kate, he had taken the opportunity to kidnap him.

Luck had been on W's side; Jasper had been so preoccupied that he hadn't noticed W's men surrounding him. His time with Kate hadn't gone the way he'd expected, and if gossip could be believed, he needed Kate to quell the Carmichael darkness that tormented him. Jasper had been off his game since he left her, and it should have been easy to recruit him into the intelligence unit. But W had been wrong. Carmichael had resisted working for him until W had threatened to imprison Kate.

Jasper was handsome, rich, charismatic— when he smiled, women fell at his feet. But only one woman had shared his bed. His love for her was legendary; he had refused to divorce her, deceiving her with forged papers.

Jasper Carmichael had skills that none of W's other operatives had. He was a chameleon; he blended in with any group of people in any place. He rubbed shoulders with some of the most wanted criminals in the world, he had a diamond network, he had safe houses dotted around the world that only he knew about and he was a master at lying and deceiving.

A bumpy landing jolted W from his Carmichael thoughts. He poked his head out of the jet door and looked up at the hilltop that had been Carmichael's prison. He briskly walked to the waiting helicopter. It was a short flight to the helipad that Gypsy, a drug lord, had constructed. He was a man who'd thought he could better Jasper and Kate Carmichael, and how wrong he had been. Gypsy and Zak Cohen, the man responsible for cutting Jasper's diamonds, had tried to take over Carmichael's shopping centre, but they had found themselves up against a Kate and Jasper on top form.

Gypsy, like so many before him, had underestimated Kate and Jasper's ability to outmanoeuvre adversaries. They were a formidable couple: Jasper with his criminal eye and Kate with her down-to-earth superior Spencer attitude. She had run rings around Gypsy and Zak Cohen, and Gypsy had paid the fatal price.

W had been consumed by greed for Jasper's diamonds, which would be Kate's when he died. She would be easy to manipulate now Bruce was out of the picture. All Jasper had to do was die. But Jasper had escaped his hilltop prison and was free. He would be like a wounded bear, roaming the wood looking for the hunter that had shot him and caused him so much pain.

The helicopter landed, and W ran to the steps that led to the kitchen and his waiting team. He followed the leader of his team to the bedroom, where W's two best female operatives lay dead on the blood-soaked bed with another of his most experienced operatives.

"Where's Manning?" he asked.

Sebastian Manning had persuaded W to give him the opportunity to get even with Carmichael after Jasper's father had shot Sebastian's.

He found him in the office, lying in his own blood, shot in the head like his father.

W stared at the wrecked radio receiver, the missing laptops, open filing cabinet drawers. This hadn't been done by a drugged man; this was done by a man on a mission.

Execution-style killings were the signature of Colin Carmichael. Jasper was sending W a message, and that made his stomach somersault. He was coming after W and his organisation.

W slumped into a desk chair, running his hand through his hair. He turned and stared at each of

15

his team in turn. Fear and confusion were in his men's eyes; they had never seen W like this. W had always been confident, but now doubt was written all over his face.

"It's her!" W said to no one in particular. "Carmichael's found out that she's grieving the loss of her lover."

He pulled his mobile from his jacket pocket and used speed dial.

"Double the surveillance on Kate Carmichael," he barked into it, before impatiently stuffing his phone back into his pocket. He turned to his team leader. "Get rid of the bodies and destroy this place. No evidence of what it has been."

W turned away from his men and briskly walked out of the kitchen to his waiting helicopter.

Chapter Three

Raised voices from the Isaacs kitchen filtered into Kate's studio. She stopped sketching and listened.

"You're not to tell her!" shouted Clare.

"She 'as a right to know," Malcolm angrily retorted.

"Tell me what?" Kate stood in the kitchen doorway.

"It's Jasper," said Malcolm.

"What about Jasper?"

Malcolm hesitated.

"Malcolm, tell me," Kate said, a little impatient.

"Some of the boys at The George 'av been working on Lord Wellsbury country estate. 'E's improved the security and needed men to do the labouring. 'E was in a mighty 'urry, didn't care where the security firm got the men from. According to 'is security guards 'e's scared shitless."

"Malcolm!" admonished Clare.

"What's this to do with Jasper?" asked Kate.

"Jasper's been working for Lord Wellsbury," Malcolm reluctantly said.

"He got too big for his boots," said Clare.

"Shut up, woman. Apparently, Jasper was working for Wellsbury *and* Jasper. If you get what I mean."

Kate knew exactly what Malcolm meant. When Jasper had controlled Carmichael and Swain, he'd invested in property for both the company and for Jasper Carmichael.

"When Wellsbury found out, 'e went apeshit."

"Malcolm, don't bring that language here."

Malcolm glared at his wife and carried on. "Jasper did what Wellsbury told 'im to, and at the same time 'is diamond network was getting bigger and Jasper richer. No one does that to Wellsbury, W, so 'e imprisoned Jasper in a Spanish hilltop villa that Gypsy built." Malcolm looked at Kate to make sure she was following. "You remember Gypsy?" Kate nodded. "'E thought no one could escape."

"Jasper has," interrupted Kate.

Malcom nodded. "Jasper's in a bad way. They drugged 'im. Starved 'im. They don't know 'ow 'e escaped, but there were four dead bodies. Shot in the 'ead. They reckon Jasper could 'ardly walk, let alone shoot four people. Anyway, where did 'e get a gun?"

Malcolm paused and stared at Kate to make sure she understood.

"W's convinced Jasper will come after 'im. Jasper 'as a rep."

Kate's eyes moved from Malcolm to Clare. "I don't understand why you didn't want me to know?"

"Jasper will come to you," Clare said.

"Jasper's stole a yacht. W's men found it. But no Jasper. Wild goose chase. The boys at The George reckon 'e's already in this country."

Kate understood what Jasper had done. He had stolen a yacht so the men who were after him would follow it while he made his way back to England and her.

"What're you thinking?" said Clare.

"Nothing," Kate lied, turning her attention to making a pot of tea.

"We've known this for some time," Malcolm said. "They kidnapped Jasper after the Mason Clarke visit. Jasper refused to work for W until you were threatened."

"Me!"

"You knew too much about Jasper's criminal ways," cut in an angry Clare. "He threatened prison."

All the colour drained out of Kate's face as she recalled the episode when Jasper had rescued her from the sea. He had said goodbye.

"Who told you this?"

"One of the men that W sacked a while back. 'E'd 'ad too much to drink. 'E was asking about you when Bruce walked in." Malcolm reddened as he realised that he had said too much.

"Bruce knew?!" Kate stood and glared, first at Clare then at Malcolm. Her eyes filled.

Clare stepped towards her, but Kate held up her hand so Clare wouldn't touch her.

A lump formed in Kate's throat. An awkward silence hovered in the kitchen until she lifted her jacket from the back of the kitchen door and took the Evoque keys from its pockets.

She drove to the cemetery in a mental haze. By the time she stood by Bruce's graveside, tears were dripping from her cheeks.

"You told me you would never deceive me like Jasper did. I fell into your tender love-making ways. I trusted you. I loved you."

Kate suddenly stumbled back as Bruce's bitter voice echoed in her mind. *"You gave yourself to that bastard. But not me. I healed you. I love you. Why do you love him more than me? Go to him. Fuck him. Love him."*

"Bruce!" Kate's broken voice cried.

But there was no answer except the wind.

*   *   *

Kate had parked on the hard sand of the beach where she had first painted, where toddler Harry had swayed along the water's edge. Occasionally he would turn and shout, and she would wave back. *Happy times*.

But today her mind was in turmoil. Bruce had deceived her when he had promised he never would. She tried to recall that day when she had told Bruce she was dying inside and she would have died if Jasper hadn't rescued her from the sea. Bruce had been jealous of how she had returned Jasper's kiss that day—and rightly so. She had never kissed any man like she had kissed Jasper. After that day she had sealed her memories of Jasper in a box and pushed it into the depths of her mind, never to be reopened. But now Bruce had inadvertently opened it.

She resolved never to lock away the happy memories of the time she had spent with Bruce. She wanted to keep Bruce's love with her in her darkest hour, his loving grin and his soft warm lips would support her, even when Jasper had resurfaced.

Chapter Four

W couldn't believe the stupidity of his men. They had waited by Jasper's yacht. None of them had thought that Jasper would see them and move on.

But where would Jasper go? He didn't know the area so he wouldn't have a safe house.

W summoned his Bentley and drove along the coastal road. He shouted at his driver to stop when he saw an Audi parked against the sea wall. His gut told him it was Carmichael's car. Jasper was on his way to England.

It was obvious that the only safe way Jasper could return to England without drawing attention to himself was by sea. Jasper was a skilled yachtsman— he even knew how to navigate the sea without GPS.

As far as W was concerned, Jasper Carmichael was in England. But where? The town of Wellsbury and Kate Carmichael would be his first stop.

***

W's company jet landed at Jasper's airfield alongside a waiting Range Rover. W scowled as he eased himself into the car.

"This is the best we could do, sir," said his driver, noting W's disapproving look.

"Where's Kate?"

"Still at home. She spent a lot of time yesterday sitting in her Evoque gazing at the beach and sea."

"Alone?"

"Yes. She never left the car."

***

The hired Range Rover stopped outside the front door of Isaacs House. The driver held his finger on the doorbell until the door was opened.

W stared at Kate. Her reading glasses were pushed back into her silver hair. Her green eyes were tired and cheeks slightly flushed.

His eyes wandered to Kate's white blouse, open to her cleavage. Her jeans rested on her hips and bare feet.

"Yes?" she snapped.

"Lady Carmichael, I assume. I would like a word about your husband. May I come in?" he said in his best aristocratic, condescending voice.

W's tone immediately riled Kate. "And you are?"

"Lord Wellsbury. But you may call me W."

Clare popped her head out of the kitchen door as Kate, followed by W, went into the living room.

Kate pointed to one of the comfortable white leather chairs.

"I'll stand," W said.

Kate leaned against the couch; she didn't want W to be looking down on her. Her eyes never left him as he wandered around the room, taking in the quality of the decor. His silence and stern features made Kate's stomach flip unpleasantly, but it was vital she remained impassive.

"I expected you to be at your office," W said, looking at one of her beach paintings, which leaned against the couch.

"I have business here," Kate curtly replied.

"I'll get straight to the point," W said. "Have you seen Jasper?"

"You know I haven't. Your employees are following me."

W was taken aback by Kate's tone. *Employees, indeed. Who the bloody hell does this woman think she is?*

He had heard about Kate's superior manner, and it was beginning to get under his skin. It reminded him of Meredith Spencer, her grandfather.

"It's vital I get in touch with Jasper." W's abrupt, aristocratic tone had returned. "He's in danger." He dropped a card onto the central coffee table. "If he contacts you, ring this number."

Kate didn't answer or look at the card.

"I can see that you're a difficult woman, Lady Carmichael. I was led to believe you were grieving."

"Grief is very personal. It isn't one size fits all."

W stared at Kate; she had managed to stir his temper with only a few words.

He scowled at Clare when she opened the front door for him to leave. His bitter voice bounced off the hallway walls. "Till next time, Lady Carmichael."

Kate deeply sighed when Clare closed the door.

"You OK, Kate?" Malcolm's rough voice was tinged with concern.

Kate turned, staring at Malcolm, who was standing in the shadows of the kitchen door.

"Make sure he's left, and close and lock the gates," she said as she walked into her studio.

"Kate!" Clare shouted, following her into the studio. "You can't put your head in the sand. That man means you harm."

"What would you have me do?"

"I hate to mention his name, but you have to find Jasper. If Jasper escaped that man's prison, he's more than a match for Lord Wellsbury and his organisation." Clare took a moment to regain her breath. "So, he comes here with the intention of frightening you. If you ask me, there's more to this

23

Lord Wellsbury than meets the eye. It's common knowledge that you're Jasper's weakness and he'll come to you." Clare paused. "Who the bloody hell is this Lord Wellsbury that he comes here upsetting you? Jasper's bloody nemesis."

Kate began to move her paintings that were stacked at the back of her studio.

"Kate! Are you listening?"

Kate lifted a painting from the stack. "I stopped painting because I couldn't paint anything else but…" Kate turned the canvas so Clare could see.

"Oh! My lord, Kate!" Clare stared at a portrait of Jasper.

"Everyone says I'm Jasper's weakness, and that's true, but Jasper is also my weakness."

"Did Bruce know?"

"Yes." Kate looked into Clare's eyes. "He would wrap his arms around me, kiss my hair and whisper *'I'm here, Kate.'* He would then love me in the most tender way."

Tears dripped down Kate's cheeks.

Chapter Five

A warm glow filled Jasper as he stepped onto the familiar platform at Wellsbury Station. He had phoned Isaacs House from a call box at Euston. Clare had told him Kate would be waiting.

He cast his weary eyes around the platform. His heart skipped a beat and a lone tear trickled from the corner of his eye when Kate hurried towards him. He didn't see Harry and Oliver following; he only had eyes for Kate. She was smiling, and happy tears spilled down her cheeks.

Suddenly he was in her arms. He closed his eyes as her warm, soft lips caressed his.

All thoughts of W disappeared. His gamble of returning to Kate in public sight had paid off. W would never have anticipated that. Jasper didn't care if W's men were watching Kate; he was in her arms and that was all that mattered.

She looped her arm in his as they slowly walked to the Evoque. It was only when she started to talk to Harry and Oliver that he noticed them. Harry was driving, Oliver sat next to him, chatting away. Kate sat in the back holding Jasper's hand.

Kate was still holding his hand when he walked into the warm kitchen at Isaacs House. He was surprised to find Clare had red puffy eyes and she smiled at him.

Malcolm was his typical unemotional self as he helped Jasper up the stairs. Jasper leaned on him taking one stair at a time.

"Which room, Kate?" Malcolm asked, stopping at the top of the stairs.

A heavy silence fell over Isaacs House as they waited for Kate's reply.

"Mine," she eventually said. "Run a warm bath. Throw his clothes away."

Even in his weak state, Jasper couldn't help but notice that Kate spoke in the soft, calm voice that he remembered.

***

Warm water lapped around Jasper's body. His head lay on Kate's chest, his back to her front.

The bathroom room door opened, and Clare's disgusted tone echoed. "What's with you? Lying in baths with men…"

Kate didn't answer.

"More towels, in case you need them—but by the look of him, a flannel would dry him."

The bathroom door closed with a thud.

A wave of jealousy flashed through Jasper as Clare's words registered. Kate had shared a bath with Bruce.

***

Sunlight bathed Kate's bedroom. The same bedroom she had shared with him, and Bruce.

Jasper was alone and naked. A smile crept across his face as he remembered lying skin to skin with Kate. Her warmth and energy had reached every part of him. Kate had a unique healing power, but her sexual healing was what he craved.

But W surfaced in his mind. By now he would know that Jasper was with Kate, and he would be planning his next move.

Jasper thought back over his escape from his hilltop prison. Jasper, like his father, was lucky, and that had played a big part in his escape.

The track from the prison was narrow and steep. The supply truck was old and didn't have power steering, and Jasper had used all his strength to control it down the track. The truck had come to rest by an old rusty road sign pointing to Perpignan. He'd parked up in the village car park, next to a Citroën that had been left conveniently open, and headed towards Perpignan.

Later that day, he had parked the Citroën at a service station with a number of market stalls arranged around the carpark. He'd bought a shirt, tracksuit bottoms and a pair of trainers that would be more comfortable than his loafers.

The services' washroom had been excellent, and Jasper had spent some time washing and changing clothes. He had bought fresh sandwiches and a carton of milk and sat in the picnic area planning his next move. It was while he was casually strolling through the car park that he'd bumped into a smart-looking businessman and deftly lifted the key fob and wallet from his pocket. An Audi responded.

It had been approaching evening when he'd parked the Audi in a quiet street in easy walking distance to the popular Old Port of Marseille, where his yacht was moored.

He'd stopped dead when he saw W's men strolling about the waterfront. He had cursed himself for being stupid enough to walk into W's trap.

He had returned to the Audi and aimlessly driven along the coast road looking for food and a place to spend the night. The sun had reflected off an old yacht tied to the sea wall of a small fishing village that looked as if time had passed it by.

He'd parked the Audi and strolled to a small café. A fresh fish dinner and a glass of house red had revived him.

It was dusk when Jasper had walked to the old yacht. It was in desperate need of repair; there wasn't an engine, but that didn't bother him. The mast appeared sound, as did the rigging.

The tide was rushing out when Jasper jumped onto the deck. He'd stowed his belongings, untied the mooring rope and let the tide take him out of the harbour. As the yacht sailed into the open sea, Jasper realised that he had overestimated his ability to handle it. The time in prison had taken a toll on his body.

It was dark when a very tired Jasper sailed into Marseille. He'd left the yacht tied near the fuel and supply depot, gathered his bags and walked to the train station. He'd boarded the only train that was about to leave Marseille. He had never been to Lyon, but he would worry about that later. He nestled into a seat, leaning his head against the window, and closed his eyes.

He had awoken to a deserted train that was in a siding. The staff either didn't know he was on the train or didn't care. Either way, it didn't matter to Jasper.

He'd found a café that was still open and sat enjoying the first cup of coffee he'd had in a long while. He decided he'd head towards the Channel coast, preferably Calais.

Luck was with him again when a family of English tourists came into the café asking the owner about Eurostar trains to Paris.

Jasper had followed them to the station and bought the same train ticket.

His recollection of Paris was very hazy; he remembered drinking coffee inside a café. He'd had to sit inside as he couldn't cope with standing at an outside table. The family he had seen in Lyon arrived at the café and were chatting about their journey back to London. Jasper thought they were angels guiding him back to England and Kate.

But he only had one angel, and she would be waiting in Wellsbury.

Chapter Six

The bedroom door opened and closed, and the bed dipped. Soft lips caressed Jasper's cheek.

"Good, you're awake," Kate said. "I've been in the attic. I'd saved some of your clothes. They'll be too big, but they'll do for now."

"Take your clothes off," said Jasper.

"What? Now?"

"Yes."

Kate hesitated. "What's wrong?"

"I need healing now! Your sexual healing."

"Probably later."

Jasper sat up, surprised. "What do you mean 'later'?"

Kate looked up into two concerned blue eyes. "I'm not the Kate you married. I'm not the Kate you left for diamonds." She paused, before adding, "And I'm not the Kate Bruce fell in love with."

"Kate!"

"Let me finish. Diamonds drove a wedge into our love. I'll remind you that it's still there. I fell head over heels for a young Jasper Carmichael that wanted to be free of the criminal world. He had ideas of sailing to different places. A new life. I would have gone with him, but he didn't ask me. I'd served my purpose and I was well paid."

"That's not how it happened, Kate."

Kate waved her hand and continued. "I was an innocent, and to some degree I still am. But when you left me, my heart shattered, and Bruce stuck the pieces back together, but over time the glue that held me together started to melt. The boys and shopping centre were my life and dear Bruce was my love, but the boys are young men now and Bruce has passed. My younger innocent self has gone." She paused as their eyes met. "However, Jasper Carmichael has never left me. When I stumbled across Zak's money and diamonds, instead of going to the police, I hid them, and to my amazement I spent some of the money."

Jasper's eyes grew wide.

"There's no need to look surprised. If I'd told anyone about Zak's money, they would have gone to the police. You would have been blamed for Zak's death, and I would have been implicated."

"God, Kate, I want to rip your clothes off you and bury myself inside you."

Kate jumped off the bed. "That's not going to happen. We have a common enemy. W must be stopped. I suggest that we start afresh as the man and woman we are now, not what we were."

"You want us to work together to get rid of W."

"Yes! I've already started. Those Carmichael journals from the London house have pointed me to your grandfather."

"I don't know anything about the old man."

"There's a photograph of him with a woman and children. He looks a lot older. The woman's looking at him."

"What photo?"

"Clare found a box in the attic. They must be from Colin's things."

"What are you suggesting?"

"What if—and it's a big if—your grandfather had another family with a much younger woman?"

"Go on."

"What if he left them penniless? Colin inherited everything. He was his only known living son. But what if he had other sons with this woman?"

"I'm not buying it. You're saying W is a Carmichael."

Kate nodded. "Let me do some more work."

"Grandfather was a bastard. But I doubt he had a secret family."

"Tell me, Jasper. Convince me. If you fell head over heels for a younger woman, had children—remember, I can't have children—would you keep it a secret?"

"Kate, that's not going to happen. I've had my fill of younger women. I didn't love them. I'm devoted to you."

"I'll remind you of that when you wine and dine other women."

"They mean nothing. I'm a sexual man. You know that."

"You're a Carmichael."

Chapter Seven

W had returned to his country estate. There was no point staying in Wellsbury: Jasper and Kate were together, his men had failed him. But to be fair, even he hadn't expected Jasper to use the Eurostar.

W poured himself a very large brandy and opened the French doors that led from his study to the stone balcony overlooking the immaculate garden.

Somehow, he had to get inside the head of Jasper Carmichael, the chameleon that always did the unexpected.

There was only one person who had seen all the sides to Jasper, and that was his wife, Kate. She had experienced his cruelty and his love. For, though Jasper may have had sex with many women, he only loved Kate. She was his only weakness; she would never betray him.

W had mistakenly convinced himself that he could control Jasper by blackmailing him and threatening her.

He cast his mind back to the time Jasper had disappeared for a long weekend. He should have suspected Carmichael's loyalty then, but he had returned fully committed to working for W. He knew now that Jasper had seen Kate and said goodbye and that Jasper had had a bigger goal in mind, one that required his total concentration.

And Jasper would have succeeded in taking over W's organisation if one of the criminals he had freed from prison hadn't been picked up by the traffic police and put in the cells for a night. When W had walked into his cell, the man had sung like the proverbial canary and told W all about Carmichael taking a cut from every mission he had been on, giving his criminal friends the nod so that they avoided prison.

Carmichael had to go.

When W had told Jasper about the diamond exchange in Marseille, Jasper had been unusually cautious. He said he didn't know Marseille, and W translated that into 'he didn't have a safe house there'.

W should have had Jasper shot as soon as he'd walked into that waterfront warehouse, but instead he had instructed his men to capture him and take him to Gypsy's old hilltop villa.

He'd allowed his emotions to get the better of him. He wanted revenge, diamonds and the money that Carmichael had swindled him out of. He wanted the names of everyone in the criminal network that Jasper led.

His plan had been working. Jasper had become weaker by the day, the consequences of a poor diet laden with drugs. But then Bruce had died, and Kate had fallen to pieces. If Jasper ever found out Kate was in emotional turmoil, he would go to her aid. And that's exactly what happened.

Jasper had seen his chance and taken it.

W had hand-picked Jasper's two female jailers, and one of his men who delivered supplies to the villa. But he had let in a rogue element. Foolishly, he'd let himself be convinced by Sebastian Manning's desire for revenge. There was no doubt in his mind that Sebastian had been responsible for the orgy that had enabled Jasper to escape, and now they were all dead, one shot to the head each.

A feat no starved, drugged man would have been capable of.

Jasper had fooled them all.

W walked back into his study and refilled his brandy bowl. He slumped into his favourite chesterfield chair, lifted his feet onto a footstool and tried to put together a plan to eliminate Jasper and Kate.

It was vital that W acted before Kate discovered the truth about his Carmichael identity. She had already been spending time in the Spencer Library reading the Carmichael journals. His source had told him she had taken a box of them back to Isaacs House.

***

While W was thinking about Jasper and Kate, Jasper was sitting in the kitchen of Isaacs House, eating Clare's chicken soup. Kate walked in, smiling, slipping her grey jacket from her shoulders and removing the tie from her hair. The top buttons of her white blouse were undone, her green eyes shone, and she smiled, flicking her hair in the manner that had captured Jasper's heart all those years ago.

Jasper dropped his spoon into the half-full bowl.

"Good day?" Clare asked Kate.

Kate nodded and turned her attention to tea making.

"Well?" Clare pressed. "Are you going to tell us?"

Jasper returned to his soup.

Malcolm had joined them, standing in the internal garage door.

Kate took a deep breath. "I'm going to take a step back from the shopping centre." She waited for Clare to sit on a stool before continuing. "The hotel will be run by a separate company; the farmers' market can have their own way and form a co-operative. I'll concentrate on the Spencer Library, book shop and gallery. Harry and Oliver can have their own jewellery shop that they're nagging me about. But I've got to think through what's going to happen to the independent shops."

"Kate, do you know what you're doing?" said a worried Clare. This wasn't like the Kate they had come to know.

"You were seen at the cemetery?" Malcolm asked.

"Yes."

"Kate, what have you done?" Clare's voice was almost a plea.

"I said goodbye to Bruce and went to the centre."

"I don't understand," said Clare.

"You all should have told me about Jasper and Lord Wellsbury. But you all decided what was good for me. It felt as if I was the prisoner."

"Don't talk stupid," Clare snapped. "Bruce loved you."

"And I loved him. I know I hurt him when I slipped into the Jasper abyss. But he healed me with the most tender love." Kate's voice quivered as memories of Bruce filled her mind.

"And this is how you repay him," Clare angrily rebuked.

"The Bruce I loved has gone. I've got to move on. Do what I want to do. And that's paint. I can't do that with the centre demanding my time."

"What about the boys?"

"There're not boys but young men. If they want to go the same way as all the Carmichaels, so be it."

Clare turned to Jasper who had sat silently eating his soup. "You've caused this. If you hadn't come back…"

"Jasper had nothing to do with this. In fact, it was you, Clare, arguing with Malcolm. You should have told me."

"Bruce was frightened 'e would lose you," mumbled a concerned Malcolm. "So, you're going to the beach 'ouse studio?"

"No. I shall buy my own retreat."

Kate poured her tea into her china mug and stepped towards the kitchen door. She stopped and turned to Jasper.

"I may need some funds from my Caymans account."

Their eyes met, green on blue, and Jasper nodded.

Chapter Eight

The atmosphere in the Carmichael household was a little strained, particularly when Harry and Oliver arrived.

Tempers clashed when they questioned their mother about Jasper staying. The fact that he was recovering from a life-threatening ordeal cut no ice with her sons.

When Oliver accused her of putting Jasper before them, Kate exploded.

Clare, Malcolm and Jasper had been listening from behind the office door. Clare put a steadying hand on Jasper's arm when he moved to join Kate.

Kate stood up from her desk chair and walked to the office French doors, gazing at her closed studio. She no longer did anything she loved; she'd given up everything to concentrate on her sons and the shopping centre.

"I gave myself to you two. I've always been there for you both. I sacrificed the love of my life." Her voice was increasingly emotional. "I should have turned a blind eye to his obsession with diamonds, but I didn't. I tried to guide you both away from the Carmichael diamond curse. But my sacrifice has been rewarded with diamond fever."

Kate paused. Her emotions were getting the better of her, and she didn't want Harry and Oliver to see her break down.

In a controlled, conciliatory tone, she continued. "You are young men. You should both be making your own way in the world. I'm still your mother, I'll always be there for you, I'll always love you." She paused, turned and stared at her sons. "I deserve a life. I've waited too long to be Kate, the woman that I used to be. I doubted myself, blamed myself for Jasper leaving. I devoted myself to you two, trying to fill the hole that Jasper had left. But I had Bruce. His love, his support. I came to rely on him—too much. And now Bruce is gone, never to return, and I must stand on my own two feet. Like I did when I ran the flower shop. I'm going to become selfish and put myself first. I'm going to paint. Spend time in the Spencer Library. Expand the bookshop."

Malcolm walked away from the office door. He didn't want Clare and Jasper to see his tear-filled eyes. But they wouldn't have noticed, as tears were running down Clare's cheeks and Jasper was wiping his own away with the back of his hand.

Harry rushed to Kate and wrapped his arms around her waist. "I won't let you down."

"Is he going with you?!" Oliver's anger hadn't waned.

"If you're referring to your father, Jasper knows nothing about this."

"W said you would be like this," commented Oliver, determined to upset his mother.

"Oliver, shut up," admonished Harry from his mother's side.

Kate stared at Oliver's stern features. They reminded her of an angry Jasper.

"You… you know W?" Kate looked into Harry's blue Carmichael eyes. "Harry!"

"He… he approached us. Wanted to know about you and dad."

"We told him you fucked like rabbits," snarled Oliver.

Kate's temper flared. She angrily strode to Oliver and lifted her hand to slap his face.

Loud gasps of disbelief echoed through the office.

"Kate! No!" shouted Jasper as he burst into the office.

Kate barged passed him and Clare. She snatched the Evoque keys from their hook and hurried outside.

Jasper caught up with her as she opened the car door. He looped his arms around her waist and held her, resting his chin on her shoulder.

"Let go of me," she said, her voice angry, strained.

"You're not driving with a raging temper."

For a long moment, he silently held her.

"Oliver's young. He doesn't understand how our love changed us." Jasper's voice was calm and soft. "Love did change us." His lips brushed her neck. Kate's body relaxed. "Kate, don't run and hide. Go back in and talk to your sons. Harry's standing in the kitchen doorway with a very worried look on his face. And from the sound of it, Clare's laying into Oliver."

Desire got the better of Jasper; he kissed Kate's neck. Kate unexpectedly tilted her head exposing more of her throat.

"I need to get away," she said, turning to look into Jasper's desire-filled eyes. "I can't think straight or rest my emotions."

"I bring you nothing but hurt. But you're not going alone," Jasper said.

Blue and green eyes danced together as Jasper stroked Kate's hairline.

"An argument with Harry and Oliver has been brewing for some time," she said. "I'm drained, Jasper."

"You are hurting, Kate. They don't understand. They've never experienced love or grief." Their lips brushed. "I want to kiss you," he murmured. "But it will have to wait. Go back. Talk to Oliver and Harry. They love you. Tomorrow, go to the centre, tie up any loose ends and come with me on my yacht. We'll be alone. No Wellsbury. No W. No sons. Just Kate and Jasper."

"You're not up to sailing."

Jasper rested his forehead against hers, and after a thoughtful moment, said, "I know a place."

"A safe house."

"A last-resort safe house. It's pretty basic. Kitchen, bathroom, bedroom. Veranda. I could watch you paint."

***

Harry and Oliver followed their mother into the living room. They sat on the couch while she curled her legs beneath her in a chair.

Oliver was bursting; he had a lot to get off his chest. He launched into a tirade that went deep into his past, to the time he was obsessed with the idea of his parents having make-up sex. He accused Kate of leaving them with Clare and Malcolm while she'd spent hours fucking Jasper.

Kate felt her face redden when his green eyes pierced her. She didn't argue with him. Most of it was true. Her love for Jasper had been all-consuming. But Oliver had failed to mention her driving them to school, her cuddles when he'd fought the school bullies and lost and the times she had slept beside him when nightmares invaded his sleep. He didn't know that Jasper had angrily complained that she loved their sons more than him. How many times had she tried to convince the men in her life that she loved her sons as a mother and Jasper as her soulmate?

Kate was more than a little uncomfortable; the living room was charged with anger.

She turned her attention to Harry, who was patiently waiting. The tension burst when Harry began to talk in a calm, measured voice. He explained that he'd been concerned about her love for Bruce. He'd felt she was on the rebound from his dad.

Maybe Harry had a point. Had she been attracted to Bruce because her marriage was falling apart? But she'd loved Bruce, and that would never change.

"Say something," said Oliver, whose voice faltered as he began to regret his tirade.

Kate stood and stared at one of her paintings that hung on the wall. She carried it to her chair. Harry and Oliver stared at one another in that "where's this going?" manner.

"I love this painting," she said. "I've captured the sea just as I remembered it. The little boy wobbling by the water's edge." She smiled at Harry. "I was happy, Harry was happy. We hadn't got much of anything except each other. I often wonder where that happiness went." She paused. "This painting and the happiness it represents have always given me the will to carry on. My love for you both has never wavered. You both have brought me happiness and sadness. I know you won't understand, but I loved Bruce." Her voice broke, and she cleared her throat. "But my love for your father was on another plane. Nothing mattered except our love. It was more than sex. Think of it as the joining of a man and a woman becoming one. My dearest wish is that the two of you experience what we did."

An uncomfortable silence drifted as Harry and Oliver waited for their emotional mother to continue.

"I'm truly sorry if the pair of you think I've neglected you. That never was my intention."

A guilt-riddled Oliver jumped off the couch and squeezed between his mother and the chair arm. "Do you love me? I couldn't …"

Kate kissed his cheek and stroked his hair. Harry moved her painting and sat on the arm of the chair with his arm around her. Tears poured down Kate's face.

"Don't you love dad anymore?" asked Harry.

Kate didn't answer.

Chapter Nine

Jasper and Kate had hoped that they could use the cover of darkness to slip out of Isaacs House undetected, but W's men had been waiting.

Kate had tried to lose them in the multi-storey car park, but another car had been waiting when they exited the car park.

Jasper didn't recognise the Wellsbury Kate was driving through. Most of the old town had been demolished. However, Kate skilfully led their pursuers on a merry chase through the remaining Victorian streets. Jasper was in awe at how she squeezed the Evoque through the narrow passages. She smiled when the chasing vehicles became lodged in the alleyways.

Jasper fell asleep when Kate joined the motorway and headed towards Carmichael Castle. As daylight broke, Kate turned into a service area and left Jasper sleeping. She returned with two lattes with an extra shot in each and two bacon rolls.

Jasper opened his eyes while Kate was reading the map. She turned her head and smiled at him.

A comfortable silence drifted by as they sipped their lattes.

"I'm not sure where we're going," she said in her customary matter-of-fact tone. "There's no road on the map."

"Trust me—the Carmichael estate goes for miles. I know where we're going."

Kate gave Jasper a wry glance.

Half an hour later, Kate checked her mirror and turned into the slip road for Carmichael Castle.

"No one is following," commented a slightly nervous Jasper as he glanced over his shoulder through the rear window. He thought Kate had been careless to stop at the service station, but she'd needed a break, and the coffee was welcome.

Kate followed Jasper's instructions and turned onto the weed-strewn mausoleum track. He leaned his head against the passenger window as Kate did her best to navigate the uneven ground, avoiding tree roots and the deepest ruts. She stopped at the end of the track and asked which way. Jasper wasn't listening; he had closed his eyes and was feeling unwell.

She sat for some time staring at the scenery, deciding the way forward. She resisted waking Jasper; he needed rest. She put the Evoque in first gear and headed towards a line of trees. She had just moved into second gear when the track started to climb. The Evoque struggled up the gradual incline. Suddenly Kate became very warm, and nervous butterflies welled inside her when the temperature gauge started to rise; there was a possibility her faithful old Evoque wouldn't make it to the top.

Wrong decision repeated in her mind as the line of trees got closer and closer. She looked for a gap in the trees to rest the Evoque and saw a narrow track through them. Without hesitation, Kate turned, and to her amazement, the sea appeared. She sighed with relief as the track started to descend to a cottage that was set into the hillside. She stopped next to the cottage's back door. Jasper was still sound asleep.

Kate sat for a long moment, settling her nerves before she walked to the cottage. Her eyes widened in disbelief; the door hadn't a lock and handle but a keypad. She turned and stared at Jasper, who was oblivious to her problem.

She walked to a small grassy mound nearby and sat staring at the sea and beach below. She was so lost in her thoughts that she didn't hear Jasper walk behind her. He put his hands on her shoulders and lowered her onto the grass. Before she could utter a word, his lips settled on her mouth.

"I need you, Kate," he murmured against her. "I need to be buried inside you. Don't push me away."

Her hands cupped his cheeks as her mouth consumed his. They kissed as if it was their first until her hands reached his hair. Desire sped through her as their kiss deepened.

A breathless Kate whispered, "Let's get you inside. I'll heat some of Clare's chicken soup."

"Only if you promise to sleep with me. Naked."

"Jasper! I…"

"I've never felt like this. I'm at rock bottom."

"Shhhhh." Her fingers tenderly stroked his forehead.

"I need your love, Kate. I need to feel the energy flow between us."

"Come," she said. "And open this door."

Jasper leaned on her as they slowly walked to the cottage.

***

Jasper slept after his chicken soup, leaving Kate to hide the Evoque in one of the outside buildings and light a fire in the old AGA that provided heating and hot water. The generator had tried her patience before starting and she gave up on organising the cottage.

It was dusk when she slipped out for a moon-light walk along the beach. She had so much to think about, but Jasper was the prominent thought. He had come back into her life when she was at her lowest.

Bruce was dead. Her stomach churned as the word lingered in her mind. She had always preferred to use the term *passed* or *gone*, as if he could come back. *Dead* was such a final word.

Bruce was no longer in her life, but he would always be part of her life. If he hadn't died, Jasper wouldn't have returned. It was highly likely that he would be dead. And the problem of W would never have risen.

She stood at the water's edge with waves gently lapping onto her trainers, gazing into the night sky, thinking of the times she had walked along a beach with Bruce. How he would twirl her round, she would laugh and then they would kiss all the way back to her studio. The studio that he had lovingly built for her and where they made love.

She closed her eyes and imagined Bruce kissing her. A familiar ache would rest at the top her thighs, waiting for his slow penetration as she adjusted to his fullness.

"Bruce…" she murmured.

She wasn't ready for sex with Jasper. But her body craved for satisfaction and Jasper knew her weaknesses. She would have to resist Jasper's seductive ways. All her energy would have to be concentrated on their common enemy, W. Why had he entered her life as if he had every right to? As if he knew her.

She carefully opened the door to the cottage, checked Jasper was still sleeping and rearranged the cushions on the sofa. She kicked off her trainers, removed her bra and opened the waist button of her jeans.

***

Lord Wellsbury snatched his mobile off his bedside table.

"This better be good," he angrily answered in a low voice. He didn't want to wake the young woman that lay next to him.

What was he thinking? She was his niece, for fuck's sake. Blackmail was a word away if his enemies got a whiff of his sexual preferences. He had never married or had children; he was a pillar of respectability.

Memories of last night drifted into his mind. He didn't need the help of Viagra to satisfy a woman. Young people today thought they knew everything about sex. They hadn't the time or the inclination to enjoy the complex female form, and not all women appreciated his sexual skill like his niece Helena had.

Words tumbled from his phone into his ear. "Kate gave us the slip."

He leapt out of bed. "Fuck!" He threw the phone across the bedroom.

"Come back to bed, unc," said a husky sexy voice. She'd pulled back the sheet that covered her firm young body. "Why so tense?"

She slid off the bed and nestled into his chest. A sigh crept from her mouth, and she smiled when his large hands cupped her buttocks.

Like a lamb, he followed her back to the bed. His soft lips caressed her ear before trailing to her neck. He felt her relax, giving herself to him.

He smiled. All those visits to the gym had paid off.

Chapter Ten

Lord Wellsbury carried his late morning coffee into his office. His bed partner had jumped at the chance of going shopping with one of his bank cards.

From his central desk, he controlled the screens that hung from the walls of his windowless office.

He touched a button, and the face of his man in charge of surveillance at Isaacs House appeared. Without having to ask, W was told about Kate and Jasper leaving in the early hours in Kate's old Evoque.

W's ears pricked when his man mentioned that a large Mercedes had also followed the Evoque. W had no idea who else would be interested in Carmichael.

He swirled his chair to face another screen, and Kate's face appeared. He had to be wary of her; she hadn't buckled to his aggressive attitude when he'd gone to Isaacs House. She didn't jump to conclusions but methodically thought things through. She might not have known the ins and outs of Jasper's criminal activities, but she knew of them. It was Kate who had made his Wellsbury business legit and had looked after it when he was in London.

W stared deeply at Kate's face.

"Where are you hiding, Lady Carmichael?"

***

Kate had had an uncomfortable night's sleep on the sofa. She tiptoed into the bathroom and splashed cold water on her face. When she returned to the kitchen, Jasper was still sleeping.

With her morning tea brewing and bread in the toaster, she rescued her messenger bag from the pile of miscellaneous things that she hadn't been able to find a place for. The cottage was more than a little bijou for two people.

She opened her laptop and spread the papers she had copied from the Carmichael journals across the only table. A photo of Grandfather Carmichael with a young woman and three children peered at her from the laptop screen.

Kate was on her second cup of tea, leaning back in the chair, staring at the photo, when she noticed that the woman was wearing a pendant. She tried to zoom in on the old, grainy photo.

Two hands gripped her shoulders and sensual lips brushed her neck.

"What are you so engrossed in?"

She hadn't heard Jasper get out of bed.

"She's wearing a diamond pendant," Kate blurted trying not to react to Jasper's kiss.

"And you can tell from that old, grainy, black-and-white photo found in an attic. Really, Kate?"

Kate was a little miffed, and without thinking, she stood and turned to face him.

"Sometimes your 'I'm always right' attitude gets under my skin."

An overwhelming surge of desire filled Jasper when her green eyes flashed and her cheeks turned a delightful pink.

"How I wish Meredith had left a journal or two," she said, changing the subject. "Instead of these Carmichael ones."

Jasper's finger traced her hair line. "Higgins gave me a box of Meredith's papers."

"Higgins?"

"You know, his trusted servant."

Their eyes met.

"Where are they?"

"I don't know."

Jasper's body stirred, and before Kate could react, he had her in his arms. His kiss was full of desire. His legs buckled when Kate's hand grabbed the back of his head and took control. All Kate's resolutions of last night disappeared as her body ignited.

"You want me," he said.

"I shouldn't."

"Forget, Kate. Just do what your heart tells you."

He lifted her top while his mouth consumed hers. Kate's pent-up sexual tension begged for release. Her hands slipped inside his boxers as they moved towards the bed. He was naked when he fell onto the sheets. Kate was atop him; her eyes were on fire, her cheeks glowing red. She took a moment for their eyes to dance.

"Don't stop, Kate," Jasper murmured as she guided him inside her.

For a long moment, time stood still while their bodies adjusted to the surge of energy that flowed between them. And then she slowly moved, he cried her name, and loudly moaned as they climaxed.

A breathless Kate collapsed onto the bed.

***

The afternoon sun cast long shadows across the bed where Kate lay awake with her legs entwined with Jasper's.

"Stop overthinking." His calm voice took her by surprise. "We needed each other."

Kate's breathing had calmed. She felt as if a great weight had been lifted from her. The tension that had been part of her for a long time had gone.

"I shouldn't have done it," she said. "You're ill. You need rest."

"I need you, Kate. Nothing else. And if I'm not mistaken, you need me."

She rolled onto her front and kissed him. "I'll heat the soup."

He wrapped his arms around her. "Kiss me, Kate. I need to know that you want me."

***

Kate sat at the table, grinning; Jasper sat opposite, eating his second large bowl of chicken soup.

"Why are you grinning?" he asked.

"You would make Clare very happy, tucking into her chicken soup."

"I'm hungry."

"Feeling better?"

Jasper nodded. "You look happy."

His perceptiveness took Kate by surprise. She did feel happy and content, and she couldn't remember the last time she had felt this good.

"Has he gone, Kate?"

Kate's expression suddenly stiffened. "How dare you!"

"Ultimately, you'll have to let him go."

"You have no idea…" Her voice quivered.

"I know enough. I've listened to you beg him to fuck you. Like we did last night."

Kate jumped up, her eyes full of anger.

"You're a complex woman, Kate. You need a man that will give you anything you ask."

"And you're that man?"

"Yes, I am! I'll love you tenderly; I'll hold on to you as you ride me."

"Stop!" Kate's cheeks were awash with tears.

Jasper stepped to her side, placing his hands on her shoulders.

"Look at me! I'm a selfish bastard. But I'm your selfish bastard. I've killed for you and I'll do it again."

"Bruce loved me!"

"He stifled you. He treated you like a princess. Over the years, he slowly controlled you into being the woman he thought you should be."

"Stop!" she yelled.

Jasper crashed their mouths together. He frantically pulled her top off, and his mouth devoured each breast in turn. She lost her balance. He took advantage and laid her next to his soup bowl. He wrenched her jeans off. She was naked. Her eyes were on fire; her cheeks glowed red. His jeans fell to the floor.

"God, Kate. Look at you. What you do to me. You're the only woman that does this to me."

Their eyes met and danced.

"Don't make me wait, you fucking bastard."

Jasper's laughter echoed. "Your wish is my command."

Chapter Eleven

The Gentlemen's Club was a particular favourite of W's where he could relax and enjoy a brandy. The club was out of his preferred brandy, but his silver-tongued companion had persuaded him to try a Hennessey. W had been pleasantly surprised, but he wouldn't admit it.

Although W had been a member of the club for many years, he wasn't a so-called regular, but he needed a change of atmosphere, and with this looming Carmichael debacle he might just need the help of the club's members.

The lounge where he sat savouring his drink hummed with friendly polite conversation and gossip. But that was abruptly changed when two names echoed.

Meredith Spencer and Jasper Carmichael.

A curtain of silence descended as all eyes turned towards two older men who were having a heated exchange about the club's two most famous members.

W held his breath and waited along with the other members. It was an unwritten rule that those two names were never uttered in such a prestigious place as the club. No one wanted to be associated with the notorious Lord Jasper Carmichael or his business lawyer Meredith Spencer after they'd dragged the good name of the club into the columns of the tabloids.

The two elderly members were oblivious to the eerie silence as they continued their heated exchange.

W couldn't hear all of their conversation, but he did hear "*Jasper Carmichael… Kate Carmichael*".

His hands started to shake as he carefully lowered his brandy bowl onto the glass table that separated him from his companion.

"You alright, old man? You've gone awfully white?"

One of the speakers stood. "I tell you she's a Spencer. She's the spitting image of Meredith's daughter, Laura—I've seen pictures." He pointed his finger at his drinking partner. "That older son, Harry, is a Spencer that looks like a Carmichael. And that Oliver is wild like his dad."

W's thoughts briefly dwelt on Laura Spencer. After all these years, some still debated whether Meredith had even had a love child. Meredith was not a nice man, and the argument went: how could he love anyone? But Grandfather Carmichael had told W all about Meredith's lifelong affair with a waitress called Helen, and their daughter Laura. Kate Carmichael was Meredith's granddaughter, and he'd left her the bulk of his fortune after meeting her only once. Kate had reminded Meredith of his Laura, not only in looks but also in personality.

The elderly club members were shouting at each other when two staff hurried into the lounge. A gentle grip on each member's arm, and the evening's entertainment was over. A low hum soon replaced the silence as conversation resumed.

"Do you remember Meredith, W?" asked his companion. "I keep expecting him to walk into the lounge in his aristocratic, superior manner."

"He's right: Kate Carmichael is a Spencer," mumbled W. "I'm convinced she's inherited her grandfather's temperament."

His companion was more than a little puzzled. "What did you say, old man?"

W was staring into space, ashen. His companion waved at a waiter. "Help Lord Wellsbury into his car. He's not feeling well."

The club members stopped their chatter and watched a crestfallen W being guided from the lounge.

He slumped into the rear seat of his Bentley.

"Where to, sir?" asked his driver as they filtered into the traffic.

"Home."

W stared out of the rear passenger window at the bright lights of London. He felt as if he had been kicked in the gut. He thought he had resigned the old Jasper Carmichael and Meredith Spencer into the archives of his mind. But his conflict with the present Jasper Carmichael and his wife Kate, both reincarnations of passed Carmichaels and Spencers, had brought the past into the present.

The old Jasper Carmichael had been a ruthless businessman. No one had bettered him and no one knew how far and wide his business tentacles had stretched.

However, as far as W was concerned, the current Jasper Carmichael was the most dangerous Carmichael of them all. He was a cross between his grandfather and father. Jasper's cleverness and ruthless business sense was the signature of his grandfather. However, he'd inherited his prominent characteristics from his father.

Colin Carmichael's covert missions both during and after the Second World War were legendary. Father and son had the same nickname: Chameleon. They both had diamonds running through their veins. Jasper may not have been a diamond thief, but he was a master at buying and selling them and hiding the proceeds.

However, the present Jasper Carmichael had a weakness his ancestors never had, and that was his wife: Kate, a Spencer.

W was more and more certain that Kate had inherited the Spencers' ruthlessness. A female version of her grandfather. He would have to be wary of the wolf in sheep's clothing.

As the old Bentley motored through the night, W reflected on his own weaknesses. He had an insatiable appetite for sex with young women, he was greedy for money and diamonds, but most of all he hungered for revenge.

It was the combination of revenge, money and diamonds that had driven him to blackmail Jasper into working for him.

W had been on the verge of having it all when Jasper had escaped his clutches. Now, Jasper was free to seek revenge.

However, time was on W's side. Jasper was hiding with Kate, recuperating from his prison ordeal.

W's car stopped by the front door of his country estate.

The front door flung open and his niece Helena came running out. She wrapped her arms around him.

"The club phoned. They said you've had a funny turn. I phoned the doctor—he's on his way."

"No need. I'll be fine," said a miffed W, shaking her off him.

He carried on walking into the house. His butler was waiting.

"I've lit the fire in your study, sir."

W nodded and turned to look at his niece, who was chatting to his driver. For the second time that night, his gut churned. Something about his niece's show of concern unexpectedly put him on his guard. He cursed under his breath. Bloody sex with young women had left him open to blackmail. Was Helena the type of woman that would resort to it?

He stared at Helena and his driver, wondering if he was fucking her. W didn't care, as long as she satisfied him as well. But alarm bells were ringing in his head. Was Helena his niece?

Old Jasper Carmichael flashed into his mind. He'd had a similar weakness, W thought. And W had been the result.

Chapter Twelve

Jasper was sleeping when Kate crept out of the cottage for a moonlight walk along the beach. She slipped off her trainers and let the water lap over her feet.

Jasper had questioned her love for Bruce and criticised Bruce's love for her. Jasper had fucked her after the inevitable argument. When he had finished, he'd left her recovering on the table while he collapsed exhausted on the bed.

He was a criminal, murderer, money launderer, addicted to diamonds—everything she abhorred—and somehow, he had captured her heart. She loved him.

She'd loved Bruce, but Jasper had taken her love onto another level. She needed to be near him, feel his presence.

Two arms snaked around her waist, and lips caressed her neck.

"What are you thinking about?" His voice was soft and low.

"Sex with you."

She felt a smile creep across his face.

"I've never had better."

"Don't lie."

"Our desire is mutual. It's a powerful emotion." He paused as she tilted her neck. Light kisses trailed to her shoulder. His hands cupped her breasts.

"I'm no longer young. I can't give you…" Her words petered out as he turned her to face him and their lips brushed.

"I want to argue with you. I want to see you on fire. I want to hear *don't make me wait.* In short, I want you, Kate."

She cupped his cheeks and kissed him.

"Death opened its door. I've looked inside. I know what's important. And that's you."

Moments passed as energy drifted between them.

"Let me love you, Jasper."

***

W had waited until he was alone before he unlocked the bottom drawer of his desk and lifted the family photo album.

His brother and sister hadn't wanted to stay in England after their mother died. They had insisted that he should be the keeper of the family secrets and it was his responsibility to avenge the family honour.

He had slowly flicked through the pages, dwelling on happier times, of photos of him, his brother, his sister and their dear mother. He stopped and stared at a face that he hated. The full head of hair, high cheekbones and a smile one never forgets.

Over the years, W had learned how to disguise his Carmichael features. His hair was neatly trimmed, he wore plain glass spectacles to hide his blue eyes and he rarely smiled. However, he had inherited the worst trait of all from that disgusting man: a sexual habit that could ruin him.

W had momentarily forgotten the reason for a trip down memory lane. He was looking for photos of his nieces. Although he had never met his brother's and sister's children when they were young, they had sent him photographs that he'd dutifully filed in the family album.

He wasn't surprised when he couldn't find a niece called Helena. Initially, he was pleased that he hadn't fucked his niece—but who was this woman?

***

While W was stressing about Helena, Jasper was carrying a mug of tea to his wife, who was sitting on the grassy mound, staring at the sea.

"Are you angry with me?"

"Yes and no." She looked into his eyes and smiled.

"I'm jealous about how you loved Bruce."

Kate looked at him sharply. "Don't."

"Kate, I need to know."

"You pushed me into Bruce."

"That's not true."

"Bruce cared. He gave me love when I needed it. When you preferred diamonds. I had the boys to support. People relied on me for their livelihood. When you didn't care. You let diamond fever take hold." She paused to sip her tea. "I'm not the woman you left. I've done things I'm not proud of."

"To survive."

"No! Because I missed excitement. I missed you."

"Were you happy?"

"In the beginning. Ecstatic."

"And later?"

"I deceived him. I deceived everyone."

"Zak's money."

"How did you know?"

"Zak would have hidden his money. I'm guessing somewhere in those Victorian buildings."

"I stumbled across it. Those Victorian buildings had become dangerous. Bruce had a team ready to knock them down. I suppose I wanted to remember the first time I met Zak, so I had a look around." She paused at memories of her first meeting with Zak. The smell, the rats and Zak with dirty hands and clothes. "The stench was worse than I remembered. I caught a loose brick in the passage wall. One brick led to two, and so on. The wall was bulging with plastic bin liners. I had a hell of a game hiding the money in the Isaacs library."

Jasper recalled the small Isaacs library. "It's in that library? Where?" His voice was a little loud.

His words hadn't registered with Kate. Her mind was focused on that day she found the money. "There were diamonds in a pouch."

"Kate! What have you done?"

"The pouch was dripping wet. I can't remember how many diamonds, but they were individually wrapped in white paper envelopes. They are with the money but in a box wrapped in white paper. I assumed they must be valuable."

She gazed at Jasper, but he was deep in thought. Who had Zak been dealing with to get his hands on individually wrapped diamonds?

"Can you remember anything else? Were they clear or coloured?"

"I didn't take much notice. I was in emotional turmoil. I didn't know what to do. I'm not like you. You would have recognised their worth and stashed them away to sell." Kate paused, gathering her thoughts. "I'm afraid you won't like the Kate I've become, but I love you in a way that I've loved no other. I've always loved you. Bruce knew that." She turned and looked into his watery blue eyes. "Bruce loved me more than I loved him."

Jasper moved to kiss her.

She pulled back. "There's more. I used some of Zak's money to buy land. It was easy. I do the accounts for the centre and a number of traders. I know their financial secrets and I keep my mouth shut. When a trader was in debt, I helped with a cash injection in exchange for an asset. Land. When the centre had a cash-flow problem…"

"You used the money to ease the problem."

Kate nodded. "I couldn't tell anyone. As you rightly described me, I was Bruce's princess. To Harry, Oliver, Clare and Malcolm, I'm the epitome of respectability. When Bruce died, it was the last straw. I felt as if I couldn't carry on. And then you turned up. Needing me. But I needed you."

Jasper pulled her into him so she could rest her head on his shoulder, his mind mulling over the possibility that Zak may have been dealing with yellow diamonds. "We need each other." He kissed her eyes, nose and mouth. "I want you by my side when I take down W and the rest of them that want me dead." He stopped to claim her mouth. "I want you all to myself. No sons or Clare and Malcolm. I want us to kiss whenever we feel like it. Make love when we want." Jasper deftly flicked open the buttons of her blouse. "Oh, Kate! No bra."

She covered his hand with hers. "I'm being selfish. I'm all about me when I should be healing you."

Jasper lowered his head to her breasts. "This heals me."

She sighed when he kissed each breast in turn.

"I haven't had a nightmare since I've been with you," he said. "My captors made fun of me when I couldn't get an erection. But you've healed that."

Her hand rested on his head, and their mouths met.

Chapter Thirteen

W was becoming increasingly frustrated. He couldn't find any reference to a Helena.

On the off chance that one of his old contacts was alive, he phoned. To his surprise, the snitch answered. W didn't want to talk about such a delicate matter over the phone, so he arranged to meet the snitch at the top of the multi-storey car park they had used in the past.

W was unrecognisable when he left his London residence. He wore a cap pulled over his face, his well-worn fleece muffled his neck and his ripped jeans caught on the pavement.

The top floor of the multi-storey hadn't changed. The wind blew litter along the concrete floor, a smell of urine lingered and used needles were discarded by the walls, along with dirty blankets and sleeping bags.

W hid behind one of the concrete pillars and watched his old snitch, who was leaning on the concrete barrier, looking down at the traffic below.

When W was sure they were alone, he walked towards him. A stale smell greeted him. The snitch had never been one for hygiene, always dressed like a tramp, but this smell made W retch.

"'Ave you brought it?" the snitch asked and began to cough.

"Tell me about Helena first."

The snitch glanced at W. "There's an 'elena Cohen. 'Er granddaddy in the gang with Colin Carmichael. When Cohen died, she went to live with some cousins and not Carmichael like Old Man Cohen wanted."

"Is that all?"

"Yo want more, it'll cost."

"Just fuckin' tell me."

"There's talk of reckoning." The snitch coughed and pulled a spliff from his pocket. "Zak Cohen's diamonds and money."

"Who's after Carmichael?"

"'Elena with 'er cousins. They blame Carmichael for Zak's death. They want what's due. Money, diamonds, Carmichael." The snitch had another bout of coughing.

W turned his nose up at this disgusting excuse for a human being. He slipped his hand into his inside pocket and pulled out a brown envelope. The snitch's eyes widened, and he stepped forward with his arm outstretched, ready to snatch the envelope, but W was too quick. He stepped away, leaving just enough space to keep the snitch's attention.

"Why me?"

"Yo know, Carmichael. Yo like to fuck 'em young." He laughed, showing his rotten teeth.

W tried to hide his angry surprise.

"Yo think it's a secret." The snitch laughed, thinking he'd got one over W.

A lump formed in W's throat as he realised this man was a liability. While the snitch was laughing, W casually reached into his fleece pocket and pulled out a knife. The snitch had put his hands on his knees, succumbing to a deep bout of coughing.

W stabbed him in the neck. The snitch's dirty hand shot to his neck, trying to stem the blood flow, but it was useless. He lost his balance and slowly fell to the concrete floor.

W stood over him, watching his body twitch as he tried to cling to life. The snitch's dark, evil eyes met W's.

He pointed his bloodstained finger at W and through a blood-filled mouth, said, "'Ee yo in 'ell."

Words meant nothing to W. He had killed better men than this. W emptied the man's pockets of anything that would incriminate him. He then wiped his knife on the man's filthy coat.

Next stop: Carmichael, he thought as he walked away.

***

Kate eased herself out of bed and tiptoed into the bathroom. She slipped a blanket around herself and walked to the grassy mound to watch the sunrise.

Sleep had evaded her after Jasper's nightmare. She had snuggled him into her breasts as he shouted her name, beads of sweat falling into her cleavage. She had kissed his forehead and stroked his hair, hoping to soothe his inner turmoil.

Jasper had instinctively opened his eyes when the outside door clicked open and closed. He was shaking. He needed her.

It took Kate by surprise when Jasper lifted the blanket and nestled beside her.

"You left me."

"You were sleeping."

"Don't leave me, Kate."

He rested his head on her shoulder, and she kissed his damp hair.

"There's something special about a sunrise. Everything is so clean and fresh. New day. New start," she said in her characteristic matter-of-fact tone. "I've been thinking—"

Jasper cut across her. "Don't overthink, Kate! We loved one another. I love you, Kate, and that's never going to change. We're soulmates and you know that." His lips brushed hers. "I want us to be together. It's not all about sex. It's about sharing a life."

"I can't go back to how things were," she said. "I need to do what I want."

"Kate, I want you to paint, expand the bookshop and gallery. Let Harry and Oliver run the centre. They have us to guide them."

"What will you do?"

Jasper took a deep breath. "I'm not well," he admitted.

Kate moved so she could see his face. "Are you in pain? Tell me."

"The only pain I have is when you move away from me."

"Jasper, don't make light of what you went through."

"I had nightmares, I was cold, the food was drugged. Unknowingly, you have soothed my nightmares with love and good food. Physically, I'm improving, but mentally, I'm not the old Jasper. If I didn't have W to deal with, I would just be with you."

"We can forget W."

"He won't forget us. He wants me in a box."

An awkward silence began to divide them.

"I've got to destroy him and others that want their pound of flesh."

"I'll help as much as I can," Kate mumbled. "I can't stand by and do nothing while they make your life hell. I'll find out who W is. I still think he's a Carmichael. I'll look into your business accounts. We can work from Isaacs."

"Kate, my accounts will name criminals."

"I know. It's best if I know who I'm dealing with."

"They are dangerous."

"My accounting skills have improved while you were away."

"What do you mean?"

"You'll find out."

"We'll go to the marina."

"I thought we'd go straight to Isaacs?"

"I have a very interested trader that wants to buy it."

"Jasper! Give me time to read your accounts."

"At this stage, it will be a handshake on a price. I'll put all my yachts up for sale, except for one."

***

Clare was making a steak and kidney pie in the Isaacs kitchen when Oliver walked in, nursing the effects of a night at The George.

"Harry's gone," she told him.

Oliver didn't bother to answer. He poured himself a coffee.

"They say he's fucking the living daylights out of her," he said between gulps of coffee. "They laughed in my face. I don't like being laughed at. How could she?"

"You don't know that, and neither do those people you drink with. Don't judge your mother. Kate is not only your mother, a wife and a businesswoman—above all, she is a woman that has needs, and I'm not talking about a fuck against The George's alleyway wall."

Oliver reddened. "Does she know?"

"Of course she does."

"She's never said."

"She loves you. Whatever you do, she'll defend you. She doesn't judge you."

"When's she comin' back?"

"She didn't say, but they're going to the marina. Then they're coming here."

"Why?"

"She didn't say. But it'll be something to do with Jasper."

Oliver finished his coffee.

An awkward silence descended over the kitchen.

"I hope she comes home soon," he said. "I need to see her."

"Oliver, you love her."

"I know." Oliver opened the kitchen door and walked towards his car. "I miss her so much."

Chapter Fourteen

It was one of those grey days that many people associate with England. Bart, Jasper's trusted Man Friday, watched over the cones he had placed around Jasper's parking space.

W had unexpectedly arrived at the marina that morning with Joanne and a young woman Bart didn't recognise. The three of them had taken residence in the comfortable leather seats in the foyer, facing the glass entrance doors.

Jasper's call had been brief; he had instructed Bart to collect the clothes he had ordered from the marina boutique. To Bart's surprise, Jasper had told him to put the word out that he was selling the marina. Gossip had it that Jasper was a changed man since his ordeal at the hands of W.

When an unusually clean Evoque drove through the entrance, Bart hurried out of the foyer to remove the cones. The car stopped in Jasper's parking space. Bart had never met Lady Carmichael, but he immediately thought she must be something special for Jasper to be in the passenger seat. Jasper was always in control, whether it was business or something as mundane as driving.

He never suspected that Jasper wasn't well enough to drive.

Jasper introduced Kate as Lady Carmichael, and Bart was surprised when she smiled, shook his hand and said, in her calm way, "Kate."

Jasper rested his hand on the small of Kate's back and guided her towards the lift, ignoring W and his female companions. Bart was a little surprised that Jasper used the lift. He thought it was for Kate's benefit, never thinking that Jasper couldn't manage the stairs.

The atmosphere in the lift was a little tense as Bart pressed the first-floor button. Out of the corner of his eye, he caught Jasper's hand searching for Kate's. He glanced at them as Kate stood on tiptoes and kissed Jasper's cheek. Jasper's complexion had turned a deathly white, and his half smile didn't reach his eyes, even as he pulled Kate into his side. For the first time, Bart considered that Jasper might be unwell.

Bart opened Jasper's office door, and Kate and Jasper hurried in. Jasper slumped into his desk chair, his hands searching for Kate.

"Bart, would you be kind enough to get a glass of water?" she softly said as Jasper rested his head on her stomach.

Fifteen minutes later, after a glass of water and soft words from Kate, Jasper's colour had returned and he began to look like his old self.

Bart was hovering in Jasper's office when they returned from having a shower in Jasper's private bathroom. He was struck by Kate's casual appearance. She smiled, her hair still wet. The designer jeans and white blouse he had collected from the boutique fitted her perfectly. However, Jasper's clothes were too big. Bart hadn't realised that Jasper had lost weight.

While Jasper stacked the contents of his safe onto his desk, Kate was giving Bart instructions on emptying Jasper's office into boxes for him to sort later.

She was nothing like what he had been told to expect. Lady Carmichael was a breath of fresh air in the plastic world where he worked.

"I trust you won't mention Jasper to anyone outside?"

Bart nodded.

"We're going to Isaacs House. Jasper will run his business from there. I'll arrange a bedroom, or probably a room over the old buildings, for you. Jasper's selling the marina and two of his yachts, but he will explain the ins and outs. Sealed offers. Nothing below four million will be considered. I would like this sale to be above board—forgive the pun—and I don't like the idea of the sale being done with the shake of a hand. I will talk to Jasper about it."

Her words tapered off as Jasper cursed and stumbled. His hand grabbed for the end of his desk, but he missed and landed on the carpet.

Before Bart had realised what had happened, Kate was kneeling beside an angry Jasper. He shoved her away, but she was having none of it. She wrapped her arms around him, nestling his head into her shoulder. Bart couldn't hear her whispers. Jasper's hands rested on her back and pulled her against him.

She was stroking Jasper's hair when she asked Bart to put the safe's contents into a holdall.

When Bart returned with the holdall, Jasper was sitting in his desk chair with his head in his hands.

"I'm concerned about Lord Carmichael," Bart whispered to Kate as he handed her the bag. "Is there anything I can do?"

"He's having a bad day. I'm afraid it will be a while before we know all the effects of his ordeal."

The office door flew open, and W stepped inside with Joanne and the young woman that Bart didn't recognise, but Kate did.

W noticed that Kate flinched—only slightly, but enough for him to realise that she recognised Helena Cohen.

"They tell me you're selling." W's words were directed at Jasper, but his eyes were on Kate.

He hadn't expected Kate to take it upon herself to answer. "Yes. Sealed bids handed to Bart. Anything less than four million will be disregarded."

His hackles rose when Kate and Jasper shared an "I love you" look.

"Letting a woman do your talking," he snarled.

"It's yours if your bid is the highest," Kate answered.

Jasper's eyes settled on Kate. His fingers circled a small box that had been in his safe.

W moved towards the desk so he could have a better look at the box that had Jasper's attention. Jasper grinned as he flicked the lid open and the Carmichael wedding rings fell onto the desktop. Kate was briefly mesmerised by the wedding ring that she had returned to Jasper. It rolled before her.

Joanne's envious eyes moved from Kate to the rings. W's body had stiffened as he recognised the rings that his family should have inherited. But Grandfather Carmichael had left them to Colin, his youngest son from his first marriage.

Helena sensed trouble and tugged on W's arm. "Come on, uncle."

W pushed her away, fighting to control the Carmichael temper that bubbled deep inside him. His angry blue eyes avoided Kate and Jasper, but he couldn't hide the tension in him or the tight clenching of his hands and whitening of his knuckles.

Kate had moved to Jasper's side, placing her hand on his shoulder. They smiled at each other, and their eyes danced. Kate leaned and kissed Jasper's hair but lifted her eyes to watch W. Her stomach flipped. She'd become all too familiar with the Carmichael temper. She'd recognise the signs of it anywhere.

Kate was convinced W was a Carmichael.

Chapter Fifteen

W stormed out of Jasper's office with Joanne and Helena at his heels. The women struggled to keep up with W's fast pace and gave up when he threw the reception doors open and continued along the walkway to the yachts.

"What's up with him?" asked Helena, confused.

"That bitch has upset him."

"Kate's not a bitch."

"You don't know her like I do. She's a wolf in sheep's clothing."

***

Kate and Jasper were watching W race towards the end of the walkway. Jasper had refused to believe that W had shown the traits of the Carmichael temper.

Suddenly W stopped walking, flung his arms above his head, and yelled.

Jasper lifted a pair of binoculars from his desk drawer. "He's visibly shaking and pulling on his hair."

"Now do you believe me?"

***

"What's he doing?" asked Helena.

"I don't like this," mumbled Joanne. "If he asks you to go with him, be on your guard."

"I think I'll phone my cousins."

"Good idea."

*****

A nervous Helena sat in the passenger seat of the Bentley. W had instructed Joanne to stop at the marina and try to seduce Jasper, even though he thought it was unlikely it would succeed with Kate wearing the Carmichael wedding ring.

"I've given the staff the week off," W told Helena. "So we'll be alone." He had grinned, giving her a sly look.

As they neared his country mansion, W's attitude changed. He was feeling restless and in need of a woman.

He parked the Bentley next to the kitchen door and tried to grab Helena, but she dodged his advances.

"You're frightening me!"

"No need to be afraid. All I want is affection."

When Helena refused to leave the car, W wrenched the passenger door open and dragged her into his study. He threw his suit jacket onto the back of a chair as he walked to his drink table. He poured a very large brandy into a crystal brandy bowl before slumping onto the chesterfield couch.

"Take your clothes off," he commanded.

Tears trickled down Helena's cheeks. She didn't recognise this man. A scowl had twisted his face and his eyes had an evil glint.

"If you don't take them off, I'll rip them off—and believe me, you won't want that."

Helena gingerly stepped in front of him.

"That's my little niece. But you're not my niece." W stood in front of her. "Helena Cohen."

He grabbed the front of her top. Helena retaliated by kicking his shins.

"You bitch!" he yelled.

She turned and ran from him, but he grabbed her arm. Helena kneed his crotch. W let go and fell onto the floor, but Helena had lost her balance. She fell heavily onto the granite hearth.

A deadly silence descended as W stared at the blood trickling from her head. He hadn't intended this to happen. He had wanted to teach her a lesson she wouldn't forget.

He stood staring at her young, limp body, waiting for a surge of emotion. None came. He had never fallen into the trap of caring for a woman. Not like Jasper, who had allowed love into his heart.

***

Jasper had his arm casually draped over Kate's shoulders as they stood staring at his three yachts. Kate had never understood why he needed three yachts, but she wasn't a yacht person, so his enthusiasm for the sailing yacht that was going into dry dock for repairs was lost on her. Her thoughts drifted to her paintings that were lying in her Isaacs House studio, waiting for the final touches.

Her happy musing abruptly ended when Jasper slipped the word "diamonds" into the conversation. Her body stiffened.

"I still have diamonds to sell, and then Zak's diamonds to consider," he said as his lips caressed her neck. He knew Kate wouldn't like him talking about diamonds, but he had to know her true feelings.

Jasper's world was shattered when Kate pulled away from him.

"Kate. Do you love me?"

She turned to look into his eyes. "What sort of question's that?"

"I'm a criminal. There's no going back. I trade diamonds with other criminals. Can your love for me overcome your dislike for diamonds and the criminal world?

Kate didn't answer.

Chapter Sixteen

W's personal mobile began to ring.

"Yes?" he snapped.

"Has that little bimbo got the better of you?" Joanne giggled.

W didn't like being teased. *You'll regret that, whore.*

"Why don't you stay at the marina?" he said softly. "Use my tab. Treat yourself in Jasper's over-priced boutique."

Joanne smiled at the thought of spending W's money.

"Of course, I'll expect a favour or two in return."

All the time W was talking to Joanne, he was staring at Helena's dead body and deciding how to dispose of it.

Joanne giggled. "You do know that she grassed on you to her cousins."

W's stomach flipped. He hadn't expected Helena would involve her cousins.

"She phoned them while she was here, so they must be close to your place."

W briskly moved to his office and stared at the security screens. There was a Rolls Royce parking next to his Bentley. He ended Joanne's call, opened his desk drawer and lifted his gun.

The three cousins stood in the kitchen. W watched, waited and listened.

"Where is she?"

"Probably fucking."

"There's no staff."

"Probably he likes looking after himself."

"She said she'd be waiting."

"Something's up."

"I don't like this."

W confidently stepped into the kitchen, pointing his gun at the three men.

"Helena won't be joining us."

The three men eyed him.

"We can take him," one said to the others.

"That's true," he said. "But one of you, maybe two, will die."

A tense silence filled the kitchen as the Cohen cousins considered which of them W might shoot first.

"Let's be civilised about this," he said. "Kick your guns over here. All your guns."

A gunshot echoed through the kitchen. One of the Cohen's had tried to get the drop on W.

"I'm an excellent shot," W remarked.

Blood dripped from the man's shoulder onto the kitchen's stone floor.

W pointed to the open door, and the Cohens slowly walked outside.

"Walk towards the little tractor and trailer."

The Cohens exchanged glances, but W was anticipating their move. Without a flinch, he fired a bullet in each of their arms.

"You're dead meat, old man!" one of them shouted. "Our family will hunt you."

When they reached the trailer, they turned to face him. W's eyes had glazed over.

"Where's Helena?" one asked.

"You'll be joining her soon."

"Where's Carmichael?"

"Looking at you."

Three shots left W's gun in quick succession. Each Cohen fell backwards into the trailer. In a slow, casual manner, W walked over and methodically emptied each of the dead Cohens' pockets before throwing their legs inside the trailer.

W manoeuvred the tractor and trailer closer to the kitchen before he dragged Helena's dead body, wrapped in his fireside rug, to the door. That had taken it out of him—he wasn't as fit as he thought. Sweat was dripping from his face; he needed to sit and rest.

Thirty minutes later, he drove the tractor towards the pit that the fencing contractors had failed to fill in. He reversed the trailer to the edge of the pit and tipped it so the bodies slipped in. Helena was the first to slide to the bottom. Her cousins covered her.

He stood on the edge of the pit, staring at the bodies. They all deserved to be dead; they had come here with the intention of killing him. Although he had enjoyed Helena's body, she'd had an ulterior motive. She'd wanted information on Jasper and Zak Cohen. She'd thought Zak's stash of money belonged to her and not Jasper. But Jasper didn't have the money, and neither did W. The money had disappeared the night Zak had drowned. For all W knew, the sacks of notes could have found their way into the river and into the sea.

***

Physical labour had always been anathema to W. He was exhausted and needed to eat and sleep, so it was much later that he returned to the dead bodies.

He sat in the small digger his gardener had persuaded him to purchase. *Funny how things turn out,* he thought as the digger trundled towards the spoil heap beside the pit. He had pretended to be interested in the digger while his gardener had enthusiastically taken upon himself to show W how to operate the machine. W could never have imagined how useful those basic instructions would be.

All he had to do was to push the spoil heap into the pit. The task wasn't as easy as he first thought, but after trial and error, plus a litany of expletives, he mastered the controls and filled the pit.

It was dark when W returned to his study and a very welcome glass of brandy. He slumped into his favourite chair and glanced at Helena's dried blood on the hearth.

One more job, he thought, *before I can deal with Joanne.*

Chapter Seventeen

They had only been back at Isaacs House a week and Jasper was beginning to feel better. He longed to share Kate's day. It didn't matter to him what she was doing as long he was with her.

He had just finished reading her summary of his accounts. It didn't paint his business in a good light. He wasn't surprised that his employees were helping themselves to his money. He'd been away for too long. Loyalties had changed.

Jasper left the accounts on his desk and walked to the French doors so he could look at his wife moving paintings from the back of the studio. He reached for the door handle with the intention of joining her when Oliver's voice pierced the silence that Jasper had grown accustomed to.

"Where's Mum?"

Oliver's aggressive tone made Jasper turn and stare.

"Oliver! Must you be so abrupt?" Harry's voice drifted into the office.

Harry was measured and calm, taking after his mother, but Oliver was a like a bull at a gate, just like a young Jasper.

"Where's Mum?" Harry's eyes rested on Jasper. "We would like a private chat."

"You're too soft," Oliver countered in his belligerent manner. "We do the telling. Not him."

"She's in her studio." Jasper nodded towards it.

Harry was more than a little surprised. "What is she doing there? I thought she was doing your accounts."

"It didn't take long."

"She's good, isn't she?" said Harry, his voice full of pride.

Jasper smiled and nodded. "What do the pair of you want?"

He looked at Oliver, expecting a typical Oliver tirade, but it was Harry who took the lead.

"Are you staying? We're concerned. You see, she was absolutely devastated when you left. But she had Bruce. And now she has no one except us."

"We didn't like Bruce," interjected Oliver.

Jasper sat in one of the comfortable chairs and crossed his legs. His two sons moved to the couch opposite.

"Kate—your mother knows how I feel."

"And that is?" snapped Oliver.

"I love her, Oliver. I always have. She's the only woman I've ever loved."

The question is: does she still love me? thought Jasper.

"Why did you leave her?"

Jasper took time to gather his thoughts before speaking. "A combination of things happened at the same time. I had diamonds galore from your grandfather. I was dazzled with being Lord Carmichael; I wanted to prove I was a worthy Carmichael." He hesitated. "And I convinced myself I would find another Kate."

"Did you?" asked Harry.

"No. You see, your mother was happy with what we had. Money, love, sons. But I wanted more."

"We weren't enough for you?" Oliver's nervous tone surprised Jasper.

He gazed into his son's watery eyes. "I began to neglect her. I let Bruce give her the love that she deserved. I knew he would look after her, protect her."

"And all that time, you still loved her."

"Yes. I tried not to think about her. I had a surveillance team report to me. I would sail to the beach studio at the weekend, just to see her and make sure Bruce was doing right by her."

"She cried a lot. I heard her pleading with him," said Harry. "We could hear her through the bedroom door."

"Your mother is a complex woman. She has needs."

"I wish people would stop saying my mother is a woman with needs," interjected Oliver. "Don't all women have needs?"

"You only think of her as Mother," commented Harry, looking at his brother.

"I'm referring to sex, Oliver," Jasper said. "Not all women need sex like Kate. She needs sex and tender love. Love that only her soulmate can give her." Jasper paused as he thought of their recent argument at the last-resort safe house. "When we argue, there's an energy that builds between us. An energy so intense…"

"…That finds its release in sex."

The three men abruptly turned to see Kate standing in the open office doorway.

Harry and Oliver blushed whereas Jasper smiled and tapped the space beside him on his chair.

"You shouldn't have been listening," said an indignant Harry.

"Why not? It involved me."

"I thought you'd be in your studio for the rest of the day," said Jasper, looking into her eyes while stroking her hair.

Jasper's mind was musing on what he would do if they were alone when Malcolm's voice broke his thoughts.

"Where do you want it, Kate?"

Malcolm stood in the doorway holding a box.

"In the studio." Kate went to move, but Jasper held her hips.

"Is that…?" Jasper asked.

"Yes. Meredith Spencer's papers," Kate said. "They were on a shelf in Malcolm's workshop."

"How on earth did they get there?" asked Jasper.

"Bruce. Dropped 'em on the gardener's 'to be burnt' pile," said Malcolm, walking towards the studio. "I had a looksee. Thought Kate might want to read 'em. So, I put 'em on a shelf."

Kate looked into Jasper's puzzled eyes. "I asked Clare and Malcolm if they could remember any Spencer papers."

"He won't be in there," Jasper said.

"W's a Carmichael, Jasper. From your grandfather's days."

Harry and Oliver shared a confused look. They had no idea what their parents were on about.

***

The studio light flicked off. From the darkened office, Jasper watched Kate walk to the small Isaacs library. Kate had gone into silent mode since she started reading Meredith's papers. Jasper had watched her run her hands through her hair and stare into the evening sky. She was more than a little concerned.

The only sounds in the house were Kate's light footsteps and the click of the library door. Jasper reached the door before it closed. He could just see Kate walk to a bookshelf and ease it from the wall. A dim light filtered through a narrow gap, which Kate squeezed through.

The thought of Zak's money got the better of him. He walked to the bookshelf and slipped through into the secret room. He was shocked to see bundles of notes crammed onto the shelves that covered the original library wall. *So, this is where Colin and Jacob Isaacs hid their diamonds.*

Kate whipped round and glared at him. In the palm of her trembling hand was an open piece of white paper. The sparkle from the diamond was mesmerising.

Their eyes met.

"It's always been about diamonds," she said as a lone tear fell from her eye. "Zak could tell the value of a diamond by looking at it. He would only hide a diamond fortune."

"Kate, you're upset. Let's sit down and talk."

"It's all there in Meredith's notes. The lust for Colin's diamonds. The ones you had, the ones that people coveted, were worth a fortune. Meredith wanted them. You still have them. Don't you?"

"I still have some. Zak cut many of Colin's diamonds. Your pendant, earrings. If you remember, too many people were showing an unhealthy interest in Zak's jewellery. They were linking me with him. I stopped supplying him."

"It looks like he was in with someone else."

Jasper carefully took the diamond nestled in white paper from Kate's hand. "Zak's diamonds might not have been Zak's. He told me he was a go-between."

Jasper took Kate's elbow, pushed the bookshelf back into place and guided her out of the library and to the Evoque.

***

It rained all the way to the beach house studio. Jasper only made one stop for fuel and a few groceries. Kate hadn't eaten since breakfast.

Kate opened her eyes as the Evoque bumped along the track to the studio.

"Why are we here?"

"To talk. To plan. To make love without being interrupted."

"Not here! I'm not ready."

"You love this place."

"I do. But the memories are too raw."

"Memories you want to cherish or memories you want to forget?"

Jasper stopped under the lean-to carport that Bruce had made to shelter cars from the inclement weather.

"I used to sneak in here and listen to your moans," he said. "One time you nearly caught me, crossing to the woods. You walked to the beach wearing an open robe. I could see all of you. How I stopped myself from fucking you, I'll never know."

"Jasper, don't try and taint my memory of Bruce."

Kate stepped onto the balcony and twisted the knob of one of the rail spindles. She lifted the knob and removed a small leather pouch. Jasper stared as she shook the door key from the pouch. She stopped just inside the studio and shivered.

"It's cold," she said.

Kate thought it was because Bruce wasn't with her, but Jasper wrapped his arms around her and whispered, "It misses you."

She knew he was right. The studio, like Isaacs House, was where her spirit rested.

"This place is your retreat," he said. "This is where you should paint. This is our alone place."

"What are you saying? I could never think of this as ours."

"Not this studio, but a beach house. Our beach house."

"I thought this land was unsuitable for another beach house."

"We wouldn't need planning permission if we build on the original footprint." His lips caressed her neck. "Think about it."

Energy sparked between them. Kate leaned her head onto his shoulder, and Jasper nuzzled her neck.

"I want you," he murmured.

"Not here."

Jasper lifted two blankets from the back of the two easy chairs and held her hand as they walked to the woods. Covered by branches and shrubs was the remains of Jasper's camp.

"I would spy on you from here."

He sat on a blanket and held out his arms for Kate to join him.

Chapter Eighteen

Loud ringing woke W from a disturbed sleep.

"For fuck's sake," he cursed to himself. "Yes!" he snapped, answering the phone.

"You better get here fucking tout de suite. Bart is beside himself. Jasper and the bitch have disappeared." Joanne paused to catch her breath. "Apparently three Cohens cornered Bart. They wanted to know about diamonds."

W sat up in bed. "What diamonds?"

"Zak Cohen's. They reckon Jasper knew all about them."

"This is nonsense. Everyone knows that Zak's money disappeared that night Wellsbury flooded. Not diamonds."

"Zak had a soft spot for Helena and he told her he had diamonds that would make her rich beyond her wildest dreams."

W took a moment for Joanne's words to sink in.

"Where are these Cohens?"

"Said they were going to pick up Helena. Have you seen them?"

"No. But I haven't been feeling too good. Helena must have let me sleep." Lying was second nature to W.

W switched off his phone and walked into the bathroom, his mind on Zak Cohen and his diamonds. He stood in the shower, letting the warm water soothe his aching body while he inwardly cursed the day that Zak had sweet-talked him into letting him take care of his near flawless diamonds.

Zak had then told him Colin Carmichael had stolen them along with Zak's own diamonds. If Colin had had them, Jasper would have had them. W had kept Jasper under a close watch to see if he tried to fence the diamonds. But that weasel of a Cohen had them all along. The question uppermost in W's mind was where Zak had hidden his diamonds.

***

Kate was sleeping, but rest had evaded Jasper. They had loved one another and then talked. Kate had tried to convince him W was a Carmichael and Old Jasper was his father. She hadn't worked out where Old Jasper's secret family fitted into the Carmichael timeline, but she knew Old Jasper's lust for young women had resulted in him having a second family.

In Meredith's papers there had been a reference to a Jasper Carmichael making an excellent candidate for the intelligence service, but she couldn't link that to W unless he had changed his name.

Then she had described to Jasper how W had hidden his Carmichael features. Glasses hid his blue eyes; a short haircut controlled the Carmichael full head of hair. He never smiled or laughed, so he never showed the Carmichael smile. He liked fucking young women—an Old Carmichael trait—but he couldn't control the Carmichael darkness that reared its head along with his temper.

"He will come after the diamonds once he works out what Zak had done," she had told Jasper.

Jasper couldn't imagine how Zak and W had met, unless it was through Gypsy, the drug-runner who fancied himself a diamond dealer. W owned Gypsy's hilltop villa where Jasper had been imprisoned, so it was feasible that they'd known each other.

But that didn't matter. What mattered was that Kate was rapidly fitting all the pieces into the Carmichael jigsaw.

She had told him that diamond smuggling explained why Old Jasper had made trips to America during and after the war. Jasper had heard stories about his grandfather's trips to America, but if this was true, where had he hidden the diamonds? An elderly Lord's story flashed into his mind.

Old Jasper had wanted a son to take up his baton, and his younger son, Colin, had been a diamond thief, not a businessman.

If Kate's theory was correct and Old Jasper had had a second family, W had been the heir apparent until Old Jasper had met Jasper and recognised himself in the boy.

Jasper had thought Kate was making too many assumptions, trying to link the whole of Old Jasper's family to diamonds. Jasper had considered the link to W to be very tenuous.

But she had countered by quoting *"Carmichaels haven't got blood in their veins but diamonds"*.

However, she had been surprised to read that Meredith, her grandfather, had lusted after diamonds. Money and greed had been his god.

Kate was awake when Jasper returned to their love nest. "What time is it?"

"I've phoned Clare. She said Bart's on the warpath. I wasn't where he thought I should be." A wicked grin covered his face. "I was buried deep inside my wife."

"Jasper!"

"It's true. Have a biscuit. You must be hungry."

"I could eat a bacon sarnie," she said, slipping his shirt over her shoulders. Smiling, she firmly gripped his hand and pulled him towards the studio.

"Lady Carmichael, are you aware that you're naked under that over-sized shirt?" He laughed.

"I'm ravenous. I need a shower and fresh clothes."

"I'm certainly ravenous, with you dressed like that."

She stopped, and her loving eyes met his. "Jasper Carmichael, you can make fun as much as you like." She stood on tiptoes and kissed him.

Jasper's hands cupped her naked buttocks as he pulled her against him.

"I love you, Jasper Carmichael, so much it hurts. I have very happy memories of us and many unhappy memories that I have pushed to the back of my mind. I have cherished memories with Bruce; they will always be part of me. The unhappy ones I prefer to forget. But I've got to move on." Her eyes sparkled with an 'I love you' smile. "This is where you kiss me."

Chapter Nineteen

W's day went from bad to worse. His first task had been to clean Helena's dried blood off the granite hearth and the Cohens' from the kitchen floor. He was soaking his soft, delicate, sore hands in cream when his work phone rang. It was his Carmichael surveillance team.

"He's at the beach house studio with her."

W dropped the bottle of cream onto his office carpet.

"Looks as if they've been here all night. She's cooking bacon. It smells—"

"Fuck the smell. Tell me when they leave."

W cursed. Initially at the mess the cream had made on the carpet, and secondly at the doorbell ringing. He hung up.

W opened the door and Joanne barged passed him. She pointed to the floor by the door for the taxi driver to drop her case.

"You weren't answering your phone," she said. "And pay him—I've no change."

The driver's eyes followed Joanne's hip-swinging walk in her tight skirt.

"She's something, guv. Look at that arse and those tits," he whispered so only W could hear. W paid him and the man grinned.

W's temper was rising. He needed to fuck. He stared at Joanne.

***

Wrapped in one of his silk robes, W lounged in his favourite leather chair, staring at Joanne's crumpled form.

Like a lamb she had followed him into his study. He'd slammed the door shut and pinned her against it. Before she'd realised what was happening, he was ripping her clothes off. When she'd opened her mouth, he had slapped her cheeks.

Her torn clothes were strewn about the room. He had raped the queen of whores, and he felt like a new man, his temper and the Carmichael blackness quelled.

"You bastard," she choked. She had been rough-fucked before, but what W had done was worse.

W hadn't bothered to look at her as he poured a very large brandy. She was lucky to be alive—he had been prepared to kill her to satisfy his rage.

"I was going to give you to some friends of mine. They are always on the lookout for sex slaves." He sipped his brandy. "But on second thoughts, you're more use to me. I have a difficult time ahead, and I'll want sexual relief. A lot of it." He paused to take a big swig of brandy. "You'll stay with me in London, keep my bed warm, lovingly hold my arm at dinners, watch me play cards, and if one of the players has need of your skills, you'll oblige. Do I make myself clear? A nod will do."

W's thoughts had moved to Jasper and the photographs he had been sent. Every day that Jasper had been imprisoned, W had received a photograph of Jasper showing his slow deterioration; it had been his idea to drug Jasper's food with small amounts of heroin. He had been surprised that the drug had little effect. He had stared at the last photograph of Jasper, taken the day before he had shot four people. How could a man who looked at death's door have mustered the strength to murder? However, he did acknowledge that Jasper had surprise on his side, and that his staff had been occupied in sexual activities.

W had moved to yesterday's photo of Jasper smiling at Kate as they walked along the beach. In a month, he had gone from a skeleton of a man to the picture of health, though a little thin for his height.

Kate had looked after him, fed him and given him the care he needed to recover, but she also looked—to quote a phrase—well-fucked.

"Come here, whore," he shouted, throwing Joanne a robe.

She tied the robe around her, but he snatched it open.

"I own you. Never do that again. Now, sit on my lap and tell me what you see in these photos."

Joanne nervously sat on W's lap while his fingers meandered up and down her spine.

"Jasper looks ill in this one," she said, pushing it to one side.

"Go on."

"He's fit as a fiddle in this one. He looks happy. He always walks with his arm looped over the bitch's shoulder."

"You're jealous."

"Of course I'm fucking jealous. That should be me and not her."

"You hate her?"

"Hate doesn't begin to describe it."

***

Jasper and Kate were happy, walking along the beach, content with each other's company.

"You know what I've got to do," he whispered into Kate's ear.

She gazed into his eyes.

"My safe houses and cars need to be checked over. I need you to take care of my business. It's all yours if anything happens."

Kate wasn't listening while he explained his business details, his bank accounts in the Caymans, his shell companies, where he hid the proceeds of his diamond deals. After examining his accounts, she already knew most of the details.

Her hand slipped under his shirt. She gently squeezed. A sigh escaped his mouth. What else did he need? He had the woman he loved, unconditional love.

They stopped and kissed.

Chapter Twenty

Jasper screamed, a loud, piercing cry of pain. Light streamed through Isaacs House as Harry, Oliver, Clare and Malcolm raced to the master bedroom. Kate had Jasper wrapped in her arms. Sweat dripped from his body onto her. They were both wet through, but Kate didn't notice. Her concern was Jasper, as he sobbed into her breasts.

Clare hurried into their bathroom and collected dry towels off the rack.

Kate mouthed "thank you" as she took the towels and gently wiped the sweat from Jasper's face, neck and chest. She covered his back with a towel and kissed his hair.

Malcolm put his arms around Harry and Oliver and led them out of the room. Clare joined them in the kitchen after she was sure Kate was all right.

"What did they do to him?" asked Oliver, upset.

"They broke 'im, lad. Poor food, only water to drink, cold water to shower, isolation and drugs," said Malcolm, pouring four cups of tea.

"Will he get better?"

"Kate's the only one that can do that."

"Will Dad go after him?" asked Harry as W flashed into his mind.

"My guess is yes. Even if it kills 'im."

"My hope is that he doesn't take Kate with him," said Clare, sipping her tea.

***

Jasper slowly walked into the kitchen, his eyes searching for Kate. In an instant, she was by his side. He pulled her into him, and they kissed.

Jasper sat while Kate poured him a coffee.

"I owe you all an explanation," he began. "I have nightmares. Last night's was particularly nasty. They started while I was a prisoner." He took a moment to hold Kate's hand and look into her eyes. "I'm going after him. The old Jasper way. Only one of us will be alive when I'm finished."

Kate tried to pull away, but Jasper tightened his grip. He looked at his two sons, one calm and measured and the other with his tendency for wildness.

"I always thought that I had the evil Carmichael temperament, but there's one worse than me. He's the one that put me in that god-awful place."

"It won't be easy, Jasper," said Malcolm.

"I have a lot of preparatory work to do." Jasper's voice was calm. "Kate will take over the sale of the marina and yachts. Initially Bart was going to do it, but my gut tells me something isn't right. Kate is impartial. Her decision will be based solely on money." He paused to drink his coffee. "I thought I would do my preparations here, but that would put you all at risk. I'll use one of my safe houses. Kate will deal with any problems that arise from my business."

"You're putting hell of a lot on her shoulders," Clare commented.

"I know. But she's the only one I can trust."

"We can help," offered Harry.

"I don't want either of you involved. That way, you should be safe."

"We will watch over her, just in case," said Oliver.

Jasper smiled and nodded.

"We're going to London," he said.

"We are?" said a surprised Kate.

Jasper kissed her hand. "Kate will decide which London property I'm going to sell."

"I will?"

Jasper smiled again, looking into her eyes. "I'll arrange for an architect to look into the possibility of building on the old beach house footprint. Transfer any money you need," he said, pulling her onto his lap. "When we're in London I want you to buy new paints, brushes, canvases, a new smock. That one you wear is way past its sell-by date."

"Jasper, I don't need—"

"Yes, you do. While we're separated, I want to think of you happy, painting with all the new things I've bought you."

They kissed as if it was their last.

***

Joanne had never been on a tour of W's London house. She was struck by how much it resembled his country home. They stopped in what was to be her bedroom.

"I'll visit you in here." W threw a credit card onto the bed. "Buy new clothes that show your tits off and that Pilates arse. I like lace half-cup bras and the smallest of thongs."

Joanne tensed when he pushed her onto the bed and lifted her dress.

"Relax. I'm just checking. A smaller thong than the one you're wearing."

Joanne started to shake as memories of W raping her flashed into her mind. She was frightened.

Chapter Twenty-One

The waves covered Kate's feet as she walked along the water's edge, thinking of Jasper.

They'd had a good day in London visiting Jasper's penthouse and the remodelled Carmichael house.

The dark woodwork had been removed. The kitchen and dining room had been combined to make an up-to-date kitchen diner. The study had been replastered and the plain walls painted.

"You don't like it?" Jasper had asked.

"Sell it," was her curt reply.

The last place they'd visited was the art supply shop. Kate had just finished loading new paints, oils, canvases, brushes into the Evoque when a shop assistant placed a large shoe box on the back seat. Before Kate could utter any words, he had returned into the shop. A *closed* sign dangled from the shop door, and Kate knew Jasper had gone.

She rolled her jeans to her knees so the sea covered her shins.

I miss him already, she thought. *He didn't say goodbye or kiss me, but it's probably for the best that I don't know where he's gone.*

***

From a first-floor window of the art shop, Jasper had watched Kate drive away.

"You shouldn't have let her go," said his old friend Henry.

"I know, but I have to make preparations."

Jasper was dressed in second-hand trainers, a sweatshirt, jeans and a fleece. The holdall contained a laptop and burner phones.

To Jasper's surprise, he was followed when he left the shop. He suspected Henry had bugged his clothes but not his laptop and burners—they were still in their original sealed packaging. He headed to Euston where he bought a new holdall and clothes from a pop-up shop, and got changed.

Jasper dodged on buses and trains to shake off any tail. Although he couldn't see his pursuer, he knew he was there.

When he was sure he wasn't being followed, he caught a bus to Mitcham. He scanned the passengers, and his stomach churned. His tail wasn't a *he* but a *she*. The bus stopped and Jasper ran off. He glanced behind him, and the blonde woman had also left the bus. Jasper didn't recognise her, but she was good.

He couldn't use his Mitcham safe house. His mind raced as he tried to think of his next move, but he couldn't concentrate.

He found himself wandering through an outdoor car park when his mind turned to Kate. He had to warn her. He pickpocketed a phone and rang her. She wouldn't recognise the number but with a bit of luck she would answer.

"Kate Carmichael."

"Dump that box I gave you."

"Jasper!"

"No questions. Just destroy the box."

He ended the call.

He jammed the phone under a car's rear wheel and dumped his holdall in a waste bin.

His blonde tail was walking through the cars in his direction.

Game on, he thought, and quickened his pace.

***

W confidently held open the passenger door of the limousine he had hired to take them to the theatre. Joanne struggled to ease herself from the car in her tight-fitting evening attire.

W's inside pocket vibrated. He tried to ignore it.

"Answer that fucking thing," said Joanne through her smiling lips.

W left her in the foyer, looking through the evening's programme. He stood motionless on the pavement as he was told that Jasper had disappeared while buying art supplies. Kate had left London alone. W had no sooner returned his phone to inside pocket when it vibrated again.

A rough voice told him that she was at the beach, they could easily snatch her.

Every bone in W's body wanted Kate, but his gut told him the time wasn't right. He wanted first to capture Jasper.

He returned to Joanne with a forced smile, controlling his anger. He caught her elbow and whispered, "We have to leave."

Joanne shivered as the words *rough sex* came into her mind, but she had no need to be concerned. W had something more important on his mind: Jasper.

He sat in the back of limo, staring out of the window. For the first time in his life, he didn't know what to do. Kate and Jasper had split up; he hadn't expected that. Jasper's next move would be difficult to anticipate, and Kate would lead his men on a merry chase. The Carmichaels had divided his surveillance teams.

He would need all his experience to kill Jasper and regain his family honour.

***

Jasper went into a jog as he exited the car park. Kate was on his mind; W would go after her once he realised that Jasper had rumbled his spy. He jumped on a bus just as it was pulling away from a stop. He turned and caught a glimpse of the woman talking into her phone. That was her mistake. Jasper had anticipated that a car would be following.

He stood by the bus driver. "Do me a favour, mate," he said in his friendliest voice. "Bloody divorce solicitor set his hounds on me. Just open the doors at the lights." He pulled a number of twenties from his pocket.

The driver didn't give Jasper a second look. He took the money, and as the bus stopped at the traffic lights, the doors opened. Jasper jumped onto the pavement and into a jog.

He followed a sign for the underground. He didn't care where the train was going; he had to shake off W's team.

A car shrieked to a halt by the underground entrance. Jasper cursed when the blonde jumped out and ran down the stairs to the platform. Jasper knew what he had to do.

A comfort break in the toilets was all he needed to regroup.

The blonde was pacing the platform. Her serious, sweaty features revealed she was under pressure. A man Jasper recognised as one of W's joined her. They stood talking while Jasper walked to the other end of the platform. He didn't like making plans on the hoof—something unexpected always happened. In this case he had two people tailing him. The couple slowly walked to where

104

Jasper was standing. As the train pulled in, he suddenly turned and raced to the stairs. He had relied on people running for the train to help his escape, and it worked.

He raced up the stairs two at a time and dashed onto the road, weaving in between the traffic. Horns blasted, brakes shrieked, drivers shouted expletives. Jasper's heart was pounding in his tight chest, but he didn't stop. He reached the other side of the road and kept running.

A loud thud echoed; the hum of the traffic noise died. Jasper caught a glimpse of the man turning away from him and running back to the road.

He knew the chase was over.

***

Loud screams woke Joanne. Furniture was being turned over, and pottery and glass hit a wall. She jumped out of bed and threw on a pair of jeans and a sweatshirt and crammed her feet into a pair of trainers. She stood outside her bedroom door, listening to W's rants coming up from downstairs.

"You're fucking dead! You and that bitch!"

She looked over the banister. W was pacing along the hallway. He stormed into his study and slammed the door.

Joanne didn't think. She raced to the front door, flipped the lock and ran outside into the early morning chill.

Chapter Twenty-Two

Isaacs House was still and silent when Kate arrived back from the beach house. She had done as Jasper requested and destroyed the contents of Henry's box by smashing every phone and laptop. They were now in a service station dumpster.

She filled the kettle and, robot-like, dropped two teabags into the teapot and filled it with hot water. She wandered into her studio, carrying her tea tray and a plate of sandwiches Clare had thoughtfully left for her.

She gave her mind to the night sky as she lay on chaise lounge, sipping tea and eating sandwiches.

***

Clare gently shook Kate awake.

"He's here. I've put him in the living room. He didn't like it."

Kate stood and walked towards the glass door. "He'll have to wait till I'm showered."

Bart had invited himself to Isaacs House after Jasper had told him Kate was going to deal with the sale of the marina and yachts.

He was drinking coffee when Kate joined him.

"I don't like being kept waiting," he said curtly.

Kate took a moment to look at Bart. He had changed since she last saw him. His features had tightened.

"Where's Jasper?" he commanded.

"I don't know."

"Of course you bloody do. He's signed everything over to you."

"That's not strictly true, Bart," she lied. "I have the final decision on the marina sale because I don't know the people concerned. My decision will be purely financial. Are those the offers?" She nodded at the file that lay on the coffee table.

Kate's soft tone and slightly superior manner immediately riled Bart, though W had warned him about her lofty ways.

"I don't understand why he's selling. The marina and yachts were his life."

"He's a changed man since his—"

Bart didn't let her finish. "Has he had any more episodes?"

"Not that I'm aware of."

"He should have received medical care."

An uneasy silence hovered between the two while Clare bustled in with a tray of tea and toast for Kate.

Bart's phone buzzed. He quickly glanced at the message while Kate was occupied.

"Take her or kill her."

Bart stared at the message in disbelief. He wasn't equipped to do such things. He was trained in serving gentlemen, not killing wives.

"Oh, Clare!" Kate said with a nervous twinge in her voice, making Clare turn. "Ask Malcolm to join us."

Clare scurried out of the living room. Kate's stomach had lurched when Bart's body stiffened while he was looking at his phone.

"Malcolm!" Clare shouted as she pushed the kitchen door open.

Bart was standing still, holding his phone, staring at Kate, when a dishevelled Jasper burst into the room. Bart stepped away from Kate and met

Jasper's angry, piercing blue eyes beneath a deep scowl.

Jasper snatched the phone from Bart's shaking hand. "When did he get to you?"

An angry tension filled the room.

Bart hesitated, but said, "While you were away." His voice trembled.

"Collect your things and leave the marina. You know what happens to anyone that harms Kate. But you have been a good loyal friend to me, so leave."

Clare and Malcolm had snuck into the living room.

"I wasn't going to do it."

"Lies don't become you, Bart. What does he have on you?"

Bart reluctantly said, "I… I was videoed with the new doorman."

Jasper had moved to Kate and pulled her into his side.

"I'll transfer money into your account. Now go. Malcolm, show Bart off the premises."

Bart had regained some of his confidence. "He'll better you. He's ruthless. He doesn't care about anything or anyone. If I could get to Kate, so can he," Bart snarled as Malcolm took his elbow.

Two long arms wrapped around Kate. Jasper desperately held on to her as she nuzzled her head into his chest.

"Kate, I swear—"

"Shhh. Not now, Jasper."

Chapter Twenty-Three

Bart never went back to the marina. He dumped his car and walked to his favourite café. He was mulling over his next move when Joanne sidled up to him. He had never seen her dressed in such a casual manner.

She drank two coffees as she ranted on about W's violent rages, how he had raped her and mentally abused her.

"He's going to kill Jasper and his bitch."

"Forget them and think about yourself," he told her. "Where are you going? You can't stay in London."

"I have some things in Sebastian's place."

"That's the first place he'll look. I'm going north. Why don't you travel with me? They won't be looking for a couple."

Joanne studied Bart for some time. Did she want to travel with him? On the plus side, he was gay and wouldn't want sex. She couldn't stand the thought of sex again after W.

"We'll spend the night at Sebastian's, then travel in the morning," she decided

"No. We'll go to the station from here."

***

W's rage worsened. As far as he was concerned, Jasper had killed his best operative. It didn't matter that she'd been following W's instructions. Jasper would pay, along with his bitch.

W had never lost control of the Carmichael darkness until he'd become involved with Jasper.

He feared Jasper was a better man than him. Jasper's talents were legendary. In certain circles he was known as the diamond king; he had the love of a woman and two sons.

Suddenly, W was overcome by a craving for everything Jasper had: his wealth, his skill at trading diamonds, the Carmichael title, but above all, the love and sex he shared with Kate.

***

Isaacs House was in darkness, except for Kate's studio, where they all had congregated. It was a safe place to talk unseen. Clare had covered the workbench with a cloth. Plates of crisps and nuts were laid out there with cans of beer, plus one glass. Kate refused to drink from a can or bottle.

Jasper sat next to Kate, holding her hand. He had been very quiet since the debacle in Mitcham.

Kate squeezed his hand. "They have had time to study you. Prepare. Safe houses, safe cars. Don't be so hard on yourself. You did what they expected. So, we now have to do the unexpected."

"I'm a prisoner here."

"I know where you could come and go without anyone knowing," said Malcolm.

Malcolm and Jasper's eyes met.

"Got an old car in the workshop looking for a run."

Harry spread photographs of men and cars across the table. "All of them were taken near Isaacs House."

Jasper picked up one photo of a man that W relied upon. "How long has he been here?"

"Bruce head-butted him," said Oliver. Harry kicked him. "Sorry, Mum, but he's been around for ages."

"He's one of W's men," Jasper said, playing down the importance of this man to W.

"Bruce knew him?" Kate's voice was unusually loud.

"I wouldn't say knew," Harry remarked, trying to ease Kate's concern.

"Why wasn't I told?"

"You know Bruce," Clare interjected. "He didn't want to worry you."

Oliver was starting to fidget.

"Oliver! What is it?" asked Kate.

"I've got to tell you. Bruce broke his nose. Blood poured down his face. The next day, Bruce and his team went away to work."

"The day Bruce suffered his heart attack." Kate's soft voice hit a chord with all of them. She stood and looked out of the bi-fold doors, recalling that day. "They cremated him before I could see him," she mumbled in a dreamlike voice. "They said they didn't want me to see him. They said his injuries were severe after the fall. I wasn't his next of kin. They had already contacted his wife."

An expectant silence lingered as they waited for Kate.

"They say love is blind. I should have realised that Bruce was hiding something back then." Her eyes had glazed over.

Jasper stood and tried to put his arm around her, but she shrugged him away.

"But how did they know about his wife?" she murmured.

"Kate, you're overthinking." Jasper's voice was calm as he tried to defuse her impending melt-down.

"She had a smug look on her face. She didn't care for him. But she wanted my money to pay for the funeral costs. I wonder how much she was paid to upset me."

Another long silence settled between them.

"All the time, that evil bastard W's tentacles were spreading into my life."

Kate didn't notice that her sons shared an uncomfortable look.

***

Isaacs House was still and silent when Kate left their bedroom. She had never felt the need for revenge before, but she was determined to hit W where it would hurt.

She closed the library door behind her and moved the shelf that hid the secret room. She opened her old laptop, the one with the NRJ bank app on from the days when the bank was hacked. Robotically, she connected it to the mains electricity and the old router. The laptop burst into life. She waited while the app updated and scrolled to the Lord Wellsbury account. She scanned the list of deposits. Ten million pounds.

Without a second thought, she opened her secret Cayman account that she used as a holding account for money she intended to transfer.

***

A week later, a man Jasper referred to as Ferret rang the doorbell. Clare answered the door and shouted for Jasper.

Kate had an uneasy feeling about the man, particularly when Jasper closed the front door and walked outside with him instead of inviting him in for coffee. She asked Malcolm if he knew this man, but he was evasive, and that made Kate feel very nervous.

"Well?" said Kate when Jasper returned from seeing Ferret out of the front gate.

"Kate, you don't want to know."

"I do want to know." Her eyes flared.

"Ferret is a snitch that changes sides."

"I don't understand."

"He wanted money for information about W."

Kate looked at Jasper. "Go on."

"W is in a private clinic. He had some bad news, and he's had some kind of relapse. There's a lot of gossip. Apparently, he was at the theatre with Joanne, and he unexpectedly left. According to his neighbours he was shouting and raving. One of them watched Joanne hurrying out of the house. Apparently, W's NRJ bank account was hacked. Millions disappeared. Ferret reckoned that had something to do with his relapse. He was fishing to see if I had something to do with the hacking."

Jasper intently watched Kate. He suspected she had hacked W's account, but there wasn't a flicker of emotion on her face.

Jasper's gut churned in that "be careful" manner. Kate blamed W for Bruce's death.

"So! This Ferret is now your snitch." There was a twinge of sarcasm in Kate's voice.

"He has information that certain people will pay for. You don't trust the guy. He'll knife anyone in the back. He has no loyalty."

"Why did he come to you?"

"He needs money, or so he says, and he knew there's bad blood between me and W."

Jasper studied Kate's stiffening features; she was in turmoil.

"Come here." His voice was calm. "I should take you to bed and let you ride me."

"Sex isn't the answer to everything," she said into his shoulder.

"I can feel your tension. It needs to be released."

"Jasper, I've done a terrible thing."

"I know. But I don't believe W's in a clinic. I think he had a bad attack of Carmichael darkness. He's trying to flush me out." Jasper paused. "Ferret did say Joanne and Bart are together."

Kate pulled away from him and stared into his caring eyes.

"Bedroom or studio. You do your best work in the studio," he said mischievously.

"W had something to do with Bruce."

"Fuck Bruce, Kate. I'm here, wanting you."

She took his hand and led him into the studio.

***

The studio was shrouded in darkness. Kate lay naked on Jasper's chest.

"What's wrong?" she asked.

"Did you do that with Bruce?"

"No. Just you."

A warm glow filled Jasper; he kissed her hair.

"Bruce wouldn't let me. Even when I was as tight as a spring. I believe he wanted me to be on the edge," she added. "That's why I looked for other distractions."

Jasper put his arms around her. "What if I suggested that Bruce isn't dead?"

Kate tried to wriggle free but Jasper held on to her.

"Hear me out. Why was the body cremated before you could get there? Everyone knew you two were an item—why was his wife there? And why was he working away? There was no need."

Jasper felt a tear on his chest.

"Are you saying he didn't love me?" Kate said. "That he played me?"

"I think his love was genuine, but someone may have been pulling his strings. No hot-blooded man would refuse what you just did without a reason."

"It's diamonds, isn't it?"

"W had me where he wanted, but he couldn't get into my money and diamonds."

"But I could."

"That's what Bruce was supposed to do. But they didn't know you had found Zak's money and diamonds, and they didn't know that you were slowly using that money to your advantage."

"You're accepting that Old Jasper had a secret family and W is from that family?"

"It makes sense."

"W is your nemesis."

"I think I have two. W and Bruce."

Kate wasn't so sure. W and Bruce may have wished Jasper harm and thought his diamond fortune was undeserved, but as far as she was concerned, diamonds were Jasper's nemesis.

Chapter Twenty-Four

Bruce stood opposite the beach house studio. The studio that he had lovingly built for Kate. For a moment, he imagined she was with him; they would exchange a smile. He thought of those happy times when they had walked along the beach, arms wrapped around each other; he saw her naked under him as he tenderly loved her.

A sudden gust of wind disturbed his memories, just as it had many times before, masking her delightful cries as he entered her.

Kate was the only woman he had ever loved; no woman had stirred his emotions like her. He missed her.

But her heart belonged to Jasper.

His biggest regret was never letting her vent her emotions. But W had wanted her on an edge. He'd thought that would make her more likely to make a mistake and lead them to Jasper's fortune.

Bruce had always been jealous of that fortune, and it was that jealousy that W played on. If Bruce worked for him, he would have all the riches Jasper had—including Kate. He had fallen into W's trap.

With a heavy heart, he sprinkled petrol over the studio. Just has he was about to drop a match onto the petrol-soaked veranda, from the corner of his eye he glimpsed a painting on Kate's easel.

Memories of that day flashed before his eyes. It was one of those summer days that stick in your mind. Blue sky, a gentle breeze, the sun glistening off the water as yachts sail by. She was painting a seascape, with only a flimsy dress for cover. She had turned to him and smiled as she flicked her greying locks. He'd caught her hand, and the paint-brush dropped on the sand. Her eyes were on fire as he lifted her dress.

"Don't make me wait."

He pulled the bi-fold doors open and lifted the painting. He held it tightly under his arm as he watched the flames gulp their food. When the flames poked through the roof, he walked back to his car, which he had left in the lane. He cursed Ferret, as it was his failure to get Jasper to say anything about W that had sent W into one of his rages, laughing at the thought of Bruce destroying the studio he had built for the woman he loved. W wanted to hurt Kate. If she was in turmoil, Jasper would be as well.

Bruce drove from the burning studio, thinking of Jasper. But Jasper was a loner; he trusted no one except Kate. W had a team watching and wait-ing for Jasper to make a mistake. Jasper wouldn't stand a chance against so many men. Then Kate would be Bruce's for the taking.

***

It was Sunday, and they were all in the kitchen, laughing at Oliver's Saturday night antics, when the special delivery arrived for Kate. Malcolm found a Stanley knife, opened the package and lifted out the painting.

"Kate, this is wonderful," said Jasper, admiring her work.

She didn't look at the seascape. The summer sun reflecting off the calm sea. Small yachts lazily sailing towards the horizon. Only Bruce knew what the painting meant to her.

She turned and ran out of the kitchen, tears streaming down her face. Her mind brimming with the memories of that summer day when she and Bruce had loved one another.

Jasper ran after her. He caught her arm as she turned into the old orchard.

"Tell me!"

"He's alive." She gulped between tears.

Jasper gripped her shoulders and stared into her teary eyes. "Tell me what that painting means to you."

An uneasy silence lay between them.

"It was a beautiful summer's day. One of those days you never forget."

"I can see that."

Kate dipped her head so she wouldn't look into his eyes. How could she look at him? He would see the love they'd shared that day.

"The bastard." Jasper was pacing up and down the orchard. "He knew you would recognise that painting. You paint with your emotions. Love oozes from the canvas. He sent it to get at me. To show me how much you loved him."

Jasper's jealous turmoil was tearing her apart. She started to walk away. Jasper caught her arm.

"You're mine. Do you understand? You love *me*." He crashed their mouths together, his tongue forcing her lips open as she lost her balance and fell onto the grass.

"God, I want to fuck you!"

"Well. Do it."

Their angry eyes flared.

With one hand, he held her arms above her head. With his other hand, he deftly flicked open the button on her jeans.

He hesitated, and she said in her calm, soft tone, "Kiss me."

***

W had smiled and almost did a happy dance when Bruce had explained his plan to get at Jasper. Bruce had rapturously described that idyllic day when he had seduced Kate from her painting. He lied about how she'd screamed when he made her come.

Kate would know what that painting meant. Jasper wouldn't be able to control his anger. All they had to do was wait for Jasper to make a mistake.

Chapter Twenty-Five

Inspector Lewis sauntered through the shopping centre office as if he owned it.

He shouted, "Kate!"

Kate looked up from her laptop to see him in the office doorway. "Lewis, this is a surprise."

Loud footsteps echoed after him.

"What do you want?" Jasper's angry voice filled Kate's small office. Neither Kate nor Lewis turned to look at him.

A heavy silence lingered.

Lewis stepped closer to Kate's desk. "I have some bad news." He paused, making sure he had Kate's attention. "Your love studio has been burnt to the ground."

Kate stared at Jasper. It had taken all of her love-making skill to reassure Jasper that she loved him, and Lewis's choice of words was undoing that.

"I thought you'd retired, Lewis," said Jasper.

"I have, except for baby-sitting you two."

Jasper moved to stand by Kate.

"The local police have been." Lewis reached into his inside jacket pocket. Six photos fell in front of Kate.

She looked at each in turn. "I'll deal with it."

Lewis was taken aback at Kate's unemotional response. "There are costs."

Kate stood. "I said I'll deal with it." Her soft tone had disappeared.

"The man, Bruce, who built it, is dead," Lewis said.

"I know who built it."

"A love present. He must have loved you very much."

The inspector's eyes moved from Kate to Jasper. Kate's features were emotionless, but Jasper's had stiffened. A half smile crossed the inspector's face. *Reaction,* he thought. The voice on the phone would be pleased.

"Make sure you emphasise it was a love gift," he had said.

"You've delivered your message." There was anger in Kate's voice now. "There's the door. Use it."

"That's no way to talk to an old friend."

"You have a strange understanding of the word 'friend'."

Kate stood and walked to the door; her hand rested on the handle. The inspector glared at her. He couldn't recall a time when she had been so uncooperative. But her stony silence unnerved him, and he reluctantly left the office.

Kate closed the door and turned into Jasper's waiting arms.

"Don't," she said, burying her head into his chest.

"I'm going to comfort my wife in her hour of despair."

"I can't believe Bruce would destroy the studio. He knew full well what it meant to me."

After a long, silent moment: "I need you to kiss me, Jasper, and tell me you love me."

His long kiss was full of passion.

"Let's drive to the beach house," she said.

"Now?!"

"I want to say goodbye."

"We'll rebuild, Kate. To your exacting requirements."

"No! It's over. Nature can have it back."

"You don't mean it. You're overreacting."

Jasper held on to her. He could feel her tension building.

No one does this to my Kate, he thought. *They have no idea what awaits them.*

***

Kate was silent as Jasper drove the Evoque to the beach house. She jumped from the passenger seat as soon as he stopped. He expected her to race to the studio, but to his surprise she threw her work jacket and shoes onto the back seat. Her white blouse was open to her cleavage, and her grey trousers rested on her hips. The tie that had held her hair back was in her hand. She flicked her head, and her hair rested on her shoulders. She smiled "I love you." He looped his arm around her shoulders, and they strolled to the studio remains.

He was surprised to feel her lift his shirt and her fingers caress his back. He kissed her hair.

"There's nothing left, Kate, except the fireplace, charred kitchen and bathroom fittings. We were lucky the trees and brambles didn't catch fire."

Her hand squeezed his side.

"Let's walk," she said.

They stopped and sat at the edge of the gully.

"He's here, Kate."

"I know."

"Wait here. Don't move."

She lay on the grass and Jasper kissed her.

Bruce and two of his team had separated and were circling where they thought Kate and Jasper lay.

Jasper hid in the bushes and waited for the man to cross his path. A blow to the man's head, and he fell unconscious. Jasper heard the familiar call whistle of W's team. He didn't have to wait long before the other team member found his friend. Silently, Jasper crept up behind him, and with his arm tightly wrapped around the man's neck, he lowered him next to his teammate. Jasper lifted the gun from his belt.

Bruce was easy to find. He was staring at Kate. His mind was so full of her that he didn't hear Jasper sneak up behind him.

"When you get into bed with the devil, expect his nemesis to seek revenge."

Bruce whipped around to face Jasper holding a gun. Before he could react, Jasper put a bullet into his head.

Jasper wiped the gun and returned it to its owner, but not before shooting the man's friend in the head. He lifted the first dead man's gun and shot the other man. The scene looked like the men had shot each other.

Jasper returned to Kate. She hadn't moved. He held out his hand and pulled her up. He thought she would mention the gunshots, but she just looked into his eyes.

"I loved this beach. It's been my solace on so many occasions. I've been happy here."

"We'll find another beach. Our beach."

"Let's not make any plans until we've finished."

Chapter Twenty-Six

"So, we're expecting the police?" Clare was more than a little miffed. "Did you see him?"

Kate guessed Clare was referring to Bruce. "No."

"He's dead, you know. Don't you feel anything?"

"Of course I do. But I've already grieved bucketloads for Bruce."

"How do you know it's him?"

"The painting and—"

Clare cut in. "Anyone could have sent that."

"It had a special meaning for us. Only Bruce knew that."

"Hello, Kate."

She turned from the office French doors and half smiled at Inspector Lewis.

"I hope you're in a better mood," he said.

Clare bustled in with coffee and biscuits. Kate pointed to the couch for Lewis to sit.

"Where is he?" asked Lewis after Clare had poured his coffee.

"Here, Inspector." Jasper strolled in and leaned close to Kate, brushing his lips by her ear.

"I was surprised to find out you two are back together."

"Water under the bridge and all that," Jasper casually replied. He sat in a comfy chair and crossed his legs.

"You look well, Jasper. Better than I anticipated," remarked Lewis.

"I've had excellent care." Jasper smiled at Kate.

Lewis turned his attention back to Kate. "Sorry to ask you, Kate, but would you identify a body that we believe to be Bruce?"

"Ask his wife," was her curt reply.

"Look, I'm sorry about the first time, but I had nothing to do with it."

Kate returned to the French doors.

"There's people in high places who want these three men identified," Lewis explained.

Kate turned. "Three?"

"You didn't know?"

"Of course I didn't."

Jasper fidgeted in his chair.

"I visit his grave, and now I'm told you've found his body. Who the fuck is in the grave?" Kate snapped as she tried to hide the emotional turmoil that was tearing her apart.

Jasper uncrossed his legs and stood. "I don't like my wife being upset."

"A bit rich, coming from you," Lewis remarked.

A dark scowl descended upon Jasper's face.

A hand gently lay on his arm.

Kate looked into Jasper's eyes and waited for her emotions to settle. "Where's the body?" she quietly said.

"London. I'll send you the address. Like I said, people in high places are interested in this case."

***

Kate leaned back in the first-class seat of the London train. Jasper sat opposite her. She smiled as she watched his eyes move over the laptop screen. Her Jasper was back to his old self.

When she'd returned from seeing Lewis to the front door, Jasper was pacing the office. His fiery eyes had met hers.

"I won't have you upset. Police or not."

His ruffled clothes and hair had stirred her. The top of her thighs ached; her body quivered as her inner self ignited. She'd stood in front of him and slowly opened his shirt. Her lips grazed his chest.

"Don't make me wait."

He'd lifted her into his arms and carried her into the studio.

Jasper was on fire. She couldn't recall their clothes falling onto the floor or lying on the chaise lounge. All she remembered was their overwhelming desire for one another. They were no longer young, but age hadn't diminished their passion.

"I'm going to make you mine," he had whispered.

And she wanted to be his, completely.

She had gasped when he marked her delicate breasts.

"No one else sees or touches these."

He was big; he had waited for her to adjust to his size. When he had moved inside her, she had moaned and slipped over the edge. Her fingernails had dug into his shoulders. He hadn't let her recover; his mouth had consumed hers as he massaged her breasts.

"Make me yours," he had murmured.

He'd pulled her on top of him. His strong hands controlled her movements. She screamed when a second orgasm had ripped through her.

She had lain in his arms, exhausted.

"Kate…"

His lips had caressed her eyes, nose, ears. He had nibbled at her lips while his fingers circled her body. Every nerve in her body had quivered as he loved her in the most tender fashion. Their hearts had opened as they moved together slowly and lovingly. He had murmured words of love as her third orgasm slowly built.

They had climaxed together while their inner selves celebrated.

Chapter Twenty-Seven

Kate sat in a darkened Isaacs House kitchen and played the day's events over and over in her mind. She lifted her favourite china mug from the cupboard and filled it with tea. She sat on a stool, elbows on the work surface, and her hands surrounded her tea.

Her mind overflowed with Jasper and their love. She thought that maybe he really did love her more than diamonds. But the London trip had put doubt in her mind.

***

A new Range Rover had been waiting for them when they left the station, a smartly dressed man leaning on the passenger door. He'd exchanged a nod with Jasper and handed him the key fob.

Jasper had smiled at Kate as she joined him with their bags, except Jasper's messenger bag, which was slung across his shoulders.

Kate's world had collapsed when they reached the morgue where Bruce lay. A single bullet to his head, Carmichael style. She had stared at Bruce's lifeless form and wondered how long he had deceived her. Was his love for her ever real? She believed at the beginning they had truly loved each other. If she had given herself to him, then this whole debacle would probably never have happened.

She'd nodded to the attendant and walked along a poorly lit corridor to where Jasper waited.

Jasper had wrapped his arm around Kate as they walked to his car. He'd planted a comforting kiss upon her cheek before he filtered into the traffic.

"I have something to tell you. It happened some time ago. It involves grandfather and his wartime activities. Diamonds."

Kate had turned and stared at Jasper when he mentioned the time when he'd been active in the House of Lords. He'd stayed in London while she'd looked after their Wellsbury business. Diamonds sprang into her mind.

Jasper had been leaving the House of Lords when a peer dressed in a Saville Row suit had walked alongside him. Jasper had refused to give Kate his name. He had said that it was irrelevant now the man was dead.

He had given Jasper a slip of paper with numbers and an address. He had told him that the paper had been entrusted to him to give to the last surviving Carmichael.

His story began at the height of the Second World War, when a group of power-hungry men had seen an opportunity to make themselves rich beyond all imagination. Diamonds had been in short supply and great demand. Their idea was simple: stockpile diamonds in a secret location. When the war ended, they could slowly sell the diamonds to the highest bidder.

They financed a railway line that disappeared underground and stopped at a natural cave—an ideal place to stash diamonds. Jasper's grandfather was key to the operation as he moved freely between the governments of Britain and America carrying diplomatic papers and diamonds.

But their plan never came to fruition. The Germans bombed the railway line and the entrance to the underground cave collapsed. But one of the team never gave up. He found the entrance to the cave and had it sealed with a steel door with a coded lock. By this time, he was old and in poor health. His name was Carmichael.

Jasper had turned off the main road, onto a weed-strewn concrete track.

"London has changed so much since the war, and still is. I believe this row of warehouses will be affordable homes."

He'd stopped and pointed to a steel track poking through the concrete outside a large derelict warehouse that was now home to rough sleepers. He drove inside and circled the damp, dark warehouse several times before the Range Rover headlights picked out the outline of a doorway that was nestled in the back. Kate had watched Jasper scrape away years of dirt to reveal a steel door. He used his iPhone torch to find the keypad. He'd punched in the code, but nothing happened. After several attempts, there was a faint click, and with the help of his shoulder, the door opened onto a flight of stairs that ended at another keypad-controlled door. It opened into a small cave.

Stale air had rushed past them, but their eyes were mesmerised by a bank of drawers that resembled safety deposit boxes. Each needed a code to open.

Kate had stood back and stared in horror at Jasper's smiling face. Like a magnet is attracted to iron, Jasper was attracted to the boxes. Kate had walked away with tears dripping down her face. She had lost him again to the Carmichael diamond curse.

The thought of Jasper being reinstated as the diamond king of the underworld frightened her.

Most of the journey back to Isaacs House had been in silence. Kate had been mourning the loss of Jasper to his grandfather's diamonds, while Jasper's mind had swirled with how he was going to become the diamond king.

***

Kate jumped when two hands gripped her shoulders and soft kisses were planted on her neck.

"We can do this, Kate."

"Do what?"

"Buy and sell diamonds on the black market."

"What about W? He'll be more determined to kill you."

"I'm too slippery for him."

"I don't like the way you're thinking."

"Look at it as the Jasper Carmichael legacy for Harry and Oliver."

She whipped around to face him, but he had anticipated her move and claimed her mouth. His kiss was deep and passionate. Whatever resistance Kate had thought she had disappeared as her hand cupped his head. He lifted her onto the kitchen work surface and pulled open the tie of her robe. Her head leaned back as he nuzzled her breasts.

"You're a bastard."

"I know, but I'm your bastard."

***

W had been dining at his club when a waiter leaned close to him. "Excuse me, sir. There's a man at the door that insists on seeing you."

W swallowed his food. "Name?" he abruptly answered, annoyed at having his meal interrupted.

"No name. If I may, he's a little unsavoury."

"What do you mean, man?" W snapped.

"He could do with a wash."

"Get rid of him, man."

"He won't leave, sir. He's making a scene in the foyer."

W glared at the waiter. With force, he shoved his chair back and marched out of the dining room.

A stale smell drifted up the stairs from the foyer. The man stood by the small counter, tapping his foot.

W stopped midway down the stairs. The man looked like his snitch, but that man was dead by his own hand.

The man immediately recognised W, and a sly smile crept across his dirty face.

W hurried down the stairs. "Outside, man. What are you thinking? This is a private club."

He lifted an umbrella from the stand just inside the street door and poked the man.

"I've got some info for yo."

W brushed his suit jacket as if the man had touched him. "I don't think so."

"Yo 'ad a meeting with 'im. The night 'e was stabbed."

W froze. He immediately knew his snitch must have told this man about the meeting. He reached into his inside pocket for his wallet.

"Yo owe me double."

"For?"

"That night, and for the black knight."

W started to walk, and the man followed.

"What about the black knight."

"'E's bin with 'is bitch."

"When."

"This after. Put numbers into the door."

"And."

"Opened another door."

Excitement was building in W as thoughts of the rumoured wartime diamonds spilled into his mind.

"What was he carrying?"

"Couldn't see."

W took all the twenties out of his wallet.

"I don't want to see you again. Understood?"

"What if the black knight comes back?"

"He won't. He's got what he wants." W turned away and then added an afterthought. "Why do you call him the black knight?"

"Black Range Rover. Carmichael always drives a black Range Rover."

The man's voice had lost its accent. W stared at him. "Who are you?"

The man didn't answer, just walked away.

Chapter Twenty-Eight

"Jasper, what do you want from me?"

He had picked Kate up from the centre office for a walk along the river. His arm was casually looped around her shoulders.

"I've told you many times. I want you, Kate. All of you. Your mind. Your soul. Your body."

"There's something else."

"W emailed me a list of the diamonds from the cave."

Kate stopped. "How did he know?"

"I suppose there were stories about grandfather's diamonds."

"But how did he know we'd been there?"

"He has spies everywhere." Jasper kissed her hair. "Come on. I'll buy you a tea."

***

W sat in an Audi Q7 parked at the Riverside Café car park, listening to his team.

"They're walking towards the café. He has his hands all over her."

"Concentrate on what they're talking about," barked W.

***

Kate sat at the picnic table by the river. She smiled at Jasper when he put her tea on the table.

"Favourite spot," he said.

She gazed into his blue eyes. "I'll never tire of this view."

"You didn't tell me the café's closing," he said.

"I'm buying Molly's share."

"Why? Sell to the highest bidder. This spot must be worth a fortune. Look at that view."

Jasper stopped and looked at Kate. She was so relaxed and happy.

"You don't get it," she said. "This is worth more to me than money."

Jasper stared at the café, imagining it demolished and a new build in its place. "Who owns the land?"

"I own most of it. The council complained that the path along the river was costing too much to maintain, so I bought it for people to enjoy." She paused and smiled. "They rewarded me by not using it."

"It's not a public path, then?"

"No. Years ago, the owner of the café owned the rights to the footpath, and then the council."

***

W cursed. Jasper and Kate were talking Wellsbury stuff. Who cared who owned the café and river path?

His ears pricked when Jasper said, "He wants to meet."

W anxiously waited for Kate's reply, but instead she stood from the picnic table and walked to the river's edge. Jasper joined her and slipped his arms around her waist.

W swore when his team confirmed that they were out of range for sound surveillance.

***

"I can't meet him without you," Jasper whispered in her ear.

"Give him the diamonds. We don't need them."

"What do you think of me becoming a legit diamond trader? Buying and selling at auctions. Being part of the diamond community. I'm sure they'd have me. I'm good at trading."

She turned so their lips touched. His fingers trailed her hairline. He was on tenterhooks, waiting for her to kiss him. Her lips hovered over his as if she was deciding if she should kiss him. Her hand reached for the back of his neck, and her mouth slowly covered his. Jasper's stomach nervously flipped. She tilted her head to one side, and he took control. He felt her passion, desire. A sigh escaped his mouth as she consumed it.

***

W glared at them kissing. He thumped the steering wheel, his dark Carmichael temper stirring. He started the engine, released the handbrake and skidded out of the car park.

It was obvious to him that Jasper and his wife were one. W would have to kill both to have his revenge. If he killed Kate first, the darkness in Jasper would surface. Jasper's revenge would be swift and painful. If he killed Jasper first, what would Kate do? She was an unknown entity, but he feared that her ruthless Spencer streak would surface.

W stopped the Audi in the lane above Carmichael's airfield and walked through the wood. He stopped and stared at the airfield. It looked deserted, but it always did. His mind flashed back to the people for whom the airfield had played a part in their demise.

Anton, the South American who wanted Carmichael dead for the deeds of his father, Colin Carmichael. There was Beth, Jasper's ex-lover, who had betrayed him and aspired to run a drug business from the airfield with Gypsy, the drug dealer. And there was Duncan, one of his own undercover men; money had lured him to work for Michaels and Manning. When Duncan had failed to kill Kate, Michaels had panicked and asked W for help. Who else could he have asked to organise a hit squad at the drop of a hat?

Memories of the past weren't helping with his problem: how to kill Jasper and his beloved Kate.

He should have finished off Jasper years ago, but he'd had to prove that he was the better Carmichael first. Then, like so many Carmichaels, he had fallen into the diamond trap. Diamonds had made Jasper rich, and W wanted those riches, particularly now that Jasper had found his father's wartime diamonds.

W couldn't get the image of Jasper and Kate kissing out of his mind. The way their bodies had melted together as their mouths joined. Her tilting her head and him taking control. The mesmerising movements of her hand through his hair.

W's hand moved through his hair, and his stomach churned. He would have to kill both of them at the same time.

He started to pace, and he started to plan, when the black Carmichael temper that nourished his soul surfaced. He tugged on his hair, his cries of despair echoed, his heart thumped with rage, his blue eyes bulged in his red face. He ranted and raved until he was exhausted and fell onto the earth, crying and shaking as the pent-up darkness flowed through him.

Chapter Twenty-Nine

It was dark when W opened his eyes. He was cold and shivering. He now knew what he should do, and that was to hire an assassin. He was prepared to pay top dollar. Half before the job, and the rest when he had seen the dead bodies. He planned to smile at the assassin and congratulate him, and when the man let his guard down, W would kill him. He could have no loose ends.

He stood and brushed down his clothes. He needed to recover from his Carmichael tantrum. He would never admit to the Carmichael demons. Did Jasper have similar episodes? W supposed he had Kate to soothe his inner soul.

He needed rest and solitude to find an assassin. He started the Audi and headed towards his country estate. He would have to open it up and re-employ his staff. He needed to be looked after and pampered.

***

While the Carmichael demons were tearing W apart, Kate and Jasper were driving to W's country estate.

Jasper wanted to familiarise himself with the layout of the estate and plant cameras and listening devices around the mansion. This was the only way he could anticipate W's next move. Now that he had his grandfather's diamonds, their lives were in danger.

Jasper reverse-parked the Range Rover in a farm gateway that bordered W's estate. He could just make out Kate's face in the moonlight. His hand cupped her cheek, and she leaned into it.

"Remember, if I'm not back within thirty minutes, you go. No waiting—and if someone tries to get you out of the car, you drive."

Jasper felt a lone tear trickle down her cheek.

He lifted his knapsack from the rear seat, slipped out of the driving seat and jogged towards W's country mansion. He stopped and listened when the outer security light didn't come on. He focused his night-vision goggles on the house, which was in darkness. He stood perfectly still, his stomach churning. Thoughts of a trap whizzed through his head.

I'm Jasper Carmichael, who always does the unexpected.

He sprinted towards the balcony that opened into W's study.

He stopped beneath the balcony. He was out of breath, and his heart thumped in his ears.

If he remembered correctly, the electrical controls were hidden under the balcony. He lay on the ground, and by the light of his iPhone torch, he found the control box. The electricity was off.

W was not at home.

Jasper raced to the balcony French doors, the only weakness in W's security system, and eased the doors open with a small crowbar from his knapsack. He was tempted to go through W's papers, but he had to stick to his plan of bugging the house with cameras and listening devices. He already had an idea where he would hide the devices: study, bedroom, kitchen, living room and W's office.

The office was normally locked, but W had been careless. The banks of computers and screens

139

were switched off. Jasper stumbled on papers that littered the floor by the desk. He collected them and stuffed them in his knapsack. He was banking on W having swept the papers from his desk in a temper fit. If W's fits were anything like his, he wouldn't remember scattering the papers.

Jasper closed the balcony doors and jogged back to his beloved. He knew she'd be waiting, even though he had taken more than half an hour.

He opened the Range Rover passenger door, but Kate wasn't there. A hot sweat swelled through him as the contents of his stomach swirled.

He whipped around at the sound of rustling hedgerow.

"You really are a piece of work." Her soft, quiet tone immediately settled his churning stomach as she stepped out of hiding. "My nerves are torn to pieces. You've been—"

He didn't let her finish; his hands cupped her face while his lips devoured her mouth.

"Kate! Kate!" he whispered as he pulled her into his chest. "My love. I thought I'd lost you."

***

W had stopped at a motorway service station. He hated these places. They were cheap, plasticky and overpriced, but when needs must, you have to swallow your pride.

He had strolled back to the Audi carrying a coffee in a plastic cup and sandwiches wrapped in plastic. He wondered how many hydrocarbons he had subjected his body to. He was sitting in the driving seat, balancing his cheese sandwich on his knees and sipping coffee when his phone rang. He pressed answer.

"What?" he barked.

"Where are you? I've been trying to get you," said Tom, who was in charge of W's security.

"Where am I? Where am I! I'll tell you where I am. I'm at some fucking service station surrounded by unclean humans parading through the car park, smoking god knows what, eating pizza and drop-ping the boxes on the floor. I'm choking on dishwa-ter coffee and eating a plastic cheese sandwich."

W's rant was water off a duck's back for Tom; he was used to it.

"We're at your country pad—"

"Good," W interrupted. "Open it up. Contact the staff and my driver. I need the Bentley, it's in Lon-don."

Tom thought it best not to ask W why he wasn't in the Bentley.

"Carmichael's missing."

"He'll be there," W said.

"There's no sign of anyone. It's all locked up."

"Have you checked?"

"Yes."

"Get some men at that beach house."

"There's nothing there."

"Trust me, he'll be there with her. Fucking on the beach. I want to know where he is."

Tom phoned his men. "Kill them."

If W wouldn't give the instruction, he would. Carmichael must die.

Chapter Thirty

Clothes were strewn along the gully that led to the sea. The only sound was waves crashing against rocks.

Jasper stood staring at the incoming tide. Kate lay on a blanket that nestled in the sand.

"What's wrong?" she asked.

"He knows we're here."

Kate sat up and grabbed her white blouse. "You don't know that."

"They'll use the tide to bring their boat close to the beach."

Jasper turned to face her and smiled as she tried to wiggle into her panties.

"If we're expecting company, I think we should leave," she said.

"You glowed in the moonlight. You're beautiful, Kate."

Kate had found her jeans and was shaking the sand from them.

"You took advantage of me. I was on an edge. Waiting for you. Terrified that W had found you." She pulled on her jeans.

He took her arm and stared into her sparkling green eyes. "I remember every sigh, every cry and *don't make me wait*."

"Jasper, do you have to?"

"It'll be something nice to remember, when I kill our visitors."

"What?! Jasper, no!"

"They intend to kill us, Kate."

"You don't know that."

He smiled. "Oh, but I do. It's exactly what I would do."

***

Kate collected their belongings and walked back to the Range Rover, which Jasper had left in the lane. She knew what Jasper was going to do; she had witnessed his ability to kill without any remorse.

Jasper was keeping out of sight in the treeline that followed the beach. He didn't have to wait too long before the outline of a boat rounded the rocks at the end of the beach. He was surprised that W's men were in a speedboat. *W must be in a hurry.*

He moved quickly between the rocks while the men concentrated on beaching the boat. He slipped into the sea and waded to the boat. When he lifted his head over the stern, the men were busy sorting their weapons. A wave of nervous energy consumed Jasper as the men checked their rifles. But he was more interested in the handguns that were sticking out of their belts.

The men stood in a line facing the beach, with one talking. This was just the distraction Jasper needed. He lifted himself onto the deck and picked up the large fishing gaff that was lying along the port side. When one of the men turned, Jasper leapt forward, hitting him hard in the throat with the gaff. Before the man landed on the deck, Jasper had sidestepped to snatch the man's gun from his belt. The shocked would-be assassins reached for their guns, but Jasper had released the safety on his and fired two shots in quick succession. They fell.

Without a second thought, he stood over each man in turn and put a second bullet in their heads.

Something had changed in W's mind; he was in a hurry to kill Jasper and Kate.

Jasper started the speedboat and gently moved the throttle, easing the boat off the beach. He slowly manoeuvred the boat so it faced towards the sea and the line of rocks that the high tide covered.

There was no room for mistakes in what he planned to do. He took a moment to calm himself before he moved the throttle to maximum. As soon as the boat moved, Jasper leapt onto the side and dived into the sea. He surfaced as the boat hit the rocks. The engine didn't cut as Jasper had expected, but caught fire. Flames ripped through the boat, and it disintegrated.

The tide was coming in fast, and the sea covered his waist. He wasn't concerned about the water but the woman racing along its edge. She splashed towards him, tears running down her face. She flung her arms around his neck and kissed him. He held her close as their tongues gently played.

Jasper's demons needed her special touch.

"I want you," he murmured.

"Take me."

"I want to fuck you."

"Do it."

He carried her out of the sea and marched to the trees.

She opened her blouse and unfastened her bra. He looked down onto her full breasts. Jasper's body was on fire; he needed to rough fuck. He pinned her against a tree and squeezed each breast as his mouth swallowed her cries. He frantically pushed her jeans to the grassy earth. He cupped her sex and lifted her. His lust for her was out of control as he forced his fingers inside her.

144

She screamed. He lifted his hand to slap her, and stopped, his hand in mid-air.

She was sobbing.

His demons were surging, but he stared into Kate's gleaming eyes. Tears were gushing down her cheeks. He touched her sex, and she screamed again.

He let go of her and she collapsed, her body shaking as she sobbed.

"Kate…" His concerned voice just above a whisper.

He was confused; his demons tried to take control—but he had hurt his Kate, the woman he loved. His love for her flooded past his demons. His hand moved to stroke her face when he noticed blood on his hand. His eyes moved to the top of her thighs. Blood.

"Oh, Kate! I'm so sorry." He lifted her to his chest. "Kate. Kate, answer me!" He pleaded.

She had passed out.

***

Kate woke in the back of the Range Rover. Her breasts hurt, her back ached, and her sex was extremely sore.

She gazed at Jasper. Tears were streaming down his face.

"I hurt, Jasper…"

"You're bleeding, Kate. Oh God, Kate. I made you bleed. I'm taking you to Max for a check-up."

She slipped back into the darkness.

***

Her eyes focused on a bright white ceiling. She blinked and tried to work out where she was. There was a smell that was vaguely familiar. The bed she lay in wasn't her own and it was small. There was not enough space for Jasper.

"She's awake, doctor!" shouted an unfamiliar female voice.

A hand gripped hers and cold lips pressed against hers. Jasper. Kate looked up into teary eyes.

"Lady Carmichael. You have a vaginal tear. You're bloody lucky that it didn't need a stitch. If I was you, I'd leave him. No man should do what he's done to you. Accident or not." The doctor turned his attention to Jasper. "Here's a bag with all the medical supplies Kate will need. Don't forget she must finish the antibiotic course."

An uneasy silence filled the room.

"This will cost you, Carmichael."

Jasper put his hand in his waistcoat pocket and pulled out a small polythene bag. He carefully opened the bag, and four diamonds dropped into his palm. "Will this cover everything?"

Max was mesmerised by the sparkling gems that Jasper had given him.

"Bloody hell, Jasper. They said you were back in business, but I didn't believe them."

"Do we understand one other?" said Jasper in a very harsh tone.

A nervous Max carefully wrapped the diamonds in a tissue and put them in his trouser pocket.

"There's a contract out on you."

Jasper nodded.

"You should leave the country. Think of Kate."

"I think of nothing else."

Jasper lifted Kate, and she put her arms around his neck. Their eyes met and Jasper kissed her forehead.

Chapter Thirty-One

Kate was dozing in the front passenger seat of the Range Rover. She was warm and comfortable, but above all, she felt safe.

"Where are we going?" she asked.

"You'll see."

"Why have you bought all this stuff?" she said, glancing over to the rear seat.

"We'll need it."

While Kate had been in Max's clinic, Jasper had been busy buying food, clothes, toiletries, burner phones, guns, cameras, listening devices—the list was endless. They might be in hiding for some time. He had no idea how long it would take to root W out, but he would succeed even if it cost him his life.

He drove for miles along deserted roads. Whenever he saw another car, he'd pull into a farm track and wait for it to pass, and all the time Kate slept.

He turned in to an overgrown track. Weeds scraped the sides of the Range Rover, and the track descended into a disused boatyard. His boatyard, Alwyn's old yard.

He left the Range Rover ticking over while he opened the workshop doors. Once they were safely inside, Jasper set the alarm.

Jasper had tried to anticipate W's next move. He would hire an assassin and suggest a place to kill Jasper. The boatyard had flashed into Jasper's mind. He knew the terrain blindfolded, and his yacht was nearby for a quick escape.

Two green eyes followed Jasper as he went about opening up the adjoining living area.

"What are you doing, and why are we here?" Kate sat on the side of the passenger seat with her legs dangling over the edge.

Jasper hurried towards her and lifted her from the Range Rover. His lips gently brushed hers.

"You can do better than that." Her hand pulled his head to hers.

"There's a bag next door. Fresh clothes. Max's tablets."

"Is there food?"

Jasper smiled; his Kate was feeling better.

***

The assassin sailed his small yacht into Jasper's harbour, which fed the channel to his boatyard.

The assassin looked every bit a sailor, in his shorts, T-shirt and boating shoes. He had made polite conversation with the old guy who sat outside the harbour hut. Of course, he hadn't mentioned Jasper.

"Just a couple of nights while I fix my yacht," he'd said and dropped the old guy twenty quid.

He had located buoy twenty-three and secured the yacht. His plan was simple: he would break into the workshops and shoot Jasper while he was fucking Kate.

He considered himself to be an authority on Jasper. The man had to have sex every day. That was no way to treat a woman like Kate. To Bruce, she'd been a princess; to him, she would be a queen. He wouldn't shoot Kate; she would be his until he'd had his fill of her delightful body.

The assassin trained his binoculars on the boat-yard. His stomach flipped when Kate strolled from the workshop. It had been years since he'd seen her, and she didn't look a day older. Her hair lay on her shoulders, her white blouse was open to her cleavage, and if he wasn't mistaken, she wasn't wearing a bra. Her jeans rested on her hips, and she was barefoot.

She's still sexy as hell, he thought.

She put her arms around Jasper's waist and pulled him against her.

Make the most of her, Jasper, for tonight will be your last.

***

"Can you feel it?" Kate whispered into Jasper's chest.

"Yes. We're being watched," he said into her hair.

"Can you see them?"

"My gut tells me there's only one and he's in the yacht that's just arrived."

Her grip tightened around his waist. "I'm frightened."

"Don't be." Jasper slipped his hands under her waistband and cupped her buttocks.

"Should we go inside?"

"Not yet. I want him to think that I'm going to fuck you."

"You're not?" said a surprised Kate.

"Good things come to those who wait."

Their lips met, and Kate didn't hide her pleasure.

***

The assassin's temper bubbled as he watched Jasper seduce Kate. Jasper had his arms wrapped tightly around her, and they slowly walked back to the workshop. The assassin cursed and threw his binoculars onto the deck.

***

Jasper locked the workshop door and walked into the living quarters.

"You can't leave me like this," Kate said. "I want you."

Jasper turned to see Kate undoing the buttons on her blouse.

"No! If we make love, we will be dead." He pulled her into him and kissed her hair. "Anyway, you're delicate down there. We'll have to wait."

Chapter Thirty-Two

The assassin sat on the side of his yacht, waiting for the right moment to swim to the boatyard. He should have surveyed the area surrounding the workshops, but he hadn't bothered—he was so confident that Jasper would be giving Kate three orgasms. His confidence was further boosted when the workshops remained in darkness.

From now on, I'll be giving her three orgasms, he thought as he slowly slid down into the water.

At that moment, while the assassin was distracted, Jasper had slipped out of the workshop's back door. He picked up a metal bar that he'd left by the door and carefully manoeuvred his way through the scrap metal that littered the boatyard.

The moon briefly appeared, outlining the assassin standing at the water's edge. Jasper swallowed his gasp of surprise. The assassin was none other than his private investigator, John, who he'd thought had been shot along with Duncan in the aircraft. He watched John kneel and scan the boatyard.

Jasper had no time to reminisce. He had a job to do, and concentration was everything.

John's gut was churning, just as it had that night at Jasper's airfield. Carmichael was watching. John tried to calm himself by taking an extra moment to scan the boatyard. His gut told him to retreat to his yacht and sail away. But he hesitated—he knew Jasper and was convinced that soon he would be fucking Kate. He stood and took a deep breath.

The moon had disappeared behind a bank of clouds, leaving the boatyard and workshops in total darkness. While John was hesitating, Jasper took advantage of the darkness and silently moved closer to John.

John could feel Jasper, but where was he? Jasper had a reputation for doing the unexpected. John erred on the side of caution and gingerly stepped back into the water.

Jasper couldn't see John, but he could hear him. In a desperate bid to hit him, Jasper swung the metal bar into the darkness.

The still night air was broken by the swish of the bar, taking John by surprise. He stepped to his side and lost his balance. He fell backwards into the water.

Jasper's ears pricked, and he moved towards the splash.

John righted himself and instinctively moved away from a menace he couldn't see. In his haste, his feet became stuck in the thick, deep mud. He clasped his hands around his thigh and tried to lift his leg, but he stumbled backward into deeper water.

Jasper heard the splashing of water as if John was struggling to right himself. Unbeknown to Jasper, John had fallen into the channel where the current was at its strongest.

***

W sat in a comfy chair in the study of his country house. He couldn't put his finger on why, but he couldn't relax. The study didn't feel right, almost as if someone had been in there. He had checked his desk, but he couldn't remember how he had left it.

He had been in a state after that episode with the Cohens.

He poured himself a brandy from the decanter he had on a small table next to his chair. John hadn't phoned him yet to say Jasper was dead.

John had argued that Jasper would never suspect him as he thought he was dead. John had known Jasper for years, doing various jobs for him and keeping a file on his dubious activities. He hadn't had to tell W that he had a thing for Kate—it was written all over his face whenever her name was mentioned.

John would never admit that he had double-crossed Jasper when he joined forces with Duncan. And likewise, W would never admit that he had secretly organised the hit that night at Jasper's airfield. When the plane had landed, W had expected two bodies, and he got them: Duncan and the man he'd sent to shoot John and Duncan. John had lain unconscious with blood oozing from his chest. W had thought he would be dead in twenty-four hours, but somehow John had escaped and survived.

W rubbed the back of his neck. He still had that feeling that something was wrong.

***

The stillness of the night had returned, and Jasper stood for some time staring into its blackness. He looked upwards, hoping the moon would appear from behind the thick cloud. He had no idea where John had disappeared to. Was he in the water? Had he made it back to his yacht?

Jasper was surrounded by the deep darkness of the night and water. He started to panic; a step in the wrong place he would be stuck in the mud.

Suddenly, Kate switched on the workshop outside light. It was as if she knew he needed her guiding light. Her special light that overcame his darkness.

She waited by the outside door until Jasper threw his arms around her.

"Jasper, as much as I like your cuddles, did you get him?"

"Sshh. It was John."

"John who?"

"The John you made eyes at."

After a long moment, she said, "I didn't make eyes at him. Anyway, he's dead."

"He is now," Jasper murmured hopefully.

***

It was early afternoon when a naked Kate strolled out of the bedroom and put her arms around Jasper's shoulders and kissed his neck.

"Thank you," she murmured in a low, sexy voice.

"For what?"

"For being so caring."

"Kate. I love you, but you're not ready to have me inside you."

Jasper pulled her onto his lap. He could count the times Kate had been happy enough in her own skin to wander around naked. He couldn't help but wonder if she had been like this with Bruce.

She rested her head on his shoulder as he trailed his fingers along her spine.

"We're going to London," he said.

"Not now, I hope. I haven't had tea." She giggled.

"Kate, sometimes you're incorrigible."

Their lips met, and one of her delightful sighs escaped her mouth.

Chapter Thirty-Three

Jasper had left Kate at the penthouse overlooking the Thames. He preferred to break into John's apartment alone.

Even though John had played dead for a number of years, he hadn't bothered to move to another apartment. Jasper thought this was a little odd. He should have gotten a new identity and moved.

The apartment was easy to break into; John hadn't changed the security code since the last time Jasper had snooped around the apartment. Jasper covered his face with his balaclava and pulled on a pair of latex gloves. He set a timer for thirty minutes on his Apple watch and moved to John's desk and computer. After a couple of tries, he found the password. 'Kate'

Jasper had come prepared to copy John's files onto a USB stick. He found the computer and set up the transfer. His eyes quickly scanned the living room, looking for a filing cabinet. He found it in the second bedroom, along with a wall dedicated to Kate.

Kate at the flower shop, Kate at his Wellsbury apartment, Kate sitting on her favourite thinking bench, Kate kissing Jasper, Kate kissing Bruce.

Jasper recoiled. John had been stalking Kate for years. If W had known, he would never have given John the contract.

In a jealous fit, Jasper tore the photographs off the wall and stuffed them into his messenger bag. *She's mine. She's mine,* repeated in his head.

In an angry state, he turned his attention to the filing cabinet. The Carmichael file was easy to find; it was at the front of the top drawer. He recorded the remainder of John's clients on his iPhone.

His watch buzzed, telling him his half hour was up. He hurried to the computer and was pleased to see that the copying was complete.

With some haste, he left the apartment and exited the building via the service entrance.

***

Jasper and Kate spent the next day in the penthouse. Occasionally, Kate would leave her drawings and put her arms around Jasper's neck and kiss his hair as he looked through John's computer files. He was studying John's detailed plans for how to break into W's country house. He didn't see Kate remove the photos of her from his messenger bag.

"When were you going to tell me about these?" she said, dropping them onto the laptop keyboard.

"I don't know. I shouldn't have ripped them off the wall, but I was so jealous. I had to do something."

"Jealous. In heaven's name, why were you jealous?"

"Jealous of the knowledge he'd been stalking you since the flower shop days. Jealous of his feelings for you. Jealous that he'd been that close to you, and I didn't know." Jasper stood and looked into her eyes. "You're mine, Kate. Right from the start, you've been mine."

"Jasper, I haven't any feelings for John."

"You had feelings for Bruce."

"Only because you shoved me away. I needed love, Jasper. Bruce gave me all the love I wanted."

"And sex."

"Yes! And sex. But I'll remind you that you had sex with many women. I had sex with one man." She stood on tiptoes and gently kissed his lips. "I love Jasper Carmichael. Only you. You fill my life with joy. Even though sometimes I want to hit you."

He pulled her close to him. "Come with me to-night."

"Where?"

"The country mansion. I don't think I can do this without you waiting."

***

W jumped up in bed. The security alarm was booming inside and outside the house. He grabbed his night robe and raced down the stairs to the old breakfast room where his security team slept. He pushed open the door; they were all sleeping. His Carmichael side surfaced as he kicked his sleeping security team one by one and stormed to the security control panel housed in a kitchen side cupboard. He glared at his cook and housekeeper, who had been preparing breakfast.

"Tea!" he barked as he switched off the alarm.

Tucked under the control box was a card that had a man dressed in black printed on both sides with the words:

All because you want what's mine.

"Carmichael!" he shouted and raced into his study. The safe was open and empty. His diamonds and cash gone.

"Carmichael!"

***

Jasper had followed John's instructions on how to break into W's mansion. He'd already been aware of the system's weak point—the French doors—but he hadn't known how to dodge the sensors dotted in the lawn, or how to open W's safe.

Jasper had emptied the safe and set the alarm off from the control box.

He had raced back to where Kate waited in the Range Rover, and before he'd started the car, he had kissed her, long and hard, and she had run her hand through his hair.

***

They had arrived at Isaacs House after midnight. Clare had left a very welcome sandwich in the fridge. Kate had retired to bed, leaving Jasper going through the contents of W's safe.

Jasper was slumped over his desk sleeping and Kate had gone to read her emails when Clare burst into her office.

"Lewis is here. I'll go and wake His Nibs."

"No need. His Nibs is awake."

Clare bustled out of the office, chuntering about Jasper.

Lewis was waiting for her at the front door.

"They're in the office," she said in a sharp tone.

Lewis walked through the house to the office where Kate and Jasper were waiting.

"Inspector! What a pleasant surprise."

"Don't give me that bullshit, Carmichael."

Jasper laughed and leaned towards his wife for a kiss.

"My wife left the marital bed without giving me her customary greeting." Jasper's voice oozed desire, and Kate went a shade of red.

"What can we do for you, Inspector?" she said, slightly nervous.

Clare, struggling with a tray of tea and coffee, pushed her way around Lewis. Jasper immediately went to help her, taking the tray and laying it on the glass coffee table.

"I'll come straight to the point," began the inspector.

Thank the Lord for that, thought Jasper.

"It's about these bodies."

"Bodies," repeated Kate.

Lewis glared at her. "Yes, Lady Carmichael! Bodies." A wave of guilt washed over Lewis as he directed his anger at Kate. "Let's start with Bruce and those two men."

Kate's eyes filled at the thought of Bruce. How dare Lewis tarnish his memory?

"You'd better leave," she said in her soft, calm voice.

"We can do this down at the station, if you prefer."

"Get the fuck out of my house!" Kate's angry tone shocked the policemen. "Malcolm!" she bellowed.

Malcolm rushed into the office with Clare, Harry and Oliver at his shoulder.

"You've married a murderer, Kate. What's he got on you?"

Kate's eyes bulged with temper. She stepped towards Lewis, but Jasper swiftly wrapped his arms around her waist, pulling her back.

Lewis turned and left.

Kate shrugged Jasper's arms from her and stormed through the French doors and out into the garden.

Harry went to follow her.

"Leave her," Jasper said, watching his wife's temper rage.

"It's Bruce, isn't it?" Clare asked.

Jasper nodded.

"Bruce was a good friend," Clare commented.

Jasper turned and glared at her. "She loved him and trusted him."

"She loved and trusted you. You left her."

"She knows I'm a bastard, but I didn't fake my death. She fucking grieved for him. I have never left her. We belong. She's mine."

Jasper walked to the French doors.

"Fucking her isn't the answer," Clare snapped. "She needs love."

"How many fucking times must I say this? I don't fuck her, I make love to her."

"And what is your intention?" Clare scoffed.

Jasper turned to face her. "I'm going to sexually heal her. It may take time, but I'll heal her, and Bruce will be a distant memory."

Chapter Thirty-Four

Two black Range Rovers screeched to a halt in the front drive of Isaacs House.

Malcolm bellowed, "Jasper!"

Jasper knew they had come for him. He collected the diamonds he had been assessing and stuffed them in the desk drawer.

Kate ran into the office from her studio just as two men dressed in black grabbed Jasper's arms.

"Jasper!" she cried. Another man in black grabbed her waist.

"Kate! Kate!" Jasper yelled as he was dragged to the waiting Range Rover.

A man forcibly held his head down and stuffed him onto the back seat.

Kate fell onto the gravel drive when the man restraining her let her go.

"What's happened?" she yelled.

"W's dead," Malcolm said.

Tears were streaming down her cheeks when the cars sped out of the driveway.

"Kate," Malcolm whispered. "No time for tears. They'll be back. Jasper said yo'd know what to do."

Kate slumped into one of the comfy white leather chairs. "What's happening?" Her head rested in her hands.

Malcolm stared at her. "Kate, you 'aven't time for thinking. Collect the diamonds Jasper was assessing and go. I'll bring the Evoque round."

"I don't understand. Jasper had nothing to do with W's death."

"For Christ's sake. The shit's 'it the fan. Don't think. Act."

Fifteen minutes later, Kate was driving out of Wellsbury towards the motorway and Carmichael Castle. Rolled in cotton were the diamonds that Jasper had been working on. His grandfather's diamonds.

The ever-thoughtful Malcolm had put Jasper's knapsack and a small bag of tools in the front footwell, and Clare had put a bottle of water in the door bin, along with a small plastic container of biscuits.

She slowly drove into Carmichael Castle and turned onto the track that led to the mausoleum. She sat for a long moment, staring at the metal doors to the Carmichael mausoleum. She recalled her one and only visit, when they'd laid Colin Carmichael to rest. She had been with Jasper, Bruce and Malcolm; she had felt safe with them. As she sat alone in Evoque, her head was spinning. She wished she had company, she wished she wasn't there, she wished Jasper hadn't been taken away.

Malcolm had said, *"The shit's 'it the fan."* She had no idea what he was referring to.

Her life with Jasper was at a crossroads. Did she want a life where they would be constantly pursued for diamonds? Jasper was already preparing her for a life with the diamond king, even though he was denying it.

Or could she live a stress-free life, painting and expanding her bookshop. She had often thought about opening another flower shop.

The ultimate question was: could she live the rest of her life without Jasper? From the back seat of the Evoque, she lifted her old messenger bag.

She looped Jasper's knapsack across her shoulders and, in a semi-daze, walked to the metal doors of the mausoleum.

The new door key that Jasper had made was in the front pocket of her messenger bag. With a forceful turn, the lock clicked.

But, no matter how hard she pulled, the doors only opened just enough for her to slide her body through. She thought her legs would give way when she stood on the top step leading down into the mausoleum. The cold, musty, smell that settles in your stomach and makes you retch greeted her.

She tried to recall Jasper's instructions, but she hadn't paid attention.

By the light of her phone's torch, she slowly walked to the end crypt where Colin lay. She used a screwdriver from the knapsack to ease a small stone from the crypt wall, revealing two metal cylinders, which she slipped into her messenger bag. She put the stone back into its place and left the mausoleum.

Kate began to feel lightheaded and nauseous. *I need sugar,* she thought as the damp, earthy air settled in her throat. Her head hit the steering wheel as tears flowed and her stomach churned. Her hand shook, reaching for the water bottle and snacks from the door bin.

After a drink and a sugar rush, she began to feel better. The Evoque engine fired, and Kate left the Carmichaels' resting place.

She set the satnav to 'Home' and let an unknown female voice guide her back to Isaacs House. Her mind brimmed over with the possible consequences of Jasper's arrest. She had to mentally prepare herself for her personal life being turned upside down. Everything she had shared with Jasper and Bruce would be examined, and she expected to be questioned about her involvement with her grandfather, Meredith Spencer, as she had inherited most of his fortune. The tabloids would have a field day raking through her past, including her first marriage to Eric and the humiliation she had suffered with him.

Kate began to feel ill. She didn't know if her emotions would cope.

***

Clare and Malcolm were waiting when she arrived back at Isaacs House.

"Jasper's kicking up a hell of stink." Clare couldn't wait to tell her. "Lewis phoned. He's coming first thing."

Kate sat sipping a very welcomed cup of tea.

"Harry and Oliver have been trying to find out where he's being held. But whoever these people are, they would only talk to you. Jasper's instructions, apparently." Clare looked at Kate, who was gazing into her teacup. "Kate, have you heard a word I've said?"

Kate looked up at her old friend and smiled. "Is there any food? I shall be up all night."

***

The text message summoning Lewis to a meeting had been brief. He knew he had to attend.

He pushed open a heavy wooden door that had a single brass plaque.

Gentlemen's Club.

Lewis walked inside to be greeted by an elderly man dressed in black trousers, a black waistcoat and a crisp white shirt.

"Inspector Lewis," he said. "They're waiting. Top floor."

A Miss Moneypenny type greeted him when he opened the double swing doors of the top floor. He followed her into a large, wood-panelled room where three men of various ages dressed in black Saville Row suits were sitting around a large oak table.

The man in the middle pointed to the wooden hard-back chair that faced the men.

Nerves gripped hold of Lewis. He had been on tenterhooks ever since Jasper had been arrested for the manslaughter of Lord Wellsbury.

***

Lord Wellsbury's body had been found by his housekeeper. He lay on the balcony that led from his study.

She had told the police he hadn't been the same since the house had been broken into and the safe emptied. He had gone into a rage, pacing around the office, shouting one minute and crying the next.

What neither she nor the police knew was that it had been the Carmichael demons that had been ravaging Lord Wellsbury.

Before the ambulance had left the estate, two black Range Rovers had arrived with men dressed in black suits. They had searched his study and his office. Computers were removed and filing cabinets emptied. Before nightfall, all of Lord Wellsbury's records had been taken away.

Jasper had been arrested and taken to London the same day.

***

Silence lingered around the musty-smelling wood-panelled room. Lewis fidgeted. He realised

165

that the silent treatment was part of a plan to make him spill all he knew about Jasper Carmichael.

The man who had pointed at his chair coughed. "Tell us about Kate Carmichael."

Lewis was in freefall; he hadn't expected to be questioned about Kate.

"Don't give us that tripe about her being the soul of Wellsbury. Is she loyal to Carmichael?"

Lewis remained silent. A cold shiver had welled inside him, and a lump rested in his throat.

"Will she lie for him? Cover his tracks? Hide his diamonds?"

Lewis remained silent.

"Speak up, man."

The men angrily stared at a silent Lewis.

"I don't know. In the past she was loyal to him. But I don't know about now," Lewis stuttered.

The man stood, pushing his chair back. He strode to a dirty window and stretched his arms on the dusty sill.

"Wellsbury was one of us. He should have killed Carmichael when he had the chance. But he became obsessed with diamonds. Carmichael's diamonds. When Jasper escaped from that hilltop prison, Wellsbury changed." He stopped and turned to Lewis. "I believe Wellsbury was frightened. He described Jasper as his nemesis. But I think his nemesis wasn't Jasper, but diamonds. Wellsbury may have been Jasper's nemesis—kidnapping him, imprisoning him—but Jasper too has a bigger nemesis. Diamonds."

He moved back to the table and fixed his gaze upon Lewis.

"You're uncomfortable, Inspector. I think it has something to with Kate." He coughed. "Jasper's in an open prison. He wants to see Kate and she has requested to see him. You will become a friend to

Kate. Arrange a prison visit. Drive her. Be attentive. Gain her trust. Find the diamonds. Jasper has them and Kate knows where they are."

The three men stood and filed out of the room.

Lewis slumped in the chair, thankful that his ordeal had come to an end.

Chapter Thirty-Five

Lewis had slept uneasily. He had heard about the nameless men dressed in black Saville Row suits, but he'd never imagined that they would turn their attention to him. He was now between a rock and a hard place. If he didn't befriend Kate, the three wise men would make life difficult for him. If he upset Kate in any way, Jasper would retaliate.

Isaacs House looked deserted when he parked his police Mondeo next to Kate's Evoque. He tried the kitchen door and it opened. Kate was sitting alone at the kitchen table, sipping tea. She looked tired. She looked up at him.

"Inspector," she said. "Coffee, tea, toast?"

"Coffee," answered Lewis, sitting on a stool.

Kate turned her attention to the coffee machine. "What do you want? Jasper's not here, but you know that."

A heavy, unwelcome silence settled in the kitchen.

"Where's Jasper?" she said, handing him his coffee.

"He had one phone call. They thought it would be to you." Lewis paused to study Kate's reaction, but there was none. "He has friends in high places does Jasper."

Kate knew who Jasper had phoned. He had called in a favour from a judge that owed him.

"He's no good, Kate. But you know that. If anyone knows Jasper, it's you. He killed Bruce and at least five other men. He'll drag you down with him."

She looked up from her teacup. "Have you proof, Inspector?" Her voice sounded tired.

"Do I need proof?"

"Why does Bruce have to be brought into it?"

"You say you loved him." He paused, waiting for a reaction. "But it didn't take you long to be back in Jasper's bed."

Kate stood and glared at Lewis, making him feel uncomfortable, but it was worth it. Kate had revealed a weak spot in her calm persona. He now had something to play on.

"You're doubting my feelings for Bruce."

"No, I witnessed the two of you together."

"What do you want from me?"

"I won't lie to you, Kate. I'm under pressure. They want Jasper, and you're the only person that can deliver him. Jasper trusts you. You know how he operates. You know where his diamonds are hidden."

"Who are *they*?"

"Nameless men in black suits."

They all wear black suits, Kate thought.

"Jasper had nothing to do with W's death."

"Kate, with all due respect, you would say that. You love him more than you loved Bruce."

Kate's green eyes pierced into Lewis. He half smiled, satisfied that he had riled her.

"All we want are his diamonds. Tell us where to find them, and you'll be free of him."

Kate glanced at her messenger bag, which lay on the kitchen table. She walked to the window and stared at the early morning.

"Have you ever been in love, Inspector? I mean a deep, consuming love. A powerful love." She paused while her mind filled with thoughts of Jasper. "Accusations are made about Jasper that are untrue." She paused again and turned to face

Lewis. "I want him back. I will have him back. Do you understand? I want the nameless men in black suits to understand. Don't underestimate what I'm capable of. If you say the name Meredith Spencer, they will understand."

Kate's features had become stern; her green eyes were cold. Lewis was in shock. He didn't know this Kate. She was fighting to control her anger. His mind flicked back to the Beth and Joanne episode, when Kate had manhandled them from her gallery after they had threatened Harry and Oliver.

Without a word, Lewis left. He'd thought the "I won't lie to you" approach would work, but to his surprise, it had had the opposite effect, bringing out steely determination that bordered on ruthlessness. Had he just experienced a female version of the late Meredith Spencer, her grandfather, who'd had the legendary reputation of outmanoeuvring the opposition at any cost?

Kate watched Lewis drive out of the gates before picking up the messenger bag and walking into the small library. She moved aside the bookshelf to the secret room.

***

Kate spent the rest of the day in her studio, the place where she could think and prepare herself for the night and what she must do.

Jasper was being held for a murder he hadn't committed. However, the men that had arrested him were not normal police. They were like men that W would employ. For that reason, she decided to visit W's country mansion.

Malcolm filled Jasper's Focus with petrol and put a small bag of tools in the boot. Clare made her sandwiches and a flask of tea. After a tearful goodbye, she left.

***

Kate cut the Focus engine and coasted to a stop along the lane that ran at the back of W's estate. Through the darkness she could just see the outline of the back entrance. Her heart hammered behind her ribs as she got out the car and walked along the lane, looking for a gap in the hedgerow she could get through.

She came to an abrupt stop when angry voices drifted towards her, making her stomach lurch. Her first thought was to return to the Focus, but curiosity got the better of her and she carefully walked towards the voices.

Four men stood in the lane, shining torches at a small hole and a severed cable. In the middle of the lane was a dead fox. Kate assumed the fox had bitten through the electric cable, killing itself and cutting the electrical supply to the house.

"Get back to the house," snapped an angry voice.

"What's the fucking point? We have Carmichael. Who's going to come to his rescue, Little Miss Frigid?"

A chuckle was shared between the men.

Kate returned to the Focus, fuming. How dare they refer to her as Little Miss Frigid. A steely determination to rescue Jasper spread through her.

Chapter Thirty-Six

With the lights switched off, Kate started the Focus and slowly moved towards the entrance of the country estate. She was thankful that the men took no notice of the sound of the engine.

She nervously manoeuvred along the dark drive that led to the house. Driving without lights was a first for Kate, but the moon was on her side, peeking from behind clouds to show her the way. She parked at the back of the house and listened. After she had convinced herself it was safe, she walked towards the back door. She was surprised to find it ajar. She took a deep breath and, with a trembling hand, pushed the door open. She stepped inside and took a moment for her eyes to adjust to the surroundings.

A passageway led to a dimly lit kitchen. The house was quiet, too quiet.

Whispers followed by footsteps drifted towards the kitchen. Kate's heart raced, her stomach churned; she had to act before they saw her.

She lifted a large metal frying pan from the overhead rack and waited behind the door. A man pushed open the door, and the frying pan hit his head. His companion tried to slam the door into her, but Kate had expected that and had stepped back, away from the door. The man jumped inside, only to have the frying pan hit him in the face.

Kate stared at the two men lying on the floor. Her whole body was shaking. She slowly walked to the only light, which shone from the open door.

"Where the fuck are you?" shouted a voice that sounded remarkably like W.

A man stepped through the door. Kate stuck her foot out, and he fell headfirst onto the tiled floor.

"What the fuck!" he yelled, and Kate hit him over the head.

She ventured into what appeared to be a study, and her eyes immediately settled on Jasper tied to a wooden chair. His head was slumped onto his naked chest. She raced towards him and began shaking his body. He was out for the count. She spotted a jug of water on the drinks stand. Without a second thought, she flung the water over Jasper.

He began to splutter while Kate freed his legs and hands.

"Kate…" he murmured.

"Come on," she said, tugging at him to stand.

They staggered towards the door and the body lying on the floor.

"Kick the bastard," Jasper said.

"I can't do that—he's unconscious."

Jasper gripped the door and kicked the man in the ribs. He groaned and rolled over. Kate gasped at the groaning W as Jasper kicked him again.

Kate took hold of Jasper's arm and tugged him towards the kitchen. Without a second thought, Jasper kicked the two unconscious men who had delighted in beating him.

"Come on. They'll have a headache for weeks."

Kate waited for Jasper outside the back door.

"Do you think I've killed those men?" she asked.

"Fuck those men. Where's the car?"

Jasper leaned on Kate as they slowly made their way to the Focus.

"I'll drive," he said sharply.

"No you bloody won't," she answered in the same tone, opening the passenger door and stuffing Jasper onto the seat.

Kate caught hold of the seatbelt.

"Forget the fucking seatbelt," Jasper said. "Let's get out of here."

As Kate was reversing the Focus, the men from the lane returned.

"Put the fucking lights on!" Jasper yelled as Kate narrowly missed their car. "Hit the fucking gas, Kate. These fuckers mean to kill us."

Kate skidded out the entrance, nearly losing the back end and nicking the grass verge.

"For fuck's sake!" shouted Jasper.

"Will you shut the fuck up and let me drive!?"

Jasper wasn't taking any notice. He had his eye on the car that was just leaving the country estate.

Jasper fell into the footwell when Kate turned onto a track without slowing down. The Focus jolted to a halt.

Kate leaned over and held Jasper's head down.

"Don't move," she said in a calm, strained tone.

A speeding car passed the track. Jasper tried to get back onto the seat, but Kate's hand held him in the footwell. After a few minutes, a second car passed the track, and then the blue flashing lights of an ambulance sped by with a police car following.

"I think I've killed them," Kate whispered.

"Let's hope it's W. Now get the fuck out of here." Jasper's voice was cold, just like it had been when he left her, all those years ago.

Kate couldn't meet Jasper's gaze; she didn't want him to see the tears in her eyes.

With each mile the atmosphere in the car thickened. Kate felt hurt. She had risked everything to rescue Jasper. She had gone against all the values she held dear. Her nerves were still on a knife edge, her stomach was in her mouth, and she wanted him to hold her, to kiss her.

Jasper couldn't look at her. W had laughed in his face when he'd told Jasper that his beloved had taken all his diamonds. W's men had followed Kate to the Carmichael mausoleum and waited for her to leave before painstakingly searching the mausoleum. They had found the loose stone next to Colin's tomb. It was empty.

Kate had betrayed him.

"Pull over."

"Why?"

"For fuck's sake, Kate. Just stop the fucking car."

Before Kate had stopped the car, Jasper had jumped out and was marching up the deserted country lane. She watched him run his fingers through his hair; she heard his cries of despair. Tears filled her eyes.

After a few moments of stillness, he turned and marched back to the car. However, instead of going to the passenger door, he pulled open the driver's door and Kate with it. She stumbled. He grabbed her and pinned her against the rear door. His mouth forcibly devoured hers. She tried to free herself, but he pulled on her bottom lip. His tongue feverishly explored her mouth. Her resolve waned and her hand reached for his hair. Their tongues danced; their passion ignited. His hand gently cupped her breast as he lifted her leg.

"I want you."

"Take me," she breathlessly said as she peppered his face with kisses.

"Not here."

He took her hand and led her to the passenger seat.

Chapter Thirty-Seven

Kate lay on her stomach with a blanket covering her. The door to the last-resort safe house was open. Jasper was talking into a phone while pacing outside. He was naked.

She felt worn out. Her body ached and she was feverish. She was thankful that Jasper had let her sleep, as she hadn't slept since he had been taken. She closed her eyes and tried to piece together how they had got to this safe house.

Jasper had driven like a madman through dark and narrow lanes. A tense anger danced between them and thickened with every mile. Before Jasper had opened the door to the cottage, he had turned on her, saying he could no longer trust her. Kate had been taken aback. Everything she had done was for him, but it seemed he had pushed that to one side, believing W's story about the whereabouts of the mausoleum diamonds.

Kate had been incensed. He didn't want to hear the reasons why she had removed the diamonds.

After a tense silence, he had asked if she had opened the metal cylinders.

She could hardly speak to him. All he was concerned about was diamonds.

"Only one," was her bitter reply.

Suddenly her old emotions—going back to the time she had given up her dream job to care for her ungrateful father, mixed with Jasper doubting her love and loyalty, Eric's humiliating comments, Jasper leaving her, Bruce deceiving her, and her sons taking her for granted— surfaced in an un-characteristic temper-ridden tirade.

Jasper had been so shocked he had moved away from her.

"I don't fucking care what's in the cylinders!" Her voice had been bitter and loud. "I've done everything you have asked of me. I've even res-cued you from your so-called nemesis. I've been worried sick. I thought I'd never see you again." She had paused to regain her breath. "And you think I've betrayed you."

Her voice was so full of hurt that it pulled on Jasper's heartstrings.

"Kate. My love…" His hand moved towards her.

She stepped away. "All my life I've done what has been asked of me. I've been there for every-one." Tears began to fall. She stumbled and reached for the table to steady herself. Her voice trembled. "I've loved. I've gone against my beliefs. I've done things…"

Her hands covered her face as she sobbed.

Jasper cradled her into his body. His hand ca-ressed her hair, his lips kissed her forehead, eyes, cheeks and mouth.

"I'm here, Kate. I'll take care of you. I love you."

And then she had slept.

***

Unbeknown to Kate, Jasper had been talking to Malcolm and Clare. He had told them firmly that in his opinion, Kate was on the verge of a nervous breakdown. He tried to convey to them the anger in her tirade. The hurt she had felt at how she was and had been taken for granted. He didn't want to hear their opinion on what he should do. He told them he and Kate were going away until Kate was better.

But Clare had bitterly retorted that he was the problem and Kate should be there with her to be looked after. Jasper hadn't the heart to tell her that Kate's life at Isaacs House was part of the problem, along with their sons, who were abusing their mother's love.

***

Jasper stood in the cottage doorway and smiled at his wife.

"I'm sorry," she said in a downtrodden voice. "I'm so tired. I don't know what's wrong with me."

Jasper lifted her from the bed and wrapped his arms around her so their naked bodies touched. "You need to rest."

"I'll be okay when I'm at Isaacs."

"You're not going back. We're going away."

"I can't go away. I've got…" Her voice tailed off and tears fell on Jasper's chest. "Why am I crying?"

"You're ill, love. If I take you back there, you will be filled with drugs, and that won't help." He kissed her hair. "You can't go back to your old life. It's destroying you."

"What about W? He'll never stop."

"I shall have to kill him, but my way."

"I've got the boys to—"

Jasper cut over her. "They're men. Let them go."

Kate sighed and nestled her head into his shoulder. "I haven't the energy to argue."

Jasper stroked and kissed her hair. "I love you, Kate. I hate seeing you like this. I'll take care of you."

"I'll be fine. I just need to sleep."

"Before you sleep, can you manage to heat a couple of tins of soup while I collect what we need?" he said with a smile.

"Only if you kiss me."

***

Jasper glanced over to his wife, whose head was resting on the passenger window.

"Where are we going?" she asked.

"Boatyard. My refitted yacht awaits me."

"Yacht…" repeated Kate. Her mind wandered back to Alwyn, the man who had taught Jasper about sailing.

Jasper glanced back at Kate, who had fallen back to sleep.

The uneven track to the boatyard woke her. "We shall have to repair this track," she said.

Jasper smiled. He liked her using the word *we*.

He lifted her from the passenger seat. "We won't stay. Just put the stuff in the yacht. I want to catch the tide."

"I need clothes. I can't wear these another day."

"It's all taken care of." He lightly kissed her lips.

"You can do better than that."

***

Jasper was alone on the bridge of his yacht. It was dark, and he was sailing without lights or a GPS.

He had let Kate sleep; he had noticed that she struggled to carry the bags and boxes onto the yacht. He had considered staying in England for her to see a doctor, but his gut told him that she needed rest.

Jasper jumped when Kate opened the bridge door holding a tray with hot coffee and sandwiches. She looked lovely; her hair was wet from a shower, and she smiled at him.

"Feeling better?" he asked.

"A little. You must be hungry."

He nodded, but the only thing he was hungry for was standing next to him.

Chapter Thirty-Eight

Jasper's Journal

This is a first for me. I don't put anything in writing as it has a habit of coming back to bite you. But I'm at my wits' end. I was so confident I could put my beloved back together, but I've failed.

I should arrange for her to fly back to England, but when I watch her walk along the waterline, my heartstrings tighten.

When I look into her tear-filled eyes, I want to hold her and kiss her.

I can't let her go.

We have been at my secret place on the Greek coast for a month. In my opinion, it's the most beautiful place in the world.

It is hidden from the sea by a narrow inlet that leads to a cove, home to a narrow strip of glistening white sand and clear blue sea. There's a small sea wall where the yacht is tied. Ten stone steps lead to my house.

I stumbled across this place many years ago when I needed to disappear from the authorities. The house was a wreck. I walked into the nearest village where I made enquiries about the house and cove.

I bought it from an old timer who was only too pleased to offload it. Over the years it has been renovated, with the help of a local builder, into a luxury retreat.

I had always planned on Kate sharing this place with me.

I envisaged we would be happy here, no responsibilities to occupy her mind.

But she is not happy and rarely talks, preferring to stare into space. When she thinks I'm not watching, tears flow.

If only she would talk.

***

Kate's sleeping. Today has been good for us.

I went into the village for provisions, and to my surprise she joined me. My heart skipped a beat when I saw the glint in her beautiful green eyes had returned. She looked lovely in a long white dress that shows her tan to the best effect. But I'm biased. In my eyes Kate is always beautiful. However, no one can deny that she has blossomed in the sun. Her long silver tresses shine, her cheeks have a delightful pink glow and when she smiles her eyes sparkle.

She wandered around the market while I did a little business. She bought fresh veg, fruit, bread and cakes from the local farmers. She smiled when she pointed at me to pay.

My friends in the café where I trade a few diamonds—we have to live—told me that questions are being asked. It was only a matter of time before W cast his net to find where I'd taken Kate. It must be common knowledge that she is unwell.

I've decided tonight I'm going to share her bed. I'm hoping she won't reject me, as I'm desperate to feel her naked body against mine.

***

I was checking over the yacht engine when she brought me a cold beer. I knew something had changed when she sat staring at me while sipping her beer from a bottle. Kate has never drunk from a bottle.

I didn't think anything of it when she followed me onto the bridge and stood behind me.

Suddenly, two cool hands slipped under the waistband of my shorts and slowly moved to the tops of my thighs.

I gasped.

My erection was instantaneous. She planted soft kisses on my naked back.

I didn't think. I turned and lifted her white linen dress. My hands cupped her full breasts as my mouth feasted on her nipples.

She sighed, that delightful sound that I had missed.

I don't remember carrying her to the bed. But that doesn't matter. All that matters is that she was naked with her legs wrapped around my waist. I kissed her body over and over; I sucked her breasts as her hands massaged my head. Elated sighs filled the cabin as my mouth caressed her most private parts.

And then the words I had prayed to hear: "Don't make me wait."

I slipped inside her. She gasped. Our mouths joined as I moved. She pulled me into her. She cried my name as her orgasm ripped through her and I drained myself.

It was later that night; we were spooning in bed when she turned to face me.

"Love me. Jasper. Love me. I need you."

I knew what she wanted, and I was only too happy to oblige.

I thought the stars had fallen from the sky as we climaxed together. Kate had opened the door to her inner self, and I willingly entered.

I would never have believed that the bond that we share could get stronger, but it has. She said to me "I love you so much it hurts," and it does.

No one will ever believe that the criminal Jasper Carmichael is in love. But I am.

***

We sat in that large, comfy chair, savouring the after-sex glow and staring at the stars.

"I loved Bruce."

I was taken by surprise.

"He was kind, considerate, and he made love to me in a most tender fashion."

My heart skipped a beat. I had no idea why Kate had suddenly decided to talk about Bruce.

Moments passed.

"I knew something was wrong. He had changed. His love-making was rushed. As if he didn't want to love me. He knew that I needed love. Sex was part of it. But I needed his tenderness."

I kissed her hair and waited.

"I can see it all now. All the pieces have fallen into place. He stood on the sidelines watching our marriage fall apart. He knew that I have needs. Love, sex, human contact. I was falling apart when you left, and Bruce stepped in, and I willingly let him."

My heart was racing as I waited for her to continue.

"You hurt me, Jasper, but Bruce hurt me even more. I knew what you were capable of. Deep down, you're a criminal and that's never going to change. To keep you, I had to change. Accept your

diamond addiction. I wasn't willing to change. To accept you as you are."

I waited for tears to fall on my naked chest, but none did.

"The hurt Bruce inflicted on me was far worse than yours. He lured me into believing his love was genuine. At first, I believed it was. He had left his past behind. Then he made excuses not to come to the studio. When life was becoming too much, I pleaded with him to fuck me. But he wouldn't."

I was becoming very nervous.

"I had to stop his access to the company bank account. No one knows. It was between me and him. He owed money—a lot of money—to a bookie. I paid it off. I think he continued to gamble, and W paid off his debts. With the help of W, he faked his death. I should have realised that something was wrong. His wife was there before me. He was cremated before I arrived. I paid for everything. I sat at his graveside and bared my soul. I cried buckets. I blamed myself for his gambling. I should have stopped his access to the company bank account earlier. And all the time, Bruce and W were laughing at me. They knew you would come to me in my hour of need and lead them to your diamonds."

Silence.

"W hasn't had it all his own way. Bruce is dead, he hasn't got your diamonds, and his bank account is a few mil short."

My heart stopped. Has she admitted that she hacked into W's account? But I'd already guessed that.

"I can't understand the attraction of the NRJ bank. It didn't take me long to find his account."

My arms tightened around her body.

"Am I a bad person to seek revenge?"

I moved her so I could kiss her.

"I wanted to kill him when he came out of his study, but I had to free you. Why didn't you finish him?"

"I would have got the blame. When I finish him, nothing will point to me."

"What's happened to me, Jasper? Who am I? This isn't who I am."

I choked. I couldn't speak. All I could think of was how that bastard W was going to suffer. No one does this to my beloved.

Chapter Thirty-Nine

It had taken W longer than he had hoped to re-cover from Kate's blow to his head. He had sent a team to find Jasper and his bitch, but they had drawn a blank. He mulled over what he knew.

His men had traced them to the Mediterrane-an. Jasper knew that coastline like the back of his hand. Over the years, he had nurtured a network of criminals there to trade his diamonds. They would do whatever he asked, and W was sure that would include nursing Kate.

His temporary London butler opened the library door and coughed.

"What is it?" W impatiently snapped.

"The inspector is here, sir."

"Well, show him in. Show him in."

Inspector Lewis nervously walked into the li-brary. W pointed at the couch opposite him.

Standing behind W was a stern-looking woman.

"Well?"

There was a tinge of anger in W's voice, but this didn't deter Lewis. He was confident he could handle W's aggressive moods.

"Excuse me, W—I thought that we would be alone."

W looked a little embarrassed and waved his hand at the woman. "This is Deborah, my security manager."

Lewis fidgeted. His gut was telling him this woman wasn't a security expert but an assassin.

He cleared his throat and concentrated on W. "If Clare, Malcolm and the boys know where they are, they're not letting on."

"What do you mean?"

"The boys are running the shopping centre and Clare and Malcolm are supporting them."

W raised his eyebrows in surprise.

"Oliver has taken responsibility in his stride. Nothing seems to faze him. Kate would be proud. But he's wild. Alcohol, drugs and sex." Lewis hesitated before adding, "Kate's put a lot of effort into nurturing Oliver."

After a tense silence, he stood and walked to the door.

"No one turns their back and walks away from me!" yelled W.

Lewis stopped, turned and glared. "You really don't know him. He was under your nose, and you still don't know Jasper Carmichael."

W stood, returning Lewis's glare. "I am Jasper Carmichael!"

"If you're the cause of Kate's decline in health, he'll come for you. Jasper, like his father, is a chameleon. You should read the Colin Carmichael archives to get a measure what Jasper's capable of."

"He's had plenty of opportunities to kill me."

"Jasper's waits until the time is right for him—and until there's no possibility that your death will be pinned on him." Lewis moved his glare to Deborah.

"He can't stay in hiding forever. Kate will need her boys." There was a hint of sarcasm in W's voice.

Lewis stepped closer to W. "I've studied Jasper from a child to a man. Jasper's been betrayed many times and now works alone. The only person he trusts is Kate. If she's ill, he's looking after her."

W slumped back into his seat. "So, he's stopped diamond trading."

"I didn't say that. Jasper trades uncut diamonds and quality diamonds that are wrapped individually in white tissue paper. He carries these to secret rendezvous in a burgundy attaché case. The poor-quality stuff is in small cotton bags. He uses these for everyday spending."

Deborah had moved to W's side. A cold shiver shot down Lewis's back as their eyes met.

"That yacht must be stuffed full of diamonds," she commented.

"I don't know that. I know they aren't in safety deposit boxes and there's no activity in his bank account."

W raised his eyebrows in surprise.

"We track any movement in Jasper's accounts," Lewis continued. "We assume all his transactions are electronic. However, we mustn't discount cash."

"Kate's accounts?"

"Nothing."

"Cash! He must be mad," exclaimed W.

"Jasper has a reputation of doing the unexpected, but my money is on electronic transfer. Particularly now that Kate's with him."

"What use is she?" scoffed Deborah.

W covered her hand with his.

"Kate assisted Jasper when he was involved with the South Americans," Lewis said.

"How so?" asked W.

"Don't know specifics, except Jasper negotiated the deal and Kate transferred the money."

"You think he's waiting for a South American deal."

"All I know is South American dealers are on the move."

"Speculate his next move."

"He won't make a move until Kate is well. We have to sit tight and hope the old Kate returns."

"For God's sake man, she's just a woman."

"A very important woman."

"Jasper's a Carmichael," W said impatiently.

"You still don't get it. Jasper is a Carmichael. But whereas Carmichaels don't love, Jasper does. Jasper Carmichael, son of the diamond thief, Colin, grandson of the power mad Jasper Carmichael, is in love."

***

Jasper woke alone. It was unusual for Kate to be up before him. A smile crept across his face. It was also unusual for her to seduce him, but she had.

He padded into the kitchen. A dim light from within highlighted Kate sitting on the balcony, holding a cup of tea between her hands. The gurgling of the coffee percolator caught his attention.

He had just taken his first swig of coffee when her calm voice broke the morning silence.

"When were you going to tell me?"

His eyes moved to the kitchen table. Diamonds were neatly laid out on their white tissue paper. His eyeglass, tweezers and prong holder were next to them.

Jasper took a deep breath.

"An idea formed in my mind when you were so poorly," he explained. "You were my main focus, but for my sanity I had to think of other things. I have diamonds to sell and more diamonds back home." He refilled his coffee mug. "Do you remember the deals with the South Americans? How we worked as a team?"

Kate nodded.

"I want to do that again."

"My computer skills are rusty," Kate said.

Jasper took his jacket from the back of a chair and unzipped the inside pocket. He dropped a small electronic box onto the kitchen table.

"These things get smaller and smaller, but this little gadget holds all the business transactions of Jasper Carmichael. I mean all of them, going back to Carmichael and Swain. It also scrambles my location. Everything is encrypted."

He walked to the linen wall cupboard and lifted a hidden laptop.

"I'll set it up for you so you can practise."

"You want me to be part of your diamond smuggling."

He turned to face her. "No! I want you to help me give it up."

"How so?"

"I want to sell but not buy."

Chapter Forty

Jasper had left Kate familiarising herself with his computer files while he went to buy fresh food. It was a beautiful day; he couldn't resist taking the steep, narrow coastal path with its stunning sea views. Kate would have loved it—she would be enthusiastically taking photographs.

As he rounded a bend, the village came into view. He sat on a large boulder and lifted his binoculars from his jacket pocket. His friend from the café was climbing the track, heading his way.

Jasper stuffed the binoculars back into his pocket and quickened his pace. He carefully approached the abandoned shepherd's hut that they used as a secret meeting place.

***

Kate looked up from the laptop screen and smiled. "That didn't take long."

Jasper dropped a week-old page from a newspaper onto the keypad. At the bottom of the page was a picture of a diamond.

The Diamond King Strikes Again

It is thought that Jasper Carmichael, of the infamous aristocratic Carmichael family, was responsible for the theft of this ten-million-pound diamond.

The diamond was on display at Carmichael's marina to celebrate the weeklong yachting regatta.

The regatta was organised by the marina's committee, who are looking after Carmichael's marina during his absence.

The Diamond King hasn't been seen since he disappeared with his wife.

It is thought that Kate Carmichael has suffered a nervous breakdown and could be convalescing in a Swiss clinic.

There have been many sightings of Jasper around Zurich, including a villa with views of Lake Zurich.

"Where do they get this garbage from?" Kate asked.

"We have to leave."

"Leave?! Surely that's what they want us to do."

"Tonight."

"Jasper!"

He turned to face her. "Can't you feel them?"

"Feel them?"

Jasper stepped towards Kate and placed his hands on her shoulders. "Do you remember the early days when my gut told me what I should do?"

"I thought that had ended."

"My gut's churning. My love. We must leave."

***

Jasper spent the rest of the day checking the yacht over while Kate collected items from the cottage to take with them.

"We leave on the night tide," he said as she handed him a coffee.

"I'm not doubting your sailing skill, but isn't it going to be a bit tricky navigating through those rocks?"

Jasper turned and smiled. "Tactfully put, as ever."

"Who's after us?"

"My money's on criminals. Bernhard wouldn't miss that clip in the newspaper. It's a typical W ploy. He must have planted that story. It's so unbelievable on so many levels. First, it's illogical for a diamond to be used as the attraction for a regatta. A yachting prize would have been more suitable. Yachtsmen are very competitive; they would like a cup to compete for. Second, who in their right mind would leave a ten-million-pound diamond on display?"

"I get the picture."

***

Jasper released the ropes that secured the yacht to the jetty. It drifted on the tide. Jasper had tried to reassure Kate by explaining he had successfully manoeuvred the yacht using the tide before, but his words hadn't dispelled the uneasy feeling welling in her stomach.

She sat on the deck dressed in black with her silver hair bunched up under a baseball cap. The outgoing tide soon guided the yacht into the middle of the cove. Kate took one last look at the cottage where she had been happy. She couldn't help but feel this was the last time she would look at her paradise.

Jasper was on the bridge, making best use of the tide.

"The trick is," he had told her, "to get through the rocks before the current gets in full flow."

When the cottage disappeared from view, she moved to the bridge to be with him just in case the yacht hit the rocks. If the sea claimed her, she'd want him to be the last thing she saw.

Suddenly, Jasper started the engine. Kate gripped the side of the bridge, her eyes firmly fixed on Jasper. *This is it,* she thought. *He never mentioned having to use the engine.*

Kate's grip tightened as Jasper spun the wheel first one way and then the other.

"Shit! There's a fucking yacht!"

Kate's gaze momentarily left Jasper. What yacht? She couldn't see a yacht.

Suddenly a high-pitched sound of cracking glass filled the confined space of the bridge. Jasper stumbled to the floor, holding the side of his head. Blood trickled through his fingers. He tried to stand, arms outstretched, reaching for the wheel, but he fell back down. Without thinking, Kate leapt towards the erratically moving wheel and steered away from the unidentified yacht. Collision seemed inevitable, even when she reduced the engine speed and pulled on the wheel. She closed her eyes and hoped for the best.

Chapter Forty-One

W was partaking in a very large brandy and polite conversation at the Gentlemen's Club when the waiter approached him with a phone.

"Yes?" he barked into the phone.

The voice on the other end was one that he'd never expected to hear again.

The raspy voice of Bernhard, Jasper's old adversary, filled W's ear. W stood, his body stiffening when Bernhard told him Jasper and his bitch had escaped. It was no consolation to W when Bernhard said, "Jasper took one to the head, but he must have given Kate some sailing lessons, because the two yachts only suffered a glancing blow."

W ended the call and slowly walked to a window so he could stare at the London traffic and try to plan his next move.

Deborah, his new security chief, had come highly recommended. When she had told him Bernhard had fallen for the newspaper story about the diamond at Jasper's marina, W had willingly accepted her plan to let Bernhard finish Jasper and Kate. But the plan had failed, and W had no idea where Jasper and his bitch were.

***

Kate was staring at the bewildering array of dials, screens and switches that covered the control panel.

"Kate. Give me a hand."

Kate turned, and Jasper took her hand. She was about to tell him off, but it would have fallen on deaf ears.

"I don't know what to press," she said as Jasper eased himself onto the bridge chair.

An eerie stillness filled the small, compact bridge. Jasper stared through the glass screen into the night's blackness. His right hand touched the broken skin on his forehead.

"We'll go to Wolf's. I need to think things through."

"Wolf's!"

Jasper paused. "Wolf and I go back a long way. We've had our disagreements. We can rest, I'll repair the boat and you'll be safe. No one in Wolf's Cove will touch Jasper Carmichael's woman. But he's dangerous, Kate," he said as Kate cleaned the dried blood from his forehead. "He deals in anything. Drugs, money, women, diamonds. He runs his operation from a sheltered cove. A few shacks are scattered along the quayside, where boats are tied up."

"Will we be there long?"

"He'll want diamonds to keep his mouth shut."

Kate didn't want to think about diamonds.

"Where are we?" she asked.

"It's best if you don't know."

The radio crackled. "Is that you, Carmichael?"

"Aye. I would like to hold up for a couple of days."

Jasper hadn't wanted to bring Kate to Wolf's Cove, but he needed to check the yacht after the collision. Jasper had a long history with the cove; he had stayed there with the Cook family, who had settled there after the war, and used their hangar. There was unfinished business between Jasper and Wolf. Jasper couldn't stomach the manner in which Wolf treated the local villagers. And Wolf wanted the diamonds that he considered Jasper owed him.

Kate had stopped cleaning Jasper's forehead while he answered the radio call. His body had stiffened, and his voice had become harsh, reminding Kate of the time when he had shot Charlie Wilson's sons.

His words came into her mind: *"I can't shoot you, Kate."*

She'd thought that Jasper was resigned to the past, but she had been mistaken. A cold, nervous shiver drifted down her spine.

Jasper's voice brought her back to the present. "Kate! Are you listening?"

Their eyes briefly met; Kate was frightened.

"Stay in the yacht," Jasper ordered, but she wasn't paying attention. Her mind was on the dark, evil place they had just entered.

Jasper had carefully eased the yacht through a narrow gap in a concrete sea wall. Lights from buildings filtered through the darkness.

Jasper followed Kate's gaze to the buildings. "They're places to sleep off a session in Wolf's bar. Alcohol, drugs and sex with whoever you fancy. This is not a place for you."

Kate turned and stared at her husband's stern, scowling face. She followed him outside and reached for his arm. Their eyes met.

"I love you," she murmured.

His hand cupped her face. "Do as I ask, Kate."

Jasper threw a rope to a man waiting at the edge of the wall.

"'E wants to see you."

Jasper jumped onto the sea wall.

"And 'er."

"No need for Kate to come."

"Boss says bring the bitch."

***

Jasper and Kate followed the man towards Wolf's bar. He pushed the door open; the room was empty. Jasper's gut told him to make a run for it. He turned towards the door just as the man turned the lock.

A scruffy, medium-height, stocky man walked from behind the bar. His dark eyes settled on Kate, and an evil grin filled his face.

"Jasper!" greeted Wolf. "And this must be your delightful wife."

"Wolf."

"Bernhard will join us. We both have a score to settle with you."

Kate and Jasper's eyes met.

Wolf sniggered at Kate's surprised expression. "He's not a doting lover, Lady Carmichael." Jasper glared at Wolf. "He's a murderer, at the very least. Womaniser. Thief. I could go on."

"Shut the fuck up," Jasper growled. "Tell me what you want."

"I want a cut of your diamond hoard. But this gentleman wants you dead."

Wolf pointed a remote at the wall behind the bar and a flatscreen appeared.

W's face filled the screen.

"I can't remember a time I didn't want you dead," W said. "I have paid for others to kill you, but you've always dodged the bullet, so to speak. But not this time. I have had fantasies of torturing you. Of you watching Kate being fucked every night by a different man. She's your weakness and your downfall. You're the only Carmichael to have loved. Carmichaels don't love. They're strong. Love has made you weak. *She* has made you weak. And now you will both pay the price. My head of security is on her way to oversee your demise."

"What about the diamonds?" Wolf said.

"I no longer care about the diamonds. He's still alive because of my diamond fever. But no more."

"We could fuck her. Here, now. That will drive him mad."

"No! I say no! Have you ever witnessed the Carmichael demons? They rise in blind fury. Their goal will be to kill anyone that touches her."

"I'll call my men in."

"He will kill you all. I know because I have the same affliction." W paused. "A younger me would have had no problem with killing so many."

The bar door burst open, revealing Bernhard, who stood staring at Kate with a lustful, evil grin.

"I smell pussy fodder." His French accent emphasised the words.

Jasper clenched his fists.

Bernhard marched towards Kate. Jasper snatched her to his side, making Bernhard roar with laughter. Jasper's body stiffened as he fought the urge to attack Bernhard.

"You're drunk." Wolf's angry voice made Bernhard stop.

"I'm not fuckin' drunk. I want his diamonds and to fuck her." Bernhard's murderous eyes stared at Wolf. He took a step closer. "Don't get in my way."

"We didn't agree this."

"I don't care a fuck. Ask him." Bernhard pulled a long-bladed knife from his belt. "That bastard"—he pointed his knife at Jasper and stared into his cold blue eyes—"knifed me. Left me for dead along with the rest of 'em."

Bernhard moved towards Jasper and Kate. Jasper pushed Kate behind him.

"There's no knifing until we have the diamonds." Wolf stepped towards Bernhard.

In a flash Bernhard turned and stuck the knife into Wolf's stomach. "There's no fuckin' we."

Wolf fell onto the floor. His large hands tried in vain to stem the blood pouring from the wound.

"It's fuckin' mine now, you piece of shit."

Bernhard suddenly stepped back from Wolf. In Wolf's hand was a small gun. Blood dribbled from the corner of Wolf's mouth as he coughed. His gun hand began to shake. Bernhard grinned and took a step closer.

With both hands steadying the gun, Wolf pulled the trigger. Two bullets hit Bernhard in the chest. He stumbled towards Wolf, his eyes staring at the bullet wounds. The next bullet hit Bernhard in the head. He swayed, and the knife fell as he stumbled backwards onto the floor.

Jasper raced to Wolf's side.

"I'm done for, Carmichael. It's yours if you want it."

Jasper lifted his hand from Wolf's bloodstained shirt. "Don't talk."

"It should have been yours." Wolf choked on his blood.

Jasper put his ear to Wolf's mouth as his words became fainter and fainter.

"Kill that evil bastard."

Jasper glanced at the screen. A dark scowl filled W's red face.

Jasper stood and stared at the dead men that had been his enemies. Kate ran to his side and put her arms around his waist.

"You're a dead man, Jasper!" shouted W from the screen. "I'll make sure the two of you will never return to England. Think about it, Kate—you'll never see your boys again."

Jasper walked to the screen. "Shut the fuck up, you piece of shit. You and your kind don't fucking bother me. I'm Jasper Carmichael. *The* Jasper Carmichael. Sleep with one eye open, you piece of shit."

A wave of fear filled W. He had never seen such a hateful stare.

Chapter Forty-Two

A week later, Kate wandered onto the yacht's deck, nursing a mug of tea. She had left Jasper sleeping. Since the horrific killing of Wolf and Bernhard, she had hardly seen him.

A group of villagers had pushed their way into the bar. They'd stared at the dead men who had terrorised them. A man called Jason had stepped forward and asked Jasper to stay. The villagers needed someone they could look to for guidance.

There were also new people sailing into the cove. Word had travelled that Jasper was back.

She lowered herself onto the comfy chair at the stern of the boat. Watching Bernhard and Wolf kill each other had affected Kate deeply. She felt that she was partly to blame. They'd both wanted to fuck her, and if she hadn't been there, they would probably still be alive. Jasper had tried to convince her that they would have killed one another anyway.

She knew that Jasper's criminal friends only wanted to fuck her because she was married to Jasper. They wanted to torture him by making him watch.

Her mind drifted to the brothel on the island run by Madam Pam, a buxom woman who had come on to Jasper. Kate had surmised that they had history.

A lone tear trickled down Kate's cheek as she recalled that morning. Jasper had left their bed before the sun rose, making the excuse that Jason wanted a meeting before the villagers started to gather. Kate had a feeling he was lying. They hadn't made love since they'd arrived in Wolf's Cove. Jasper was always either too tired or too busy.

She had found the real reason why he had left early that morning. Jason's wife had warned her against a woman named Deborah, who had unexpectedly arrived on a superyacht. Deborah and Jasper had a turbulent history. Kate had watched Deborah fling her arms around Jasper and plant two red-painted lips on his cheek.

Kate's emotions were fraying. She was losing Jasper to his past. She needed a change of scenery; she needed to walk and think.

Jasper had left Deborah when he'd glimpsed Kate walking away from the village. He went into a jog after her. Kate had set a fast pace and it had taken Jasper longer than he'd anticipated to catch up with her. He caught hold of her arm, but Kate had freed herself when her eyes settled on the red lipstick on his cheek.

The stony path forked. Kate had stopped, unsure which path to take.

"It was after I left you in the dinghy that I found this place," Jasper blurted "I owe you an explanation."

Kate stopped; she wanted to hear his explanation.

"This way," he had said, taking the right fork.

They had walked in silence until a house appeared. Jasper had explained that the house was built during the war. The Allies had used it to house escaped prisoners and suchlike.

He had unlocked the double front doors and they had walked into the living room and kitchen. There were two rooms and a bathroom at the back.

Jasper had opened the back door to a neglected vineyard.

A couple by the name of Cook had settled here after the war and developed the vineyard and wine-making business. There were two large sheds that Kate assumed were used in the wine-making process.

Her eyes had lingered on a hangar very similar to the ones at the Wellsbury airfield.

"That's where I keep my plane." Jasper's voice had taken on a matter-of-fact tone, as if it wasn't a big deal. But it was a big deal for her. Jasper had failed to tell her about this before.

"I've been wanting to tell you for ages. But there seemed no point, as I never intended to come here."

Kate had carried on to the hangar. The doors were open, and she walked inside. A man had shouted to her from inside the plane.

"I told him to tell you! I'm Hank by the way. I look after Jasper's plane."

Kate turned but Jasper had gone.

Hank had a lot to say. How Jasper had saved him from the evils of drugs. How Jasper used to fly to Wellsbury to see her even though she was with Bruce.

"Thought he'd come here when he left the hill-top villa, but he went to you."

Kate had remained silent. There was something about Hank that put her on her guard.

"Has he told you about his dalliances?" Hank asked. "It would be best for everyone if you just accepted them."

"What dalliances?"

"The red lipstick is Deborah. Ex-CIA. Jasper was on their most wanted list, but they thought that they could capture him during diamond dealing.

No one gets one over Jasper where diamonds are concerned. She got the sack and set up her own security firm. She now works for W."

"Are there more?"

"Dalliances? Yes. Jasper's a good catch. Good-looking. Rich. Gives a girl a good time. But you would know about that."

It wasn't a surprise, but the words had sat heavy over her all day.

Kate was still on the deck, staring at star-filled sky, when the night's tranquillity was broken by Jasper's cold voice. "How long have you been here?"

Not so long ago, he would have joined her on the deck, complaining the bed was cold without her. Kate looked at him, he was still dressed in his work clothes.

Her silence unnerved him. "Is an argument brewing?"

"No. It's too dark to work, though. So, I assume you're visiting one of your dalliances."

Jasper stiffened. Hank must have been gossiping—he always referred to Jasper's women as "dalliances". But in this instance, Kate was correct. He was going to a meeting with Deborah.

"Deborah's keen to know what my plans are for the cove."

"Don't give me that bullshit. Just go."

As he was walking towards the bar, where he'd arranged to meet Deborah, Kate said in an unusually loud voice, "Remember the Cayman Islands."

Jasper stopped. He didn't need to be reminded of that night. Kate's temporary job with him had been ending and he had taken her to the Caymans, partly as a reward for being a loyal employee and partly to spend days in bed with her. However, he had been concerned that she would become too clingy. So, he had left her for Chloe. When he had returned to the suite, Kate had gone.

That was the biggest mistake he'd ever made. He'd fallen into a deep depression—he missed her. His mental state had worsened when he couldn't find her, and when he did, she'd had his son, Harry.

Jasper glanced at the bar. Deborah was standing outside. Even under the dim lighting, he could tell she was scantily dressed.

He returned his gaze to the yacht, but Kate had gone. He couldn't trust Deborah. She had a hidden agenda: revenge for losing her high-profile CIA job. However, he could trust Kate. Her only agenda was love.

Love for him.

Chapter Forty-Three

Jasper never had his meeting with Deborah. Much to Kate's surprise, he had spent the night sleeping in the comfy chair on the deck.

"Come," he had whispered as he grabbed her hand and snatched a blanket from the back of a chair. His grip upon her hand had tightened as they marched past an astonished-looking Deborah.

Kate tugged on Jasper's arm, but it had no effect. He was on a mission. She thought they were going to the Cook house, but he turned onto an overgrown path that gently meandered towards the sea.

When he finally let go of her hand, Kate walked to the water's edge and stared at the sea as the early morning sunrays skated over the rippling waves.

Two strong arms pulled her against his warm chest. "I knew the view would captivate you."

He waited until she smiled, then his soft lips caressed her neck. "Come," he said in a husky voice that was full of desire.

***

The sun was climbing when Jasper walked out of the warm sea. Kate was lying on her stomach, her head propped on her hands, admiring her husband's naked body. She was happy. Jasper had loved her in a most tender manner, igniting her senses with a slow rhythm that had deepened her orgasm.

He lay down beside her and rolled her atop of him. "Happy?"

Kate smiled and kissed him.

"I love the way you show your appreciation with a slow, passionate kiss," he playfully said, his hands squeezing her buttocks.

At that moment there was a blast from a ship's horn.

Deborah's state-of-the-art yacht had sailed from its safe anchorage to the reef-ridden mouth of the inlet.

***

Deborah had just finished a call with W. She was extremely angry. Her day had shown promise until Jasper led Kate away from the village to this isolated inlet. What Jasper saw in that woman was a mystery to Deborah.

The captain of the yacht had argued with her about moving it. They were anchored too close to the reefs that surrounded the inlet. The sea was calm at the moment, but a storm was brewing and that put his yacht in danger.

Deborah didn't care about the storm or that the yacht would be blown onto the reefs. All she cared about was Jasper and Kate.

***

W lay on his four-poster bed in a complete state of calm. He couldn't remember the last time he had felt so much peace. His expensive London doctor had been brutal in his health assessment: unwind or die.

The doctor had suggested a sexual therapy, prescribing Viagra and enjoyment. W had willingly agreed, expecting two young women to satisfy his sexual need. He couldn't have been more wrong.

Two mature ladies had been shown into his bedroom, and W had thought, *I don't need Viagra for this.*

Candles had been discreetly placed around his bedroom. His robe had been slipped from his body, and he had lowered himself naked onto the bed. His mind had drifted as the candles' intoxicating aroma wafted around the bedroom. The naked women had danced around his bedroom, holding long, flowing silk wraps. Drops of cool oil dripped onto his body and a pair of soft hands massaged his chest. He wanted to touch her, but his hands had been tied to the bedposts. Relaxing music filtered into his ears as the women slowly massaged his body, setting a rhythm that moved the Carmichael demons living deep inside him. The demons slowly moved through his body, locked in the rhythm.

W fell into a deep sleep.

When he had opened his eyes, his bedroom was in darkness, his naked body was covered by a sheet and his hands were free.

He couldn't remember if he'd had sex, but the warmth he'd felt when one of the women lowered herself onto him was very real, as were the soft hands that had massaged his aging body.

W felt a peace that he hadn't felt before.

He couldn't help thinking, *Is this the peace that Jasper feels when he's inside Kate?*

Chapter Forty-Four

The storm had hit Wolf's Cove during the early hours. Jasper had secured his yacht, but he hadn't allowed for other boats breaking their mooring and smashing into his.

If the storm had wrecked boats that were moored relatively safely in the cove, he wondered what it had done to Deborah's superyacht, anchored too close to the reefs. The captain should have sailed away from that part of the coast. No anchor would have secured the yacht in that storm.

Two arms stretched around his waist. "Is she done for?" asked Kate as she gazed upon the damage a motor launch had inflicted upon their yacht's starboard side.

"I'm not sure. She'll have to be towed to the nearest boatyard."

"She didn't sink like some boats."

"Most of what you see is scrap."

"But they're insured?"

"None of the owners will admit to being in Wolf's Cove. Insurance won't touch them."

Hank sidled up to them and spent a brief moment looking at Jasper's yacht. "There's a lot of wreckage washing up around the point."

Jasper didn't answer.

"The fishermen are picking up bodies."

Hank waited for an answer, but Jasper's eyes never left his yacht.

"Don't you care about Deborah?"

"No!" came the sharp reply.

Kate let go of Jasper's waist and stood at his side. But Jasper needed her close; he pulled her back to him.

"What's wrong with you?" snapped Hank.

"Deborah was working for W. He wants us dead." Jasper paused. "And you expect me to care?"

"We need your help. You know what to do. We don't."

"I know," Jasper said to Hank. He turned to Kate. "Stack whatever's salvageable and put it on the quay. Anything, Kate. Food, clothes, bedding, electronics. We will stay in the Cook house."

Jasper had begun to walk towards the bar when he stopped and shouted, "Kate! For god's sake, be careful."

***

W was in the study of his London house when the police arrived. They were a new team that had been assigned to him since Inspector Lewis had decided to go back into retirement, citing his age for his inability to catch Jasper. But W thought Kate was the reason Lewis had returned to his garden. W had recognised the look of love on Lewis's face whenever Kate had been mentioned.

"Well?" W snapped, looking his young team up and down.

"We have received a report."

"Get on with it, man."

"Your team in the Mediterranean was caught up in a storm. The one that's on the news. We believe they're all dead."

W's ashen face shocked the police team. "All of them?"

"We are waiting for confirmation, but bodies have been seen on the beach."

W walked to his drinks table and poured a very generous brandy.

"Keep me informed of any developments," he said in a dismissive tone.

***

Wolf's Cove was still buzzing with people clearing storm damage while Kate sat with the pile of salvageable items from the yacht. She was holding a welcome cup of tea, pondering what to do next, when a car horn caught her attention. An old Defender Land Rover was chugging towards her. Jasper was hanging out of the side where the driver's door should have been. The car gradually came to a stop next to Kate's pile. Jasper leapt out. His beaming Carmichael smile made Kate's heart race. He lifted her in the air and kissed her.

"Meet Betsy," he said, gently tapping the front wing. "Isn't she wonderful?"

Kate had difficulty sharing Jasper's enthusiasm for the old rust bucket. "Is it safe?" she gingerly asked.

"No!" Jasper laughed. "But with a bit of luck, it will move this lot."

"Where did you find it?"

"Tucked away at the back of one of the wine sheds. It's wartime, at least," Jasper said proudly. "She didn't start first time, but with a bit of encouragement, she fired up."

Why are yachts and cars always referred to as "she"? thought Kate as she started to stack their possessions into the old jalopy.

***

Life at the Cook house was suiting Kate and Jasper. They had fallen into a routine. After breakfast, he would set off to the village and she would do chores. When he returned for lunch, he would kiss her. Not a peck on the cheek, but a full-on kiss. After lunch he would disappear into one of the sheds or the hangar. On occasion, he wouldn't go outside, but spent the afternoon loving her. There was never a dull moment with Jasper, and she loved every minute.

Her musing was abruptly interrupted by shouting.

"Missy! Missy, come quick!" An out-of-breath boy from the village was standing at the front door.

Kate grabbed a knife and ran to the village. She pushed her way through the crowd that had gathered outside the bar.

She burst through the door to find Jasper sitting at a table, facing three men she had never seen before.

One of them turned and grinned at her. "Your pussy's here, Carmichael," said his rough, coarse voice.

Kate's temper flared. She hated being referred to as *pussy*. Her angry eyes met an evil black gaze. She stood her ground as she tried to weigh up the predicament that Jasper was in.

The men's attention had momently turned to Kate.

"Kate! Run!" shouted Jasper as he jumped onto the table.

Before the men realised what was happening, Jasper kicked each in the head with such force that they toppled onto the floor unconscious.

"Who are they?" Kate asked.

"Pirates!"

Kate turned and stared at Jasper. "This is the twenty-first century, for goodness' sake."

"You think it's any different from any other century?"

And to think, I was so happy here... Kate thought.

Chapter Forty-Five

Jasper was late returning from the village. Kate suspected he was trying to avoid her. But she could wait, while her temper simmered.

He stood in the open front door of the Cook house. The angry tension that filled the room turned towards him. His eyes fixed upon Kate's stiff back, her hands on her hips. She was more than angry.

Without meeting his gaze, she said, "Jasper, I want to leave this place."

Jasper slowly stepped inside. "I thought you were beginning to like it here."

"I was, until a group of wannabe Blackbeards…"

Jasper had to smile. Only Kate would describe them as wannabe Blackbeards.

"They weren't Blackbeards," he said. "They were twenty-first century pirates. Plundering the innocent."

"You could have fooled me. Weather-beaten tanned faces, evil eyes, missing teeth, no shirts, waistcoats, bandanas, knives, swords. I bet they had just captured a Spanish galleon with cannons sticking out of the sides!"

Kate's tirade was abruptly ended by Jasper's hands on her shoulders.

She tried to shake him off, but Jasper's grip was firm and her body was weak. The tension in her slowly lifted.

"They were going to kill you," she said. "I suppose they wanted diamonds."

"And money. And women for slaves. You were worth a lot of money to them. English, silver-blonde hair, with beautiful breasts." His hands gently cupped them.

He slid her round and rested her head on his shoulder.

"I have the horrible feeling that something's wrong with the boys," she said. "I miss them. Harry's calm voice and loving blue eyes, Oliver's bounding energy, Clare's roasts and Malcolm's knack for knowing when I'm in need of tea and biscuits."

Jasper's hand caressed her head. "They love you, Kate."

"I don't deserve it. I've treated them very badly."

"You were ill, my love. All of us were guilty of not recognising it. You are the glue that holds us together. We rely on you." Jasper kissed her hair. "We all need you. Harry and Oliver need your guidance and support. Clare treats you like a daughter, and Malcolm, never one to waste words, loves you."

"And you?"

"You're my life, Kate. You rest deep inside me, giving me the love that I've always needed. You make me whole, Kate. Without you, I would be a cutthroat—"

Kate's words cut over his. "No. You wouldn't. Deep inside you, there's goodness that no other Carmichael has had. All I did was love you. Our love turns your darkness into light."

***

The next day, Jasper was up before the sun rose; he had left Kate sleeping. He opened the hangar doors and walked to his Cessna 182. He ran his palm along the fuselage to her name, *Kate*. He had named it after her because she was the reason he owned the plane.

If it hadn't been for Bernhard's yacht waiting for him to leave their cove, he would have never gone to Wolf's Cove, and Kate would never have known about his plane and what he used it for. He now had to decide what he should tell her about another secret.

You could count on one hand the people who knew about Jasper's plane and pilot's licence. Kate had settled into a life with Bruce, and although Jasper had had a surveillance team, he'd needed to see her. He'd been in contact with Malcolm, just as he was now, and Malcolm had told him there was no interest in the Wellsbury airfield. All he needed was a plane and a pilot's licence and he could see Kate whenever he wanted.

But that wasn't the only reason he had it. There had been too many people interfering with his diamond network, and Jasper—just like his father, Colin—operated alone. His double life with Lucinda in America, superyachts and his secret diamond flights around Europe had all been running smoothly until he had given into his desire to see Kate.

The trip to London and then to Kate's gallery had ended in disaster. There had been hatred in Kate's eyes; he couldn't have been more hurt if she had kicked him in the crotch. He had left the gallery in a daze, and as he'd entered the airport, W had kidnapped him. His days of flying around Europe had come to an abrupt end.

"What are you doing?"

Kate's calm voice made him jump. She stood in the hangar doorway, wrapped in her see-through silk robe. Desire filled him. He wanted to carry her into the plane and have his way with her, but after yesterday's tense exchange, he controlled his desire.

Kate strolled to the plane and lifted his hand from her name. Her eyes widened and she stepped back.

"Kate, meet Kate," Jasper light-heartedly said.

Kate was not impressed. "Why is my gut telling me you're hiding something?"

Chapter Forty-Six

Jasper's day had gone from bad to worse. He could see in Kate's eyes that he should have already confessed his diamond-running days.

Kate had gone into quiet mode.

"Kate. Talk to me."

She turned her back to him and carried on preparing dinner.

"Kate! I won't stop until you talk."

Kate whirled round to face Jasper. He was shocked to see watery, bulging, angry eyes.

"You're lying to me."

"I'm not!"

"You run diamonds in that plane."

Jasper stopped dead in his tracks.

"I can see through you. Running diamonds. That's what made you so rich in such a short time. What else do you have to tell me?"

Jasper sat at the table with his head in his hands.

"When we get back to England, you'll start again."

Silence descended like the Sword of Damocles. There was only one way that Jasper could win this argument.

"How much did looking after me cost you?"

"I love you," he mumbled.

"Love! Love!? You call deceiving me *love*?"

Kate was on fire; he had to extinguish it. He leapt up and grabbed her. His open mouth consumed hers. She tried to push him away, but he lifted her dress and with one hand cupped her bare buttock.

He felt her mouth open.

"I'm going to fuck you until this madness is driven out of you," he said.

She moved to slap him, but he caught her arm.

"I love you. That will never change."

"You hurt me. My emotions are in tatters. It must stop. I can't continue."

Guilt swept through Jasper. He wanted to fuck her against the wall and on the kitchen table, but that would cause her pain. He picked her up and carried her to the bedroom. "You're not going to leave me. You're mine. I need you."

His strong hands tore her dress. He pushed her onto the bed and took a moment to admire her naked body before he entered her.

He swallowed her gasp as he moved inside her. Her resistance waned. She wrapped her legs around him and threaded her fingers through his hair.

***

Jasper may have won this battle, but Kate had won the war. They were going back to Wellsbury.

Kate stared at the aircraft, mustering up the courage to climb inside. Jasper had reassured her that the plane was safe. He couldn't guarantee that, but the plane had completed several test flights without incident. It was also the only way back to Wellsbury now that the yacht needed extensive repairs.

Jasper knew Kate was nervous about flying, so he tried to ease her nerves by teasing.

He tried to hide a playful grin. "Next to me, re-member!" he shouted while Kate manoeuvred into the co-pilot's seat.

He climbed into the pilot's seat, put on his pi-lot's cap and saluted. "All secured. House locked. Hangar locked."

Kate turned and met his smiling eyes.

"Don't you dare."

"Dare what?" Jasper laughed. "You know the procedure." He picked up his pee bottle and waved it in the air. "If you want to pee, lift the hatch at the rear and—"

"Shut the fuck up and fly this bloody plane."

Jasper bent over with laughter.

He leaned over and pulled her into him, plant-ing a soft kiss upon her lips.

"Relax, my love. We'll be in Venice in no time."

Jasper had made this diamond run to the old World War One and then World War Two airfield many times. It had been abandoned after the sec-ond war because the runway was not long enough for large aircraft to land.

While Jasper had been diamond running from Wolf's Cove, one of his contacts had told him about the old Venice airfield that a group of businessmen were extending. They needed a cash injection to complete the work. Jasper had immediately real-ised how the airfield could complement his dia-mond network.

He had successfully completed many diamond deals in the derelict building, but he hadn't told Kate that. The least she knew about his past dia-mond dealing, the better.

His plan was to fly to Venice and refuel. Kate could use the bathroom facilities and buy food and water. The flask of tea and sandwiches she had made wouldn't last them to Wellsbury. He was hoping he'd find people who remembered him, as he hadn't the cash for a full tank of fuel, but he had diamonds to trade.

***

The plane circled the airfield while Jasper communicated with the control tower. The landing was a bumpy affair, and Kate thought Jasper needed to refine his landing skills.

As instructed, Jasper taxied towards the refuelling area. While he was sorting the paperwork, Kate made a dash for the smart-looking glass-fronted main building.

She was in desperate need of a bathroom, but she wasn't going to admit that to Jasper.

Her trainers squeaked on the polished stone floor as she followed the signs to the ladies'. With some urgency, she pushed open the door and hurried to the first empty cubicle. She locked the door and dropped her bag onto the floor.

Suddenly, the main bathroom door burst open. Kate froze; angry male voices echoed off the tiled walls. She stood perfectly still while the men argued in a language she didn't understand. However, she did recognise the words *diamond* and *Carmichael*.

Her stomach churned as she silently waited for the men to leave. When she thought the coast was clear, she carefully unlocked the cubicle door and peeked into the bathroom. She sighed with relief; she was alone.

She turned and flushed the toilet. The water gushed into the bowl with such force that the ceramic lid moved away from the wall. She tried to push it back, but a polythene bag peeked from behind the cistern. Kate shoved it back behind the cistern, but it wouldn't fit into the narrow gap. In desperation, she pulled the bag out. It split, and euro notes fell onto the floor.

Nervously, she stepped back into the bathroom and checked she was still alone.

Whoever the money belonged to would return. They wouldn't be interested in how she'd stumbled upon it; all they would want was her life. She panicked; she had to get out of the bathroom.

The bag the money was in had split. She couldn't just leave the money on the floor; she couldn't involve the police as they would want her to stay, and she couldn't do that because she wanted to see Harry and Oliver. So, she hurriedly stuffed the money into her bag.

Heavy footsteps echoed outside the bathroom door. Kate nervously waited for the men to enter.

"Kate, are you in there?"

Her legs buckled and she knelt on the floor.

Jasper poked his head around the door. He rushed to her side and lifted her up. His eyes settled on the money poking out of her bag. He didn't ask questions, just closed the bag. Kate stood at the sink, splashing cold water on her face.

"Kate, we have to go."

He put his arm around her.

"I can walk."

Kate was thankful that the few people in the foyer were only interested in the football match they were watching and not them.

Jasper had his arm looped across Kate's shoulders.

"I'm having second thoughts. We should hand that money to the police," she said.

"You think they will believe you?"

"Jasper, it's probably stolen."

"It's drug money. You stumbled across their pickup place."

Kate looked behind her as she climbed into the plane. Jasper was taking rolls of money from her bag.

"Be back in a mo," he said. "Going to pay for the fuel. The old crew have gone, and these new boys will only take cash."

Chapter Forty-Seven

While Jasper was paying for the fuel, Kate wandered to a pop-up stall just outside the airfield perimeter to buy sandwiches and bottles of water for their flight back to England.

When she returned, Jasper was checking the plane's engine. A warm glow spread through her. She was secretly very proud of her husband—he had surprised her with his flying skills, and she knew he was an outstanding sailor. Though she wasn't impressed with his diamond reputation, he was an exceptional diamond dealer—and most of all, he was a very skilful lover. He knew her body better than she did; he read her moods. She grinned. Jasper was not only the diamond king but the orgasm king.

"Kate!" Jasper shouted as he wiped his hands on a cloth.

She walked towards him, eyes shining and cheeks slightly flushed.

"You have that look in your eye."

"I love you. I feel like together we can cope with whatever life throws at us." Kate planted a kiss upon his cheek.

"We have to leave, or I'd let you show me how much you love me."

***

It was dark when Jasper circled his Wellsbury airfield.

The Cessna bounced along the grassy runway before coming to a halt facing the far hangar, which had been used many years before to hide Beth's drug-running plane. Jasper taxied towards the hangar doors and pressed a small button mounted upon on the instrument panel. There was a loud clang and the hangar doors began to roll upwards.

"I thought the doors opened inwards," Kate commented.

"If you want to stay alive in the diamond business, you work alone. Just like with the yacht, I made changes so I could work alone," said Jasper as he waited for the doors to fully open.

Red lighting filled the hangar as the plane came to rest. The doors clanged again as they closed.

Jasper took Kate's hand and led her to a small partitioned area at the back of the hangar. There was a single bed and a work surface with a microwave, toaster and kettle.

Jasper slumped onto the bed and pulled Kate with him.

***

Kate abruptly woke with Jasper's hand covering her mouth.

"Shhh," he murmured into her ear.

Kate could hear voices, one of which was Oliver's. She tried to push against Jasper.

"Listen. Just listen."

"Who's this bloody lowlife?" Oliver snapped.

"Some tramp. He said he heard a plane," answered a rough voice.

"He's dead."

"He was still alive when I found him."

"Professional job?"

"Difficult to say."

Kate and Jasper's eyes met.

"Get rid of the body. W's flying in."

Jasper pulled Kate close to his chest.

The hum of a plane engine filled the airfield. Jasper took Kate's hand, and they slipped out of the hangar's side door. They dodged across the back of the hangars until they reached the first one, which Beth had used for stashing drugs. Jasper opened the back door, and they nestled behind racks of boxes.

They overheard Oliver's voice. "I was surprised that you flew up here," he said meekly.

"I have a lot of money riding on this deal," W snapped. "You're the last Carmichael. But too young. Everything has to be done yesterday for you. Sometimes things have to be done slowly."

"Everything's set. The buyers are on their way."

W continued as if Oliver hadn't spoken. "I thought your dad would follow me and continue my work. But Colin thwarted me. Jasper has all the instincts to be the best Carmichael, but he met your mother. He fell in love. Carmichaels don't love. Remember that." W paused. "You should know your mother and father are missing."

"Missing? I thought—"

"There was a storm. Lots of damage. People dead, including the team I sent to kill them. If they're alive—and my gut tells me they are—you must kill them. Your mother will hug you. That's when you knife her. Jasper will go berserk. You must shoot him before he reaches you."

"You want me to kill my mum and dad."

"If you don't… Believe me, Jasper will get the upper hand."

At the sound of approaching diesel engines, W stopped talking.

Jasper and Kate couldn't hear the verbal exchange between the buyers and W. However, they did hear the sound of a single shot and W's angry voice barking instructions.

"Get the coke!"

Jasper peered between the free-standing racks that must have been installed for drug storage as the men began to move boxes. When one checked behind the rack where Jasper and Kate were hiding, Jasper wrestled him to the floor and lifted a knife from his belt. With the skill of an assassin, Jasper stabbed the man between the ribs.

Jasper glanced at Kate. She was in shock. He hadn't the time to console her; he had Carmichael business to settle. He picked up an automatic gun that the dead man had dropped. He marched from behind the racks, blasting anything that moved.

It was a massacre. The drug runners were taken by surprise and were no match for Jasper's demons.

"Carmichael!" shouted a voice.

Jasper pointed the gun at the cab of a truck and opened fire. Two drug runners jumped off the back and started to run away. They fell dead onto the runway. Jasper was in no mood for prisoners.

The air was thick with gunshots when Kate ran towards the open hangar door. Oliver's body lay limp next to a winded W.

She sat on the concrete floor and cradled Oliver's head, rocking him back and forth, back and forth, while Jasper checked that the drug runners were dead. Jasper couldn't look at her in case she saw the tears gushing down his face. He dropped the gun into a water butt in the corner of the hangar.

W's evil eyes were wide open, waiting for Jasper. In his hand was the gun he had shot Oliver with, one shot in the head.

"How does it feel, Jasper? Your son's dead." He managed a nervous grin, for he knew he was a few seconds from joining Oliver.

W hadn't anticipated that Jasper would be back in England. What were the odds that Jasper would be at the airfield the same day he had organised a drug deal?

He had let Oliver believe that he was in charge, but the plan had always been to shoot Oliver and then, after a satisfactory deal, fly away with the money.

But now W was looking into a pair of cold blue eyes. The life drained out of him as he realised that Jasper was the better Carmichael. He mustered some energy and lifted the gun, but Jasper stood on his hand and took the gun.

Jasper glanced at a distraught Kate, sobbing her heart out.

"Bastard," Jasper's voice was cold.

A single shot pierced W's head.

Kate looked up into Jasper's tear-filled eyes. His heart broke. He felt her pain. He sat behind her, and she nestled her head on his shoulder.

"Jasper," she pleaded. "I can't go on." Her hands stroked Oliver's blood-spattered face.

Jasper kissed her hair. "Lean on me, my love. I'm here for you."

***

Jasper had no idea how long he had cradled Kate as she sobbed. He kissed her eyes, lips, nose, ears. He lost count how many times he had whispered "I love you."

He tried to ease her away from Oliver's lifeless body.

"No! He needs me."

Jasper kissed her lips.

"I need you, Kate, and you need me."

Their eyes met.

"Don't shut me out, Kate. Let me grieve with you."

Chapter Forty-Eight

The sound of sirens was getting louder. Jasper searched Oliver's jeans pocket and pulled out his mobile phone.

"What are you doing?" yelled Kate "That's Oliver's!"

"Shh." Jasper stroked her head.

Jasper looked towards the airfield's main gate. He had never been so pleased to see Inspector Lewis striding towards him. He wondered what Lewis was doing here—after all, he was retired—but he knew Lewis had a soft spot for Kate. He would go along with Jasper's story just to protect her.

"What the bloody hell happened here?" Lewis's voice was stern, but his eyes softened when he saw Kate.

"Call Clare," Jasper said. "I can't leave her."

***

The old Evoque rattled along the airfield's grassy runway and came to a stop behind rows of police and forensic vehicles. A tearful Clare pushed past Lewis, but he caught her arm.

"Hold on," he said, trying his best not to be emotional. "We can't separate her from Oliver. She's lying in Jasper's arms, sobbing. We need to look at his body."

Malcolm nodded.

"It's bloody carnage, and just my luck to have a green forensic team. Most of them are coughing their guts up." Lewis paused. "Malcolm, it's vital I talk to Jasper."

"Jasper would never do anything to upset Kate."

"I'm guessing that Kate and Jasper stumbled across a drug deal. They shot Oliver and W."

"W? What's 'e doing 'ere?"

Lewis continued, ignoring Malcolm's questions. "Jasper flipped. The Carmichael demons went into overdrive."

Malcolm shook his head and strode past, heading towards Kate. Dead bodies were strewn about the airfield; boxes of drugs lay open where they'd been dropped. White powder mingled with blood.

Carnage, Malcolm thought. *Carmichael carnage.*

Jasper was staring at W's body, running his hand through his long grey-and-black hair. His blue eyes had a wildness that Malcolm hoped he would never see again.

"Jasper…" Kate mumbled.

Jasper knelt beside her; his hand caressed her face. "I'm here, my love."

Kate looked up into Clare's caring eyes.

"Come, Kate, love," Clare pleaded.

"I can't leave him. He doesn't like the cold."

A tear fell onto Clare's cardigan. "Harry will be waiting."

"It's Oliver, not Harry."

"Come on, Kate," said Malcolm. "Tea's brewing."

"He doesn't like tea."

"I've made his favourite biscuits."

Clare and Malcolm gradually lifted Kate.

233

"He'll like that." Suddenly Kate stopped and looked back at Oliver. "They'll keep him warm. Won't they?"

***

Harry stormed through the kitchen door. "What's happened? Where's Oliver?"

A heavy silence filled the kitchen as a tearful Malcolm and Clare stared at Oliver's empty seat.

The silence was broken by the studio door creaking open. Jasper stepped outside, facing the night sky.

Harry, Clare and Malcolm tiptoed to the studio door.

"Jasper…" said Kate.

"Not now, my love. I'm evil."

Kate stood behind his tension-filled back. "I know. But I've come to share your grief." Her arms circled his waist.

"Kate, have you any idea what I've done?"

"Yes. I was there. You held me while my heart cracked. You were my strength." She rested her head between his shoulders. "You asked me not to shut you out. Now I'm asking you not to shut me out."

Jasper turned around and pulled her into his chest. "Oh, Kate! Oh, Kate! I hurt. I feel empty, numb…" His voice broke as tears gushed onto Kate's blouse.

Jasper Carmichael—murderer, diamond dealer, money launderer—had been brought to his knees by his son's death. He had avenged Oliver's death the only way he knew, but it hadn't lessened the pain.

Chapter Forty-Nine

Inspector Lewis sat alone in his office nursing a large Famous Grouse. He had broken police procedure on so many levels because of his desire for Jasper Carmichael's wife. It seemed that every time that Jasper caused mayhem, he was called upon.

He had arrived at Isaacs House early and without his sergeant. The family had been in the living room, drinking tea and nibbling at toast. Lewis didn't know who looked the most devastated: Harry, Clare, Malcolm, Jasper or Kate.

"I'll come back later," he had croaked. The emotionally charged atmosphere had got to him.

"No!" said Jasper. "Sit."

Lewis had lowered himself into the only empty soft leather chair. Clare offered him tea and toast while they waited for Jasper to speak, but to everyone's surprise, Kate took the lead. She stood and gazed out of the window that overlooked the garden.

"We were trapped in Wolf's Cove. That's where Jasper kept his plane."

So, she already knew about the plane. Lewis diverted his gaze to Jasper, who was staring at his bare feet.

"The storm had damaged the yacht. To cut a long story short, Jasper worked on the plane so we could return to England. We refuelled at Venice and from there flew to Wellsbury."

Kate had paused and returned to her seat between Jasper and Harry, taking their hands. Her teary eyes met Harry's. Understandably, Harry was a mess; the brothers were unusually close considering their age gap. Oliver always had hit above his weight when protecting Harry.

Hold it together, Kate, Lewis had thought. *They both need you.*

"We heard voices. I recognised Oliver straight away." Her voice had quivered, and she wiped a lone tear off her cheek. "I wanted to run to him, but Jasper stopped me." She squeezed Jasper's hand. "I think Jasper recognised W's voice.

"It was obvious they were talking drugs. Oliver's voice appeared confident, but Oliver never lacked confidence. He told W that the deal he'd arranged was foolproof." Her voice broke and she put her head in her hands. Jasper put his arm around her and kissed her hair.

"My gut told me something was wrong," Jasper had said. "We heard trucks that we now know belonged to the drug dealers. There were voices and two shots. I don't know what was said to cause the raised voices, but all hell broke loose. Kate and I huddled together behind some racks and waited for the gunfire to stop." He squeezed Kate's shoulders. "Kate didn't wait, she ran to Oliver. The rest you know. It was a massacre. Dead bodies, blood, cocaine, the stench of gunfire, and our son dead."

Lewis sipped his Grouse as he recalled Jasper and Kate's story. He knew Jasper had killed those men. They had killed his son, a Carmichael, and they'd had to pay.

At that moment, two men in grey suits walked into his office. They each pulled up an uncomfortable plastic chair and sat opposite him.

"I'll have one of those," said the elder of the two. "I don't mind a cup."

Lewis poured him a drink.

"How's Carmichael? In shock?" asked the man as he sipped Lewis's whisky. "We need Carmichael back in the diamond trade."

"He has a stabilising effect upon those criminal types," said the other man. "Do you need anything to prove Carmichael didn't massacre those drug dealers?"

"We knew there was a deal going off," said the elder of the grey suits. "One gang hadn't the cash, so they joined forces." He swished the whisky around the cup. "We now have two less drug gangs."

"Is Kate going to be a problem?"

Lewis reddened. "He'll do nothing against Kate."

"Do you think he can deal diamonds without her?"

"You've seen what he's capable of. Leave Kate out of this."

The two men stared at Lewis.

"If you harm Kate, he'll come after you. And then…" Lewis stopped and stared at the men. "My guess is he'll then run a criminal network like you've never imagined."

An awkward silence developed while the two grey suits considered their options.

The elder put the empty whisky cup on the desk. "I think you've got the measure of things. We'll let the dust settle with this Oliver business."

Business. Oliver's death is not a bloody business, Lewis thought.

"Don't stand in Carmichael's way. He's an important asset."

The men stood and walked out of his office.

Lewis sat staring at the empty chairs, when an old friend from the forensic department appeared in the doorway.

"Got a minute?"

Lewis nodded towards the empty chairs. He shared the last of his Grouse between them.

"I've been going over the airfield massacre. I know this is old tech, but look at these diagrams. This shows the different bullets used."

Lewis stared at the paper diagram with blue crosses showing where the dead bodies had lain. His friend placed a plastic film over it.

"The red crosses are types of bullets used to kill the men. Notice anything?" He paused while Lewis studied the diagram. "The red crosses are all from the same gun. The team worked through the night on this."

Lewis couldn't believe what he was hearing. "There must be a mistake."

"No mistake. W was an important man—and then there's the two drug gang leaders. I've had my arse kicked to get this done. There's only two men killed by a handgun. The Carmichael kid and W. No prints on it."

A heavy silence lingered as Lewis considered the most probable explanation.

"W shot Oliver and Jasper lost it."

"Lost it! That's putting it fucking mildly. He's a maniac. He should be locked up and the fucking key thrown away. Those men were no pushovers."

And neither's Jasper, thought Lewis.

"He shot the bloody lot of them. He took no prisoners."

"Have you found the gun?"

"Of course we bloody have. At the bottom of a barrel of water."

"No fingerprints then."

"Just bring the bastard in so we can test for gunshot residue."

"Can't do that. In a roundabout way, I've just had my arse kicked as well."

"The suits?" the forensics man asked.

Lewis nodded and emptied his whisky glass.

Chapter Fifty

Harry walked into the Isaacs House kitchen, looking for his super. Clare and Malcolm sat there with very worried expressions.

Angry voices were coming from the office. Harry moved to the kitchen door, but Malcolm stopped him.

"Let them be."

***

"My son is not going to be laid to rest in that dark, cold mausoleum!"

"He's my son too."

"What's that got to do with it?"

"Everything. He's a Carmichael."

"He's half me."

"No! Harry's you. He walks like you. Talks like you. He's calm and measured."

"Leave Harry out of it."

"Why? You don't like the truth. You've always favoured Harry over Oliver."

Kate's cheeks flushed. "That's a lie. Oliver always demanded my attention and he had it. I slept with him, nursed him and lately, paid his fines. You weren't there, Jasper."

It was Jasper's turn to feel uncomfortable. He knew Kate was telling the truth.

They stood facing each other like two boxers, neither willing to give an inch.

After what seemed like an age, Kate turned and moved towards the French doors.

"Where are you going?" Jasper bellowed.

Kate turned the door handle.

"Don't fucking walk away from me!"

"Did you love Oliver?" Kate said in her calm voice.

"Love him? Of course I loved him! I shot the evil bastard that killed him and every fucker that was there. No one kills what's mine."

Kate stared into her husband's wild eyes. "Jasper, you can't go around killing people because they've upset you."

"Upset? Fucking upset?! He killed my son. He deserved to die. Those lowlifes were using my airfield to traffic drugs. They deserved everything they got."

"Jasper…"

"Don't *Jasper* me, Kate! My demons have been raging since Oliver's death. I'm not like you. My Carmichael demons demanded revenge."

Kate's anger slowly turned to compassion. "My love, come here. Sit next to me."

"I can't look at you." Jasper started to pace, his hands running through his hair.

"Jasper. I can't get through this without you. I need to feel you inside me. I have this dull ache deep inside me. Arguing makes it worse."

Jasper stopped and stared.

"I need your love."

"Kate, I can't."

Kate sat silently, staring into space.

"Okay."

"Okay what? Kate, fucking answer me!"

"This is pointless. You've just said you don't want me. So I'll go."

"Go where?"

"Wherever the car points." Kate stood and walked away from Jasper.

"You're not driving. You're not fit."

"Fit?"

Jasper caught her arm while she was in the hallway.

"I said you're not driving."

In one swift move, Kate was pinned against the wall. Jasper was so close she could feel his breath.

"Am I interrupting?" Lewis's voice took everyone by surprise.

Lewis had joined Harry, Clare and Malcom watching Jasper and Kate. He had followed the raised voices.

"What do you want?" Jasper's angry voice echoed.

Lewis staggered into the hallway, holding the diagram of the airfield massacre.

"You're fucking drunk."

Lewis leaned against the hallway wall.

"I've had one of those days," he slurred, dropping the diagram.

"I'll make coffee," said Clare, walking back into the kitchen.

Malcolm took Lewis's arm and guided him into the living room.

"This isn't over," Jasper whispered into Kate's ear.

"Oh yes, it is."

Jasper picked up the diagram and followed Kate into the living room. Lewis sat hunched over his knees, holding a cup of black coffee.

"This must be a social visit," Jasper said sarcastically while looking at the diagram.

"Do you know how many you shot?" Lewis said in a thick whisky voice.

"What do you mean?" asked Kate.

"Had a visit from two suits. Drank my whisky. It seems Jasper is a very important man. If I had my way, I'd lock him up and throw away the key," Lewis said between swigs of coffee.

Jasper was silent as he continued to stare at the diagram that could put him in prison.

"The crosses are dead men. The red crosses are the same bullets that killed them."

Kate took the diagram from Jasper's hand.

The coffee seemed to be having an effect on Lewis as he put his case together. "You heard the single shot that killed Oliver and you snapped. You got a submachine gun and shot anything that moved. Except W, who must have gloated to your face that he'd shot your son right under your nose. The Carmichael demons went out of control. You took the gun from W and shot him, Carmichael style, one bullet in the head. Then you wiped the guns clean. Put the handgun by W and dropped the automatic in the barrel of water. Only cold-blooded killers behave like that. Then—this is the bit that makes my stomach churn—you joined Kate cradling Oliver as if nothing had happened."

"Have you finished?"

"No! The only way I can prove this is by giving you a gunshot residue test. But you know that, and it doesn't matter anyway. The men in grey suits have a job for you. A very important job. W was a very important man." Lewis stared into Jasper's eyes. "But it seems you're more important than him. All is not lost. You eliminated two London drug gangs. For that, we're thankful."

Lewis stood and swayed back into his seat.

"How many people have you shared this cock-and-bull story with?" said Jasper.

Lewis laughed. "Scared?"

Jasper stared at the diagram that was still in Kate's hand. "Your forensics buddy, I'd guess. Only another old timer like you would use a paper diagram."

Chapter Fifty-One

The night was slipping into dawn, and Jasper was sitting alone in the office. He'd been there all night. After Lewis's visit, he'd decided to give Kate some space.

He didn't expect to hear the kitchen door open and close, then the Evoque start. He hurried outside, but he was too late. The Evoque, with Kate behind the wheel, was driving out of the gates.

"She's had no breakfast," said Clare in her disgruntled fashion.

"I'll go to her, but she needs some alone time," Jasper said as he walked out of the kitchen.

***

Malcolm was in the driver's seat of the Isaacs House pickup. "'Ow do you know she'll be at the beach 'ouse?"

"I know Kate. She needs space to think," answered Jasper. He wasn't going to tell Malcolm that the beach house was a very special place for Kate.

His mind flashed back to the times he had watched her at the studio Bruce had built. She'd been alone; her relationship with Bruce was changing, and the sea and beach had been her solace. He had fought back the desire to go to her. He'd been in W's clutches, and he couldn't put Kate in danger.

"She's 'ere," said Malcolm, looking at the Evoque parked by the beach.

Jasper collected his bag from the back of the pickup and walked towards his old hiding place opposite where Kate's studio once stood. He left his bag, threw his trainers next to it and walked towards the gully and the beach.

Kate stood facing the sea, the water gently lapping over her feet. Jasper waited and opened the waistband of his jeans, just the way Kate liked it. He slowly sidled up to her.

"Fancy company?"

She leaned back. "Who's offering?"

Jasper stepped closer so he brushed her back. "A man that misses you." His lips caressed her neck, and a sigh drifted from her mouth. "I'm sorry about Lewis upsetting you."

"My emotions are very raw."

"Let me soothe them."

Kate didn't answer.

"Are you mad at me?"

"That evil bastard deserved it. But Oliver, but Oliver…" Kate's words disappeared into the wind. "When I think what Oliver could have achieved, and he threw it all away for drugs…"

Jasper wrapped his arms around her waist. "Even as a child, he fought boys older than him, and he wouldn't rest until he bettered them. And he had so much energy. I should have recognised the Carmichael demons, but I thought it couldn't be happening."

Kate rested her back against Jasper's chest. "I loved him, but he dismissed it. I know now it was the Carmichael darkness."

"There's something you must know."

"About Harry?"

"Those important men in grey suits Lewis mentioned want me. Or they want a Carmichael diamond legacy."

Kate turned to face him. "Not Harry."

"For my freedom, they want me to be a bridge between the diamond black market and the legit market. I know all the players. I know what to buy and when to sell."

"How do you know this?"

"Because I was approached before we left." He stroked her forehead. "You were more important."

"Harry!"

"They want a Carmichael diamond dynasty. Their first choice was Oliver. But Harry is the one. He's intelligent, calm and measured, just like you. He knows diamonds. He had a good tutor in Zak."

"This can't be happening. I'm losing you both to diamonds."

"Talk to Harry. Let him tell you what he has planned."

She nestled into his chest. Jasper took advantage of her vulnerability and flicked open the waistband of her jeans. He slipped his hands inside.

"Tell me what you have planned," she said.

"Accept our diamond scheme. You don't have to know any details or meet any people." Jasper moved his hands, gently caressing her skin. "You'll still have Harry close and me in your bed."

"Where will you run this business from?"

"Isaacs House."

She pushed away to face him, their lips met, and Jasper took advantage. His kiss was full of desire while his hands kneaded her buttocks.

"I want your legs wrapped around me," he told her. "I need to feel that glow that flows through me when you sigh and you whisper *don't make me wait*."

"You're asking a lot."

"You can have everything, Kate. Bookshop. Beach house for your painting. Harry. Me to keep you warm. That rattling old Evoque. Just accept the diamonds." Jasper paused. "The bit I've missed is that I'll need a lot of loving."

Kate giggled.

Neither Kate nor Jasper noticed that a yacht had dropped its anchor in the bay.

Chapter Fifty-Two

It had been a trying few weeks since Oliver's death. Kate had been distraught when Wellsbury council had refused to allow her to bury Oliver in the cemetery. The letter she had received had been signed by all the council members. They had claimed that Oliver Carmichael had become an activist against authority and had been travelling around the country organising demonstrations. The council members didn't want such a person in the cemetery, where the grave could become a focal point for activists to congregate.

Kate exploded and went in search of Harry. He was shocked to see tears streaming down her cheeks, her red, sore eyes and drawn face. Harry's heart broke. He wrapped his arms around his mother and rested her head on his shoulder. She begged him to tell her the truth about Oliver, but he couldn't. It would break her heart.

He waited until her tears had subsided to gently tell her that Oliver had changed. He had no longer been that happy boy she remembered. He took a gulp and held her tight when he told her that Oliver had suffered from the Carmichael demons.

"If only I'd been here," she said, and walked away.

***

Kate was alone when she pulled the Evoque into the Riverside Café carpark. The café was boarded up with a 'To Let' sign nailed on the door. The once manicured grass was overgrown; the picnic benches had become victims of the wind that blew off the river.

Kate walked to the river's edge, thinking of Oliver and Harry bounding down to the water, tip-tapping and laughing as they collected stones to skim. Oliver would turn and smile that infectious Carmichael smile that filled his face.

Tears fell when Kate recalled Oliver marching through her shopping centre office, cap to one side, tie pulled away from his collar, dragging his school bag, grinning at her. He would jump on a chair, swing his legs and playfully complain that she never spent quality time with them. When she'd tell him they would go to the Riverside Café, he would jump from the chair and march out of the office, thumping the air.

***

The Evoque was filled with a heavy silence as Kate drove to the Riverside Café. Jasper sat next to her holding Oliver's remains in a wooden casket in the shape of a boat. Clare, Malcolm and Harry were squashed in the back of the car.

They all solemnly walked to the river's edge. Jasper handed Oliver's ashes to Kate. She turned and tried to smile at the people that were most precious to her. Her legs felt heavy and didn't want to move for her to say her final farewell to her beloved son.

Suddenly, Kate was surrounded by Harry, Clare and Malcolm. They huddled together, thinking of Oliver.

The water lapped around her knees as she placed Oliver's casket into the river. She stood awhile as the casket floated from the shore. She couldn't believe that she wouldn't see her son again on this earth.

See you on the other side, my darling boy.

Chapter Fifty-Three

Grief had been consuming Kate. Jasper tried to ease her pain, but he only knew sexual healing, and Kate wasn't ready for that.

Inspector Lewis had unexpectedly arrived and made himself at home in Jasper's office.

"Kate's not here," Jasper said as Lewis lowered himself into a leather chair.

"I know. Some problem at the bookshop."

Jasper was immediately put on guard. Lewis was obviously having them both watched.

Lewis smiled at Clare when she brought in cake and coffee.

"You look pleased with yourself," said Jasper as he sat opposite Lewis.

"You'll be pleased to know that you're innocent of any killing at the airfield. It seems that the rival drug gangs were responsible," Lewis said smugly, sipping his coffee between bites of cake.

Jasper remained silent, preferring to study Lewis's expression. He could tell Lewis had more to tell.

"I've been to London, met some acquaintances of yours. They were very pleased with my conclusions about the airfield shooting. It's a shame Oliver and W died."

"Get on with it."

Lewis smiled in that peculiar cocky manner he had when he thought he had the upper hand. "I know what's expected of you."

"Thought you'd retired."

"This assignment is far more important than retirement. This is the opportunity I have been waiting my whole life for. I will oversee the diamond dealing of the diamond king. I will know the names of your criminal friends."

Jasper's cold blue stare sent a shiver down Lewis's back.

Lewis's smile dropped. "They want a progress report."

"They'll have to wait. I've been preoccupied with Oliver's funeral. Kate needed me. Anyway, I can't just conjure up a diamond network. Most of my contacts are dead or retired. I'm working on using Isaacs House, but that depends on Kate. Harry's keen on opening a jewellery outlet in the shopping centre."

"Don't tell me it all depends on Kate."

"I lost her once through diamonds and that's not going to happen again."

"They're impatient."

"Well, they'll have to fucking wait. Kate's emotions are too raw to cope with me being a diamond dealer."

"Do you need money?"

"I trade diamonds. I don't buy them. If your masters want progress, give me diamonds."

"They're your masters too."

At that moment, Kate returned with Malcolm, who was carrying a box of books.

"Am I interrupting?" she said as she planted a kiss on Jasper's cheek.

Malcolm put the box on Kate's desk.

"You want all of them 'ere?" he said, nodding at the space between her desk and the French doors.

"Yes." Kate smiled at Malcolm then turned her attention to Lewis. "Do we have a problem?"

"Kate, what's going on?" asked Jasper, his eyes fixed on the box of books.

"She should sack the bloody lot of them. Bloody useless lot." Malcom's voice drifted as he left the office.

"Kate! Answer me."

"It's nothing I can't handle. But not today."

"I'm going to add to your problems then, Kate," Lewis commented.

"Lewis has a new job," interrupted Jasper.

"The council is gunning for you." Lewis's choice of words had Kate's complete attention.

"I broke no laws or council bylaws," she said. "I own the Riverside Café and the land. I checked."

"That's the problem—you own too much land."

Kate eased herself next to Jasper. "Go on."

"The council want to build affordable housing. But you own large swathes of suitable land."

"You mean Hopes' Farm and Hill's Garage. The council refused to help the Hopes and Mr Hill."

"That may be, but you own the lot."

"You need a history lesson, Lewis." Kate's calm voice had suddenly taken a firm tone. "My property ownership started in a small, emotional way. The Hopes had a cash-flow problem when the price of milk fell. I do their books—for free, I'll add. I injected cash into their business. The Hopes are a proud family; they don't accept charity, so I accepted the land adjacent to Isaacs House in exchange. I'll also add that the land wasn't used by the Hopes. It wasn't suitable for dairy farming."

"But you saw a business opportunity."

"Yes. I have always thought that market gardening was a good long-term investment. As it turned out, I was right."

"More money in the Carmichael coffers."

Kate didn't rise to Lewis's sarcastic remarks. "I felt sorry for Mr Hill. His family had given so much to Wellsbury, and the council just let his business fail instead of stepping in and helping him."

"So, you own the garage and Jasper owns the airfield. Whatever next?"

"I admit I did see the possibility of a future business between the airfield and the garage. But at the time, Jasper and I were having problems."

"What about the other pockets of land?"

"If you're referring to the Riverside Café, I have always been a silent partner." Kate paused for Lewis to catch up before she dropped her bombshell. "The Victorian buildings have always been owned by Jasper and I." She hesitated as her eyes moved to Jasper. "The George pub I inherited from Eric."

"What?!" exclaimed Jasper.

"I suppose your London masters have been digging into my various dealings." Kate stood and walked to the French doors. "I used a London law firm. They received any money and dealt with any paperwork. Any papers that required my urgent attention, I would make an excuse and go to London. I was shocked when they contacted me about Eric's will." Kate nervously laughed. "The ultimate humiliation. His frigid ex, owner of his pub. I did nothing. The George just carried on being the dive it has always been. How ironic that it now stands in the path of redevelopment. Or, should I say, *I* stand in the path of redevelopment."

"Kate, why?" Jasper's concerned voice filled the office.

"I've told you. I was bored. I was very emotional." She turned and stared into his blue eyes. "Life was dull. I needed to feel adrenalin pulsing through me. I missed you. It was just something that took my mind off you. I never intended for the property business to get this big. It seems to have taken on a mind of its own."

Unbeknown to Kate, Clare, Malcolm and Harry had slipped into the office.

"Your wife has her fingers in so many pies— she's rich," Lewis commented. "Not as rich as you, Jasper, but rich nonetheless. Did you know that she has outmanoeuvred your property company in an auction stand-off?"

"I'd do it again. They're lazy, overpaid and over-confident." Kate's voice had suddenly changed into that of a no-nonsense, strong, determined woman.

Clare, Malcolm and Harry looked on in surprise, but Jasper was filled with pride. His trousers tightened; he wanted to be inside her, satisfying her emotions.

"I insisted on anonymity," Kate continued, unaware.

"That may come at a price," Lewis remarked.

Kate swiftly turned to face him. "Are you blackmailing me?"

"Not yet, but it's a possibility you may want to keep at the back of your mind."

Kate's green eyes turned cold.

"I'll make tea," said Clare, expecting an angry outburst from Kate.

"My relationship with Bruce was changing," Kate said. "He was changing, or I was changing— it doesn't matter. But the day I was told he was dead, I felt as if my foundations had been pulled from under me. Somehow, I had to carry on. Then my health started to decline."

"You don't eat enough," said Clare, returning with a tray of tea.

Kate couldn't help but smile. "Then Jasper appeared, and I needed him to recharge my inner strength."

"Is that what you two call it? Recharging," said Clare.

Kate smiled. "I'm afraid I haven't given my properties much thought."

Lewis stood, declining Clare's offer of tea. "I suggest that you give them your complete attention, Kate."

Chapter Fifty-Four

Kate sat facing Jasper in the first-class carriage of the early train to London. Jasper had suggested he accompany her to her solicitors, and she had agreed.

Later that day, Jasper had a meeting with his anonymous masters, which Kate would also attend.

Kate closed her eyes as she reflected on the days since Oliver's passing. Oliver had always brought her happiness, and now she had to face making a new life without him. She'd needed something to occupy her mind, and felt the deterioration within the bookshop could be the answer, along with the expansion of the shopping centre and her reorganisation of Isaacs House. A quick look at the bookshop accounts had revealed discrepancies with some orders.

The bookshop had been on her mind ever since Lewis had left. It was midnight when she'd lifted the Evoque keys from the kitchen rack. She'd been surprised when Jasper slipped into the passenger seat.

The moment Kate had unlocked the bookshop door, she could tell something was wrong. Jasper had stayed back, preferring to stand at the door.

Kate had slowly walked between the bookshelves, and the tears had begun to flow. She'd picked up books that were lying on the dusty wood floor and put them back on the shelves. The sofa reading area had empty cups left on the carpet. The desks with computers had half-filled cups left to the side. Computers were left on.

Kate had opened the small office door but didn't go inside. She placed her head on the wall and cried. Her once pristine bookshop was a mess.

The next morning, she had been waiting for the bookshop staff to arrive, along with a small gathering of disgruntled people who'd complained about the state of the bookshop. The staff were late, and she was told by the folk outside the shop that this wasn't unusual.

A stern Kate had ordered her staff to stand just inside the shop. Those that were fifteen minutes late were immediately dismissed and told to go to the shopping centre main office to collect any outstanding wages. Her voice had taken an angry tone when she assigned the remaining staff tasks to clean up the shop. Some decided to leave, but Kate had expected that and had employed a team of contract cleaners. The staff that remained were given tasks of reorganising the books into categories and author. Kate then went outside and told the gathered crowd that they would be opening in half an hour.

Jasper had rescued her from the bookshop office for lunch, but somehow, they'd ended up in the gallery's small bathroom.

"You need this," he had said as he lifted her onto the bathroom counter.

Kate had spent her daylight hours at the bookshop, making it into the premier bookshop it used to be. Her evenings had been spent with Harry and his scheme for a diamond shop. Jasper always joined them and sat silently listening.

Harry had given the shopping centre a makeover, including an extension where his diamond shop would be. His scheme was to expand the centre from the back of the units that backed onto the present car park. The new car park would be on the plot that The George occupied.

Kate had asked about deliveries, and Harry had his answer prepared. Delivery vans would be allowed into the shopping centre at certain hours. Automatic bollards would prevent access during peak shopping times.

Kate hadn't told either Harry or Jasper, but she liked the idea, particularly the design of the extension with an arched, covered walkway with upmarket shops that included Harry's diamond shop.

When she was alone, she thought about Clare and Malcolm. Running Isaacs House was becoming too much for them, but the last thing she wanted was to hurt their feelings. They had given their lives to her and they had become her trusted friends, but they needed help. She was working on how she could introduce her new staff, Rosie and Sam, into the Isaacs House family.

Rosie's energetic personality was just what Isaacs House needed. Kate had had a soft spot for the girl after Oliver had raped her. He had claimed that Rosie had consented to sex, but Kate had her doubts. Kate feared that Oliver had inherited the Carmichael rough sex gene from his great grandfather.

She then turned her mind to Sam; he was her gardener and Malcolm liked him. But she had plans for the garden that involved the reuse of the large greenhouses that Hopes' farm was replacing. Her plan was to have them erected in the field beyond the Isaacs House orchard. Her goal was to produce sufficient food for the house. She wondered if this would be too much for Sam if he was helping Malcolm as well.

The train began to slow. They were coming into London Euston.

***

Kate couldn't hide her smile. Jasper had changed into the Lord Carmichael role as he strode ahead of her and the porter he had summoned to take their luggage to the waiting limousine. Of all Jasper's chameleon roles, Lord Carmichael was the one that Kate hated. However, she had to admit he did look every inch a lord. He was immaculately dressed in designer clothes that fitted perfectly. His greying hair lay on his collar, as Kate liked it, and the rimless glasses gave him a distinguished look that turned heads.

Jasper had insisted that Kate wear a dress, but she had insisted on the brown knee-length boots and a brown coat that brushed her calves. He was a little miffed when she had refused to have her hair coloured; she'd kept her natural silver hair with blonde streaks.

Jasper held the limo rear passenger door open for Kate while the driver and porter secured their luggage in the boot.

The driver filtered into the traffic, and Jasper gripped a nervous Kate's hand. He slipped his hand into her coat and gently caressed her leg. Their eyes met.

"I love you, Lady Carmichael, and don't forget it," he whispered.

Kate tried to smile but London always made her nervous.

The limo stopped in front of the glass doors of Jasper's apartment block. The porter rushed out to collect their luggage, and the apartment block agent greeted Jasper with her plastic smile. She didn't even look at Kate, only at Jasper's hand holding hers.

Kate's body relaxed when they entered the penthouse apartment.

"Any requests, sir?" the porter asked.

"We're eating in. I have work to do. There will be visitors. Just ring."

Kate casually dropped her coat onto the back of the leather couch and walked to the coffee machine.

"Oh! I didn't realise you would be coming—I didn't buy tea," said the agent, who had followed them into the apartment.

The agent's words went over Kate's head; she had brought her own tea. Jasper smiled at Kate, who lifted a packet of tea from one of their bags.

"I'll have a cup of that, Kate," said a familiar voice.

Inspector Lewis walked into the apartment as if he owned it. "I want to be alone with Lord and Lady Carmichael."

The porter and the agent scurried out through the apartment door.

"Lewis!" said Jasper impatiently as Kate handed Lewis a tea and Jasper a coffee.

"Biscuits?" asked Lewis, and waited for Kate to offer him one of Clare's specials. "You two have got to be careful. There's a lot of interest in the pair of you. People are prepared to pay for information."

"Why are you here?" asked Kate.

"Your meeting, Jasper, is at the club. Turn left at the main door; it's just along that passageway, so Kate can join you. And Kate, your solicitor is sweating cobs. Have you caught him fiddling?"

***

It was late afternoon when the hired Range Rover sped towards W's country estate. Kate glanced over to Jasper, who had the Carmichael scowl fixed upon his face.

Jasper's meeting with his new masters had been cancelled, and he'd been instructed to go to W's country estate. W's brother was waiting to discuss W's will.

Jasper had argued, but his new boss had insisted he was required to attend the reading of W's will.

Kate's mind settled upon her solicitor, Mr Goldberg. To quote Lewis, she *had* caught him fiddling, although she preferred to say that she had found discrepancies in her account.

Mr Goldberg's office was in walking distance from Euston; that was one of the reasons she had opened an account there. She hadn't done due diligence on Goldberg; she'd just put twenty solicitors' names in a hat, closed her eyes and picked out his name.

On one of her visits, when she had intended to leave the deeds to her properties in his safe, she had met his son, a new partner in the firm, and something about him had set her on edge. The son had brought up the subject of the deeds, and she had lied, telling him they were in a safety deposit box. When he had asked which bank, Kate had given him one of her "none of your business" smiles. In fact, thanks to him, she intended to keep the deeds in a hidden cupboard in the Isaacs library, along with Zak's cash and diamonds, as well as some of Jasper's diamonds.

Mr Goldberg had been alone when Kate introduced him to Jasper. He had been unusually nervous and was continually wiping his brow. When his son joined them, Mr Goldberg's unease increased. His son, in a somewhat aggressive tone, queried why Kate and Jasper were visiting. In his opinion, Kate's account was running smoothly. The atmosphere in the office tensed when Kate lifted a folded piece of paper from her small messenger bag and handed it to Mr Goldberg.

She cast her eyes to the strongroom that was behind Goldberg's desk and then politely asked for all her account transactions.

"All of them?" asked a surprised Mr Goldberg.

Kate nodded. "I'll wait. You see, I can't remember some transactions, and according to my records, some are missing."

"No way you've gone through all your account," said Goldberg's son.

Jasper had stood and glared, first at the son and then at the father. "If my wife says she has checked her account, then she has."

"Well… er… I don't think…" Goldberg stuttered.

"Open the fucking safe and hand over Kate's account records." Jasper's patience had been wearing thin.

Goldberg stood and clicked the dial of the strong room. Jasper pushed him to one side and pulled the door open. His keen eyes quickly scanned the box files, which were arranged in alphabetical order.

Jasper whipped round to face Goldberg and his son. "How fucking much?!" Jasper grabbed Goldberg by the collar.

His son raced from the room, shouting for help.

Kate touched Jasper's arm. Their eyes met, and she tugged on his coat sleeve.

"This bastard…"

"Was a bad choice and a lesson learnt."

Jasper had let go of Goldberg's collar when Kate, in her calm manner, told him she'd be closing her account.

Jasper had raced from Goldberg's office, his Carmichael temper simmering. Kate had to jog to keep up with him.

"Jasper, stop!" she pleaded. "I urgently need a computer. Do you have a contact I can use?"

Jasper had abruptly stopped at the kerbside to hail a taxi. "How can you be so calm?"

She linked her arm in his and smiled.

Jasper had taken her to a seedy-looking place just off a main road. Kate hadn't bothered to ask where they were going, as her mind was whirling with the possibility that Goldberg and his son had accessed her bank accounts.

A man who reminded her of Zak—scruffy clothes that needed a wash and a face that needed a razor—greeted them. Kate had been briefly mesmerised by the interaction between Jasper and Mr Scruffy; they obviously had a past.

Kate had eagerly taken the laptop from Jasper and settled into a private corner of the shop.

She delved into her messenger bag and pulled out her encrypted USB. She impatiently waited for the USB to secure her files. She highlighted the Goldberg account and opened the file. Her fingers skated over the keypad as she closed Goldberg's account and the associated bank account. As a precaution, she changed passwords on her other accounts.

"Finished?" Jasper had asked and promptly picked up the laptop.

Kate was a little surprised that he kept hold of the laptop as they walked out of the shop.

"Lord Carmichael?" shouted a tabloid reporter who had written false stories about him before.

Jasper turned towards the voice and slung the laptop into a passing bin lorry.

Chapter Fifty-Five

It was W's brother, who had flown over from America, and had requested Jasper's attendance at the will reading. Kate had an uneasy feeling about this. She thought it was a ruse to get Jasper to the country estate. Jasper dismissed this by explaining that W's brother wasn't the same man as W. Kate had retorted that they'd come out of the same mould.

Trouble was waiting for them at the country estate. Even dead, W was going to haunt Jasper.

***

Armed guards were patrolling the estate. One stepped out of the new gatehouse and waved for Jasper to stop. The guard leaned inside the Range Rover and took a photo of Jasper's face.

After a few moments, the guard sarcastically said, "Important man, Jasper Carmichael. Park at the front."

Kate could feel the tension rising in Jasper. "Stop along the driveway," she told him.

"What for?"

"Just do it."

Jasper stopped on the country house driveway where they had the best view of the house, which was lit up like a Christmas tree.

"Come," she said as she opened the passenger door.

Kate walked to the front of the Range Rover and leant on the bonnet.

"Look at me. Jasper."

Jasper turned to face his wife. Her soft hands cupped his face as she kissed him.

"I love you, Jasper. Not the lord, or the diamond king, but Jasper. My Jasper."

He had leaned into her, drawing their bodies together and deepening their kiss.

***

A butler that Jasper hadn't seen before opened the house's wooden front doors. In silence, Kate and Jasper followed him to W's old study. The butler opened the door and stood inside.

"Lord and Lady Carmichael, sir."

Jasper cast his eyes around W's once immaculate study. Paintings had been removed from the walls and lay on the floor in a pile. W's precious books were stacked next to empty boxes.

A man turned from the French doors and set his eyes upon Jasper.

A cold shiver passed down Kate's spine, and she stepped closer to Jasper so their arms brushed.

W's brother's American accent echoed through the room. "You didn't come to the funeral or the official reading of the will. My brother was very thorough in every detail, and that included you. He hated you, but you know that. Right from the moment that our father came back from visiting you and announced that he had at long last met the true Carmichael."

The American's words riled Jasper. *He's W in an American cloak,* Jasper thought. He aggressively stepped forward, and Kate gripped his jacket sleeve.

"I can hardly remember Grandfather."

"But you see him every time you look into a mirror. My brother said you're the spitting image of him."

Kate tugged on Jasper's sleeve.

"I was a child when he visited me," Jasper said. "He just stood and stared."

"But he knew you were the one. My brother was your grandfather's favourite until then. He left us penniless. If it wasn't for Meredith, we would have starved. My brother stayed behind for revenge, but the rest of us went to America. Meredith had contacts."

"You mean you lived off the Carmichael name."

Evil blue eyes clashed with evil blue eyes.

"I'll get straight to the point. We want my brother's diamonds. That's the only reason you're alive."

"There're no diamonds."

"You owe us. There's not much cash. His account was hacked. The stupid cops over here haven't found the hacker."

A wrathful silence descended.

"I haven't much time. I have to empty this place. My brother never owned it."

"What do I call you?" Jasper asked.

"I'm Mr Carmichael to you."

"Well, Mr Carmichael, your brother lived a luxurious life, so there must be money. Have you opened the other safes?"

Mr Carmichael's evil eyes penetrated Jasper.

"There's the study safe, the office safe, the bedroom safe," said Jasper. "There might be one in the kitchen. Don't forget the passageway. I always thought that was a good place to hide money or diamonds."

Mr Carmichael's eyes rested on the butler. "Find them."

"I could help," offered Jasper.

***

Jasper and Kate were sitting silently, waiting on two uncomfortable, hard-backed chairs when the study door burst open. A guard marched across to the desk and dropped small hardback books and USB sticks onto the surface.

Jasper's keen eyes noted six A5 notebooks and six USBs. W didn't like computers—he only used them because he had to—so he had handwritten copies of his accounts.

Another guard appeared with a box and spread the contents over the coffee table.

Jasper glanced at the photographs and grinned; he guessed that the box contained a record of W's sexual activity.

Mr Carmichael leafed through the box of photographs. He glared at Jasper before turning to the guard. "Show me where you found these."

Chapter Fifty-Six

Kate and Jasper were left alone in the study.

"I don't like this, Jasper. We should leave."

"Not yet," said Jasper, fingering the photographs of W's young sexual partners. Underneath the photos was a small sealed polythene envelope of memory cards, which he dropped in his jacket pocket.

"Come on."

Kate followed Jasper out of the study and into the hallway. He hurried into the kitchen and stood by the door, turning his head from side to side as if trying to remember something. His gaze settled upon an old kitchen cabinet that you wouldn't normally give a second glance. Jasper ran his fingers along the edge of the cabinet that abutted the wall. A sly grin spread across his face when he found a matchstick-sized lever. He carefully pushed the lever, and the cabinet moved outward.

"Jasper, come on," Kate whispered. "Let's go before we're caught."

Jasper ignored her as he concentrated on the contents of the cabinet. "Kate, find a bag."

"What?"

"*Kate*."

"Okay. Okay."

Kate handed Jasper a couple of plastic supermarket bags, which Jasper promptly filled with cash that was in neat piles on the shelf behind the cabinet. Excitement flowed through him when he ran his fingers through the glittering contents of a canvas bag.

If he added these to the diamonds that were in the Isaacs library, he'd have enough to start trading again.

His eyes met Kate's, and he smiled.

***

Jasper and Kate were miles from W's old country estate when Mr Carmichael discovered they were missing. His men had reported that Jasper was still on the premises as his Range Rover was still parked outside. It wasn't until Lewis arrived that Mr Carmichael realised that Jasper and Kate had gone.

Lewis was furious. He'd been the one to spin the lie that Jasper was mentioned in W's will and had to attend the reading.

Ever since Lewis had been instructed to hide Jasper's guilt in the airfield massacre, he had sworn that Jasper would pay for what he'd done. He had convinced Mr Carmichael that Jasper had shot his brother and must pay. Mr Carmichael willingly agreed; he was consumed by the same hatred for Jasper as Lewis.

***

Kate's frayed nerves were making her extremely argumentative. Her arms and shoulders ached from carrying carrier bags of money. She hadn't slept for twenty-four hours and was thirsty and hungry when Jasper parked the stolen Land Rover Defender in the workshop of Alwyn's old boatyard.

They had left W's country house by the kitchen door. Kate had hurried towards the Range Rover, but Jasper had walked towards the estate's Land Rover Defender.

"What the hell are you playing at?" she had angrily whispered.

Jasper ignored her and threw the bags of money in the back of the Defender.

"Get in and wait."

Jasper had jogged back to the kitchen and turned in to the narrow passage that led to the room he had originally been imprisoned in. At the end of the passage was the weapons room. The key was hidden on the top of the door jamb. Once inside, he searched for the small incendiary devices cupboard. He carefully lifted two sealed packages off the self and put them in one of the canvas bags that hung from the back of the cupboard door. Jasper was familiar with these mobile-phone-controlled incendiary devices, as W had insisted that he use them.

Kate had been fuming when he returned. He ignored her to fiddle with wires under the steering column. The car fired, and Jasper floored the accelerator.

Kate clung to the passenger seat as the Defender bounced across fields and through woodland.

"Jasper! What—?"

"Not now, Kate."

And the rest of their journey was spent in silence with a stewing tension between them.

The tension exploded when Kate walked into the workshop living space.

"What the fuck are you playing at?"

Jasper walked away, unable to face her. His temper was also bubbling. His mind was on fire; he had been outmanoeuvred. There had been no reading of W's will but a ruse to murder both him and Kate. He had deliberately set the seed of W having safes in other rooms to make Mr Carmichael think there might be hidden money, and to give himself time to plan their escape. Jasper had always suspected that W had a secret hiding place for his valuables. It was a Carmichael trait to hide valuables in more than one place. For some reason, the day he had caught W sheepishly hovering by the kitchen cabinet had flashed into his mind.

He turned and looked at Kate. "I want to fuck you."

"Go fuck yourself."

"They were going to kill us."

"You don't say, Sherlock."

"How's the adrenaline? Can you feel it settling just above your thighs?"

"Shut the fuck up."

"I could rape you."

"Wouldn't be the first time."

Jasper's demons had surfaced and they needed satisfaction. "That was under the belt."

"You're not the only one who can fight dirty."

Jasper clenched his fists. "Take your fucking clothes off and lie on the fucking bed. I swear, Kate, I'll fuck you until you bleed."

"Wouldn't be the first time."

Jasper yelled. His angry blue eyes met defiant green eyes. But Kate didn't move.

"Go on. Rape me," she taunted, daring him.

He marched away from her, tugging on his hair. "No one defies me." His demons were in full flow.

"Get used to it."

He growled, gripped her shoulders and threw her onto the bed. He was astride her, holding her hands above her head with one hand. His free hand yanked the waistband of her trousers open.

"You're my wife. You do as I say."

"You're my husband. Show me some respect."

Jasper had raised his hand to slap her. "I'll shut that mouth of yours."

Their raging eyes met, and a lone tear crept from the corner of Kate's eye. Jasper watched as the tear slowly meandered down the side of her glowing cheek. Her angry, defiant façade was cracking, and his heart flipped. For a long moment, he hesitated, doubt flashing into his mind. Did he really want to hit her and make her bleed?

Her mouth opened and she took a deep breath as if she was preparing for the worst. Jasper had always delighted in the tingling sensations from her mouth. He could feel her warm breath upon his face, tempting him closer. Her eyes glazed over as she lifted her head. Their lips were so close he could almost taste her.

His anger melted as he consumed her mouth. He released her hands as their tongues danced and she threaded her fingers through his hair.

She needed him as much as he needed her. They needed each other.

Chapter Fifty-Seven

Kate propped Jasper's folded jacket against the window of the Defender and closed her eyes. She was in desperate need of sleep, but yesterday's sex wandered in and out of her mind. The pent-up tension in both of them had fired a sexual desire so intense that she craved for more. Just thinking about it, a heaviness settled at the top of her thighs.

She opened her eyes. Jasper was smiling at her with that charismatic Carmichael smile, and a warm glow built inside her. She wanted to feel his fullness, his kisses, his love.

Jasper stopped at a service station. "Tea, coffee, sandwiches?"

Kate managed a smile and nodded.

Jasper returned balancing the food and drink and a pack of disposable panties. "Thought you would appreciate these," he said with an enormous grin that stretched across his face.

***

Kate felt a lot better after a drink, sandwiches and a trip to the service station facilities.

"Where are we going?" she asked when Jasper turned off the main road.

"I've just had a text message confirming that my offer has been accepted."

"Offer for what?"

"You'll see."

The Defender eased its way along a level grassy track that stopped at a house. Kate stared, taking in every detail.

"Rooms either side of the front door, kitchen at the back, along with a dining room, four bedrooms—although one is very small. Needs a refurb," Jasper said.

"How do you know?"

"It was one of W's safe houses. After we finished a job, we came here."

"You've bought it."

"Dirt cheap. W has probably left Mr Carmichael with debts. Come on—I'll show you my bedroom."

Jasper had a twinkle in his eye when he grabbed Kate and kissed her.

***

A contented feeling filled Kate as she lay on the clean white sheets at Isaacs House. She had shared a roast dinner that Clare had cooked just for her. Then, while Malcolm and Jasper had disappeared to hide the Defender, she had lain in the bath until the water went cold. She was glad to be home.

She drifted off to sleep knowing that she was loved.

***

Kate felt someone shaking her awake.

"Kate, wake up."

"Go away."

"Open the cupboard in the library."

"No! You do it. Let me sleep."

"If you don't come, I'll show you what you mean to me."

Kate opened her eyes. "You wouldn't dare."

"Wouldn't I?"

Kate slowly moved off the bed and slipped her robe over her shoulders. After opening the secret cupboard, she padded into the kitchen to make tea. With her hands wrapped around a steaming cuppa, she peeped into the office, but Jasper was oblivious to her, staring at the diamonds from the library spread over the desktop.

She settled in a comfy white chair and sipped her tea. She still felt a twinge of hurt that Jasper preferred diamonds to her company.

***

The morning didn't go as Kate expected. The market stall holders were up in arms about the rumoured changes to the shopping centre, worried that a rent increase would put them out of business. What they always forgot was that Kate did their accounts, so she knew what they could comfortably afford.

She wandered into the Isaacs House office, hoping for a kiss and cuddle from Jasper. The last thing she expected was to be confronted by Lewis and two grey suits.

"Kate!" said a surprised Jasper. "You're back early." He leaned into her, pecking her cheek. "What's wrong?"

"Nothing," she replied, downcast.

She dropped her work briefcase onto her desk and hung her jacket over her chair. Sam, the gardener, caught her eye, and she opened the office French doors and walked outside to share a chat.

Clare bustled into the office. "What's she doing back?"

"I don't know."

"She left the Evoque by the gallery, so she must have intended to go there." Clare went to open the French doors.

"No! Leave her," said Jasper in a very concerned voice.

Clare looked up at him. "You're worried."

"Yes."

"Look here, Carmichael," said Suit One. "We've come for a meeting, not to witness a domestic."

"W warned us about this," said the other. "Everything stops when she's around. Get rid of her. She means to destroy you and our business."

Jasper whipped round and glared at the suits. "Understand this: without her there's no fucking business."

He returned to the French doors and watched Kate smile at Sam while shaking her head and pulling the tie from her hair.

***

It was late afternoon when Kate returned from the garden. Jasper was sitting in the kitchen talking to Clare and Malcolm. He smiled at her. She looked happy, with flushed cheeks and shining green eyes. To Jasper's surprise, she balanced on his knees, hooking her arms around his neck, and kissed him.

"I'll make the tea," said Malcolm cheerfully.

Kate stood and stared out of the kitchen window. "Everything has changed since Oliver."

She had their complete attention.

"I thought… I thought I could carry on. Just pretend that he would bounce through the door. He had so much energy. So much to live for. So much to share."

An awkward silence built until she continued.

"It was after our argument and make-up sex that I realised I must change. Life must go on without him."

"I knew it. I knew it—sex was to blame," interrupted Clare.

"I thought about selling the Riverside Café. At the moment, I can't go there. Oliver is everywhere. Running along the water's edge, throwing stones in the river. But they say time is a great healer, and some day, when I need to connect with him, I will go there and share our happy times."

Jasper's stool scraped along the kitchen floor.

"No! Don't come to me."

Another awkward silence developed.

"The beach house has so many memories, some happy, but many are sad. And that includes Bruce." She paused as happy times at the beach house flooded her mind. She turned and faced Jasper. "It has always been my place of solace. It's where I do my best work. But as much as I liked that house by the sea, I can't see me there. I can't see us there." Her eyes filled. "I would like us to build a new beach house on the footprint of the original 1920s build." She smiled. "I miss the sand between my toes and the sea lapping against my feet. But above all, I want a house where I can be Kate the painter and you can be plain Jasper. Not Lord Carmichael or the diamond king."

He rushed to her. His passionate kiss swept her off her feet.

Chapter Fifty-Eight

The hall clock chimed three a.m. while Kate waited for her tea to brew. Jasper had wrapped himself around her as if she was going to run away. The thought had crossed her mind after he had told her about the meeting with Lewis and the Suits.

The Suits had had a change of heart. Locked in the airfield hangar were the drugs and cases of money from the debacle that cost Oliver his life. The police had cleared away all evidence of the massacre except the drugs and money.

The Suits wanted Jasper to trade the drugs instead of diamonds. They even had a list of drug dealers he should contact. Kate was so incensed that she couldn't sleep. She'd waited until Jasper was asleep and eased herself out of bed.

She reached for her china mug and filled it with tea. Two arms circled her waist, and warm lips caressed her neck.

"Do you love me?" Jasper murmured between kisses.

"If you don't know by now…"

"I need reassuring words."

Kate carefully placed her mug on the surface and turned to face him. Her fingers traced his hairline. "You have my heart, mind and body. You always have. There isn't a word that fully describes my feeling for you. Just because I argue with you doesn't mean I've stopped loving you. I shall always argue with you."

She stood on tiptoes and claimed his mouth.

"I don't want you to ask questions when I disappear," he said. "It's for you own safety. You're the only person I listen to. The only person who can change my mind. But no one tells Jasper Carmichael what to do, least of all Lewis and his masters."

"Kiss me."

"Only if you come back to bed."

***

The guard on the airfield gate was surprised to see Jasper. After a brief chat, he opened the gate and Jasper drove to the hangar that housed his aircraft. He had convinced the guard that he was collecting his belongings off the plane. He left the hangar doors open so the guard could check up on him.

Hidden under the pilot's seat was a gun, a phone, tracking devices and ammunition. Jasper meticulously laid them onto the rear seat of the Range Rover, picked up the bag with the incendiary devices, slipped out of the rear door of the hangar and ran to the hangar with the drugs.

He didn't have much time. He slipped through the rear door and ran towards the boxes of drugs. He inserted W's incendiary devices between the layers of cocaine. There was a case of money he didn't recall seeing before, but he had more important things on his mind.

Before he left, he double checked that the mobile timers were on, and he had the control mobile in his pocket. One call from him, and the inferno would ignite.

***

A speeding police Mondeo caught Jasper's attention. His gut told him it was Lewis, driving like a madman with the blue light flashing. Jasper turned around and followed Lewis. With each mile, Jasper's nerves welled inside him.

He turned onto the lane that led to woods above the airfield. From there, he had a clear view of the drug hangar. Two men were leaning against a BMW parked beside it, and to Jasper's surprise, one was smoking. His hands started to shake when Lewis joined the men—the guard would be telling of his earlier visit to the airfield.

The guard managed to push the drug hangar doors just enough for Lewis and the men to squeeze through. Lewis and his two companions pushed the guard out of the way and disappeared inside. The guard continued to push the door, widening the gap before he followed them through.

Jasper waited, and then his fingers touched the control mobile in his pocket. Flames streaked through the opening in the doors, and he stumbled back. He regained his balance and returned to his observation point, but promptly fell onto the grass as a large explosion rocked the hangar.

Jasper lay on the grass, trying to control his shaking body. Those small incendiary devices couldn't have caused such a large explosion.

Chapter Fifty-Nine

Jasper needed Kate.

"Where are you?" he said into his phone.

"What's wrong?"

"Kate!"

"Isaacs."

***

Kate opened the kitchen door; she had taken to locking it when she was alone. Jasper rushed in, lifting her off her feet and pinning her against the kitchen work surface. His mouth consumed hers, his hands cupped her breasts, and his knee caressed her sex.

"Jasper!"

"Oh! Oh! Kate!" he gasped as her took her hand, pulling her towards the stairs.

***

Kate gazed at their clothes that littered their bedroom floor as she stroked Jasper's hair. His open mouth was resting on her breast while his hand cupped her sex. He had marched her into the bedroom and flung her onto the bed.

She didn't remember the sex, only Jasper crying, "Forgive me. It was an accident."

Kate wanted to know what had sparked Jasper's behaviour, but she had promised not to ask questions.

"Do you love me?" he asked.

"I can't believe you keep asking me that."

"Did I hurt you?" His voice was full of concern. She kissed his hair. "No, my love."

"I don't want to cause you pain. But I need to feel your love."

"Take what you need."

***

The headlights from Malcolm's pickup filled the kitchen. Kate sat alone sipping tea. Jasper weighed heavily on her mind. It had been many years since she had seen him in such turmoil.

The kitchen door bounced open, and Clare switched on the lights, making Kate squint.

Clare stopped and stared. "No need to ask you what you've been up to. Look at the state of you."

"Not now, Clare."

"You haven't heard…"

"Heard what?" said Jasper, pouring a glass of water.

"There's been an explosion at the airfield," said Malcolm, filling a mug from Kate's teapot. "You're not answering your phone."

"I switched it off. Didn't want to be disturbed." Jasper's eyes settled on Kate.

Kate insisted they should go to the airfield.

"It will be expected of us," she told him.

***

Jasper joined the chief fire officer and the chief constable staring at what was left of the hangar. Both officials were curious as to what Jasper knew about the hangar's contents in light of the drug gang massacre. Jasper couldn't add to what they both knew except that he had neglected the airfield in recent years.

The chief constable was interested to know the details of the airfield security. Jasper explained that there were cameras, and twenty-four-hour guards that patrolled the perimeter. Jasper was surprised to learn that the security cameras had been disconnected.

When the fire and police chiefs were finished with Jasper, he looked around for Kate.

He marvelled at his wife's compassion as she talked to the crowd that had assembled just inside the airfield. He wished he could be like her.

It was mid-morning when an official Rolls-Royce with flags on the front wings stopped on the road outside the main gate. Two Saville Row suits strode towards Jasper.

"Carmichael, I presume," said a stern voice that projected from a similarly stern face. "You won't remember me. I'm Lord Blackthorn, and this is my assistant, Johnson."

Of course you are, thought Jasper.

"Let's walk. A wartime airfield—have you the original plans?"

"I have nothing. It was a gift from an old friend."

"Yes, yes, we know all about your association with the Cohens." Blackthorn paused. "Well, during the war, we had several secret fuel dumps. Large underground fuel tanks. We had decommissioned most of them, but this little airfield got overlooked." Blackthorn stopped and stared at the runway and the dead grass surrounding it. "Nothing has grown in this field since Anton's plane caught fire. Don't look so surprised—we know all about Anton and your father. Anyway, I digress. The field is slowly being poisoned by the underground tanks leaking.

Nothing to worry about, until the concrete floor of that hangar began to crack and break up.

"Before we could do anything, W had organised a drug drop. I'm surprised it didn't explode when you went on your shooting spree. Then Lewis and his interfering associates turned up. Something must have ignited the bloody stuff. I believe the guard pushed the door open. There must have been a few sparks from the rusting metal rail. I don't have to spell it out—spark from the rail plus possibly a cigarette end mixed with cocaine. Boom."

Jasper followed Lord Blackthorn to the rear of the demolished hangar.

"Notice that there's a dip in the ground. I wouldn't walk on it if I was you."

"I don't know what to say. I knew nothing about this."

"Of course you bloody didn't. This was a top-secret airfield during World War Two. Need to know basis."

An uncomfortable silence lingered between the men.

"You say nothing," Blackthorn said eventually. "Not even to your attractive wife."

Jasper followed his gaze. Kate was talking and smiling to the sandwich man while sipping tea.

"Is she worth it?" Blackthorn said. "Got Spencer blood. It shows."

"What do you think?"

Another awkward silence fell between the men.

Blackthorn broke it. "You have no choice in the matter. We are taking over the airfield. Barbed wire fencing. Soldiers guarding the place. In a nutshell, you no longer own the airfield. It won't be an airfield. We are also going to confiscate Hill's Garage. What will the delectable Kate say about that, I wonder? I have a feeling that in the scheme of things, she won't mind about Hill's Garage, but she will mind about her other Wellsbury business interests."

"What do you mean?"

"Let me put it this way. We have taken a special interest in Wellsbury. It needs to be brought into the twenty-first century. But the problem we have is that your wife owns the land that we want to develop."

"What do you mean, develop?"

"Houses, industry, newcomers."

Jasper's gut churned. Lord Blackthorn was lying. Whatever they had stored in the underground tanks was dangerous and harmful and he didn't want Jasper poking his nose in.

"Let me give you an alternative," Blackthorn continued. "If you both cooperate, you can expand the shopping centre with your diamond centre. Kate can keep her books and gallery."

"But you want the rest," Jasper interjected.

"Ah! You get my drift. On the other hand, if the pair of you cause trouble. All three of you will disappear."

"Including Harry?"

"Of course. Just take Kate to Wolf's Cove. I'm sure she'll cooperate, particularly if Harry's included."

"Kate will never leave England."

"Then I can't protect you. Make her understand that there're people that want the pair of you dead. You both know too much. They won't pussyfoot around like W. They won't get diamond fever." Blackthorn paused. "However, there're a number of us that think that this country owes the Carmichaels. Your grandfather and father. We also owe Meredith Spencer. He prevented many a scandal."

"We're being exiled?"

"I'm offering an idyllic life. Mediterranean life-style. Kate will appreciate the warmth. You can deal diamonds as long as you don't get in our way. Kate can paint, and restore a vineyard. And the pair of you can fuck as much as you like."

Kate was walking towards them. Knee-length boots and a long coat suited her. Jasper stepped towards her and kissed her cheek.

"Be good," Jasper whispered to her.

"Absolute pleasure, Lady Carmichael," Blackthorn said, kissing her hand. "I'll be in touch, Carmichael."

Chapter Sixty

Two weeks had passed since Jasper had told Harry, Clare and Malcolm about Blackthorn and Johnson. Kate had gone into silent mode.

Jasper concentrated on the sale of his marina; he had moved his two yachts to the mooring by Alwyn's old boatyard. He was at the yard when he received the call from Malcolm. Blackthorn had singled Kate out.

***

Kate had been at her desk in the office at Isaacs House, dressed in blue jeans and a white blouse, her feet bare and her silver-blonde locks held from her face with her reading glasses, when Blackthorn and Johnson bustled their way into office.

"Lady Carmichael, I presume," Blackthorn said in a condescending manner.

"What do you want?" Kate's impatient tone betrayed her simmering anger. She hated strangers interrupting her.

"Lack of progress. Jasper's started, but you…" Blackthorn raised his voice. "*You*. Have done fuck all."

Kate's mouth filled with bile as her anger surfaced. Blackthorn had let his calm façade slip. Kate glared at him.

Stay calm, stay calm, rise above his taunts, she repeated in her head. *Remember, when the enemy swears, they're losing the battle. Stay calm.*

***

Clare and Malcolm had been joined by Harry as they huddled over Jasper's secret listening device that was still wired up to the kitchen recorder.

"She's too quiet," said Clare. "She'll explode. Put the kettle on, Malcolm."

***

Kate closed her laptop and pushed away from her desk. She slowly stood, taking deep breaths, and walked to the French doors. She gazed at her closed studio. It was Sunday, the day she normally spent with her family in the studio. Oliver had been very protective of the Sundays he spent in the studio with his mother.

The image of her cradling him and staring at the bullet hole in his forehead flashed into her mind. Her eyes filled and the angry bile changed into a nervous lump in her throat. She dared not turn and meet Blackthorn's eyes; he would see that she was emotionally wounded, and that was just what he wanted.

"I'm not leaving," her voice was controlled and calm. She heard Blackthorn move and imagined his face reddening. "I'm not leaving Harry. He needs me."

***

Harry sat on a kitchen stool and leaned on the work surface with his head in his hands.

***

"Take him with you," barked Blackthorn.

Kate turned and faced him. "No!" Her calm voice struggled. "No! Harry deserves to be his own man, to forge his own path through the jungle of life. Do what he wants, not what I or you want. And I intend to be here for him." Kate stepped closer to Blackthorn so she could read his eyes. "My family will stay where we belong, here at Isaacs House. We all need each other. We need a family's support. We need to grieve Oliver as a family."

"The three of you can do that anywhere."

"No!" Kate's anger surfaced. "Oliver was part of us. Clare and Malcolm are part of the family."

"They're staff. Sack them."

Kate snapped. "Who the hell do you think you are?"

Blackthorn stepped back from two angry green eyes.

God, the Spencer temper, he thought.

"Clare and Malcolm are part of this family. They have shared happy and sad times. They're loyal. But you wouldn't understand that."

"Do you know who you are?" His change of tack took Kate by surprise, momentarily breaking her train of thought. "You're a fucking Spencer. That's why he left you his fortune. He saw himself."

There's that word again, thought Kate. *He's scraping the barrel. Stay calm, Kate, you've got this.*

***

Harry moved towards the kitchen door.
"No, lad. Your mother's got this."

***

Kate's silence started to unnerve Blackthorn.

"Meredith Spencer's granddaughter. His precious daughter opened her legs for a married man and you popped out. Not Reynolds."

Blackthorn read Kate's silence as him gaining the upper hand.

"You sound familiar with the Spencer bloodline." Kate's voice was calm once again as she stepped towards Blackthorn. "But you didn't know him. No one did, except my grandmother and then my mother. Understand this: I'm Kate Carmichael. My own woman. My Spencer blood won't let the likes of you pull my strings."

***

Harry gasped, and Malcolm smiled at Clare. "She's back," he said.

***

"I'm not moving from Isaacs House. I shall run my own business as I see fit."

"What about Jasper and his diamonds?"

"What about them?"

"He won't stop."

"Do you think I don't know that? Jasper's also a brilliant businessman—that, you all seem to forget."

"He's haemorrhaging money."

"If you referring to the marina, I believe it's sorted."

Blackthorn reddened.

"If you think I'd let my husband sink to borrowing, you don't know me or Jasper. We're a team. A powerful team."

"We'll finish the pair of you. You'll have nothing."

"Try. You and your like think we need money and diamonds to survive. But you're wrong. We share a love that cannot be destroyed."

"You'll regret this, Kate Spencer." Blackthorn moved towards the door. "We'll destroy you and him."

He slammed the office door behind him.

***

"She stood up to him," said Harry.

"Of course she did, lad. Your mother is quite a woman." Malcolm's voice was full of pride.

Chapter Sixty-One

The Range Rover shrieked to a halt by the kitchen door. Jasper leapt from the driving seat shouting Kate's name.

"Kate! Where's Kate?"

"Pacing the garden," said Malcolm matter-of-factly. "She's left 'er tea, and she never does that."

But Jasper didn't hear him finish as he raced out into the garden.

He pulled Kate into his arms and peppered her hair with kisses. "My love. I'm so sorry. I had no idea that he would single you out."

"He shouldn't have used the f-word at me. I lost it after that."

"What?" He stared into her glistening green eyes.

"Your nemeses are not getting their own way with me. I'm not going to Wolf's Cove. I'm staying here with my family."

Jasper's hands cupped her face, and he planted a kiss on her lips. "I gather you gave Blackthorn a run for his money."

"How do you know?"

"My phone hasn't stopped ringing. They want a face-to-face."

"I tried to stay calm."

Jasper kissed her again.

"I'm not leaving Harry," she said. "He had a deep bond with Oliver. He needs our support.

So do Clare and Malcolm. We all loved him. We should grieve together."

Jasper stroked her hairline.

"He brought up Meredith. Even said Reynolds wasn't my father. But I already knew that."

"They will drive a wedge between us, my love."

"They'll try. I did tell him our love cannot be destroyed. I don't care about diamonds. Losing Oliver has taught me what really matters is the love of a family."

***

Jasper had opened the unused Carmichael House offices for this meeting. Four identical men dressed in Saville Row black suits, all with dark glasses and beards, sat opposite Kate and Jasper.

The men had all refused the offer of tea or coffee, preferring their own bottled water. They each half filled a glass with water and waited.

"I'm X, and the spokesperson for this meeting," said one of them. "I don't approve of involving women in such important matters, but you, Lady Carmichael, have proved to be the exception."

"Oh! Stop being so melodramatic, 'I'm X'. This is the twenty first century not the nineteenth. Let's get on with it." Kate's voice was more than a little irritated. She'd had enough of secretive men.

"Carmichael, control your woman."

"Kate's my wife, not my woman. She is her own person. I wouldn't have married her otherwise. Anyway, I agree—let's get on with it."

X took a moment to stare at Kate, then Jasper.

"We can't trust you, Carmichael." He began in a calm, authoritative voice. "You're more than capable of controlling the diamond black market, and we can't let that happen. We've tried to guide you, but you've resisted."

"If you're referring to Lewis, I had nothing to do with the hangar explosion. They wanted me to trade the drugs instead of diamonds. The airfield has been confiscated by the military. But you know that."

"We know you have diamonds and probably cash. And you, Lady Carmichael, are the one that has hidden them. It's got to be you. We know every move Carmichael has made. No safe deposit boxes. No bank accounts. You two are so squeaky clean it's unbelievable. In fact, you're becoming a security risk."

An uncomfortable silence shifted about the room until:

"What a load of codswallop."

All heads turned to Kate; her little outburst had taken them by surprise.

"What you mean is that you want to control both the diamond black market and the…" She hesitated. "Let me put it another way. Jasper has the wherewithal to influence the diamond black market. He has the ability to flood the world with diamonds, having a detrimental effect on the price of diamonds. And you and your associates want to control that price." Kate looked between the four men. They looked extremely uncomfortable. "You do realise that my scenario is fictitious."

"You're a dangerous woman," said X. "That is why the two of you must be where we can control you."

"So you're making Wolf's Cove a prison," said Jasper.

"Yes. No internet. No phones."

Jasper laughed. "But Wolf's Cove is run by criminals."

"Not anymore. They've moved out."

An angry tension developed. Suddenly, Jasper jumped up and pushed the heavy wooden table into the men. Their eyes widened, and beads of sweat dripped from their foreheads.

"Enough!" Jasper leaned on the table, his angry blue eyes fixed on the men. "I'm not playing your silly fucking mind games. I'll fucking finish your control on the diamond black market. Any agreement you thought we had is over. You want the diamond king? You've got him."

"You're bluffing," said X.

"Bluffing, am I? Watch."

"You need millions. You haven't that many diamonds."

"Ha! You think so, do you? Are you that confident of your intelligence?"

"You won't pull my strings, Carmichael," one of the men said defiantly.

"Won't I?"

"Let's take a break," said X. "Calm down. And reconvene in half an hour."

"You think I'm stupid?!" yelled Jasper, his temper bubbling. "That's more than enough time for the police to arrive."

Jasper snatched Kate's hand and marched out of the conference room and up the stairs to the penthouse.

"Jasper!"

"Not now, Kate," he snapped as he locked the internal door to the penthouse.

He opened his office safe, which was hidden behind one of Kate's beach paintings. Jasper's temper was brimming over as he drummed his fingers on his desk while waiting for his computer to boot up. Kate knew when to keep her mouth shut, so she lowered herself onto the leather sofa that filled the wall opposite Jasper's desk.

Kate watched Jasper's fingers fly over the keyboard. His face reddened as a scowl descended. A wave of nervousness flipped her stomach.

Their eyes briefly met when he stood to look out of the window at the changing landscape of Wellsbury.

A loud ping from the laptop, and Jasper returned to his desk. His scowling gaze moved to Kate as he closed the laptop lid.

"I need to be inside you."

She stood and slowly walked towards their bedroom, dropping an item of clothing with each step.

Chapter Sixty-Two

Kate lay staring at the ceiling of their Carmichael House penthouse bedroom. The door creaked open, and Jasper walked in carrying a cup of tea.

"You must be a mind reader," she said, lifting herself to take the tea.

Jasper leaned and kissed her hair. "Thank you for loving me," he whispered.

She smiled.

Jasper sat on the bed and trailed his index finger along her hairline. "I can't do this without you. I know I've said it before. But this time I've got to finish it. I thought with the demise of W it would be over, but they won't leave me alone." He paused to kiss her forehead. "Jasper wants a life with Kate."

"Will you win?"

"With you beside me."

"Yes, but there's Harry, Clare and Malcolm. We can't just abandon them."

"They can come with us. I can make enough money for all of us."

"Diamonds?"

"That's what I know."

***

It was late morning, and Jasper was drumming his fingers on his desk.

"Are you doing this on your own?" asked Kate, putting a coffee beside him.

He nodded as his eyes moved over the laptop screen.

"Kate, don't go," he said, and patted his knee.

She settled on his lap and gazed at the laptop screen. "I don't understand what you're doing."

"People are always on the lookout for cheap genuine diamonds. There're lots of fakes and dealers, and the public lose out." He nuzzled her neck and murmured, "My diamonds are all genuine. They'll pass any test. All I need is interest from a buyer or buyers." He paused to kiss her neck. "It's times like this that I miss having Zak around. He knew where to sell diamonds."

"How so?"

"All you need to know is that those greedy men will leave us alone if I can prove that I can control their profit margin."

"You can't do this on your own." She hesitated. "I hate to admit this, but you need another Zak."

Jasper's fingers glided up and down her back as he tried to concentrate on the screen. "I do have another Zak. With practise, his skill will surpass Zak's. He's clever and has diamonds running through his veins."

"No!" She jumped off Jasper's lap. "Leave Harry alone."

"You're the one that said he could do whatever he wants and you'd support him."

"I thought he'd run the shopping centre or go back to uni to complete a PhD."

Jasper walked to her and rested his hands upon her shoulders. "But what if he wants to carry on the Carmichael diamond business? Would you be prepared to support him?"

***

Harry Carmichael sat at his mother's desk in the Isaacs House office. He was working on the new upmarket extension to the shopping centre. His thoughts flashed back to Zak's one-person windowless office. The cramped workshop and the old, worn equipment he used for cutting diamonds. Harry's workshop was going to be large enough to fit the latest diamond-cutting equipment. He closed his eyes and imagined himself adjusting a computer-controlled cutting machine.

Zak had let him remove diamonds from pieces of jewellery. By eye, Zak would masterfully alter the diamonds to fit new pieces of jewellery: pendants, rings, earrings. Harry had never asked where Zak's diamonds came from, but he suspected his dad had something to do with it. Zak was old school and his skills had died with him, except the ones he had passed onto Harry.

Harry stood and looked out of the office French windows to his mother's studio. She had virtually stopped painting, and he wondered if she would ever return to it. Oliver's death had affected her more than him and his dad. He didn't want to add to his mother's grief, but when he had revisited universities with the intention of committing himself to a PhD, he'd realised he had no wish to return to university life.

Oliver had always told him to stop being a stuffed shirt—there's more to life than a PhD. Get the adrenaline running. Harry had argued back, saying university life wasn't for stuffed shirts.

But walking around the campus hadn't got the adrenaline running.

However, the prospect of running a quality diamond jewellery centre did. His long-term goal was to have the good and famous wearing necklaces, pendants and earrings he'd designed. Harry wanted to leave his Carmichael stamp upon his generation, just as his grandfather had, and his father. Harry was a Carmichael.

But his diamond centre would have to be put on hold until the cracks in his mother's heart had healed. His dad had broken her heart and Oliver had shattered it, and Harry had no desire to join their club.

***

Kate stared aimlessly out of the Carmichael House penthouse window.

"I must go to Harry. He'll be worried. He needs me."

"Harry's his own man, Kate. You must let him go."

"I can't let him become another Carmichael that's addicted to diamonds."

Jasper wrapped his arms around her, her back to his front. "Kate, my love, he has too much of you in him to be that."

Chapter Sixty-Three

Jasper's Saville Row suits had asked for an urgent meeting. All four of them had a sheepish look about them, as if they had had their backsides well and truly kicked. The man called X had suggested a gentlemen's agreement—Jasper would not interfere with their diamond network, providing they did the same for him—and held out his hand to Jasper. Kate thought that Jasper should have pressed for the agreement in writing, but he had agreed to a handshake. *All that drama,* Kate had thought, *for a handshake.*

When they had arrived back at the house, Harry had wrapped his arms around her.

"I was worried," he had said, but Kate's gut told her that she should have been the worried one.

Clare had cooked Kate's favourite: chicken roast with lots of vegetables, followed by apple pie. Conversation and banter flowed easily over dinner, but Kate had a feeling that something had happened while she had been with Jasper in Carmichael House.

She slipped on her jacket and shoes and went for a gentle night-time stroll around the garden. Inside, she could see Jasper and Harry with their heads together, staring at a computer screen. She felt unwanted and left out of this new father-and-son bond. She had a feeling that it involved diamonds, and it hurt.

***

Kate was up early the next day. Jasper and Harry were both asleep in the office when she left Isaacs House.

She had accepted a tea from the shopping centre's early morning coffee vendor. He had tried to make polite conversation, but it was lost on her until he casually mentioned the extension. Harry had been seen taking photos of the car park that lay between the shopping centre and The George.

Kate just smiled at the vendor and continued walking round the deserted centre. She stopped and stared at the Spencer Library, admiring Bruce's workmanship. She quickly turned to her gallery, where there were so many happy memories with the boys, Jasper and Bruce. She had enjoyed talking about and selling paintings. But the gallery had a neglected appearance. She vowed to reopen it after she had sorted the bookshop.

The finances of the bookshop lay heavily on her mind, but lurking in the background was the new relationship between Jasper and Harry. She knew it would be diamonds—after all, Jasper had mentioned Zak and his skill with cutting diamonds. Zak had been like a father to Harry, eager to pass on his diamond cutting skills to an impressionable young lad.

Kate couldn't lose Harry. She would swallow her pride and let him have his diamond centre.

***

Kate hadn't bothered with lunch. Her morning had been interrupted with resignation letters from four members of staff. She was sorry to see them go, but it was probably for the best.

It was mid-afternoon when she left her desk for a change of scenery. While she sauntered through the marketplace, her thoughts hovered on the bookshop. She was happy with the new cleaning crew, and the remaining staff were doing a good job organising the books. She had stabilised the finances; however, there was a possibility that the shop would need an injection of money to prevent bankruptcy.

Without paying attention, she wandered into one of the new marketplace cafés. She sat in a window seat so she could people-watch. Conversation and banter flowed easily between the café's customers, and Kate looked like just another customer, dressed in blue jeans, knee-high boots and a long jacket.

"Have you met Kate?" asked a customer sitting on a bar stool.

Kate's ears pricked.

"You should talk to her about the extension."

Kate's gaze settled on two men sitting at the bar. Nervousness welled inside her—one of them had a notepad.

"She owns The George. She was left it."

Kate couldn't hear the questions that the notepad man was asking.

"That's right, by her ex. She's going to knock it down. Her son Harry's been round there all week… No, Jasper doesn't own Wellsbury, Kate does. Diamonds is Jasper's game, and by the looks of it. Harry will follow in his footsteps."

Kate coughed as her tea tried to go down the wrong way.

***

On returning to Isaacs House, Kate made a mug of tea and walked into the office. Jasper and Harry sat huddled over a computer at Jasper's desk. Kate slowly wandered over to the French doors, nursing her tea.

The atmosphere thickened and Harry and Jasper stopped talking. Jasper knew Kate's body well, and he could see she was controlling her temper.

"When were you going to tell me?"

Jasper and Harry remained silent, unsure of what to say.

"I overheard two men talking. One of them had a notepad."

Harry rose and took a step nearer to his mother. "I was frightened that you would be mad. I don't want to go back to uni. It seems dull compared to what I can achieve with the shopping centre."

Kate turned to look into his blue eyes. "Diamonds."

"I can't explain it. Zak saw it—I'm attracted to diamonds. It's not just their sparkle. It's… it's…"

"The adrenaline rush when they're nestled in your hand after they have been cut into your own design and clasped into platinum." Kate paused. "Zak told me all about your skill with uncut diamonds."

"He used some of my jewellery designs."

"I know."

"Are you mad at me?"

"Yes and no. I'm disappointed that you're going down the diamond route."

"Uni's not for me, Mum."

"It's not about uni."

"It's about diamonds," Jasper interjected.

"I've lost you both to diamonds."

"You haven't lost me, Mum. I'm not Dad."

"Your dad can't leave them alone. I bet he's already planning how to sell or trade your diamond jewellery." She stopped and looked Jasper in the eyes. "Before he converted Carmichael Castle into luxury apartments, I imagined he would use the castle for diamond parties."

"He's already mentioned hiring the hotel for that purpose."

"Enough said." She walked to the office door. "I've had an exhausting day. I need food and sleep."

"Kate! We have to talk."

"Not tonight, Jasper. Maybe tomorrow."

Chapter Sixty-Four

It was a Sunday, and a comfortable contentment flowed through Isaacs House. Kate was in her studio, with every intention of sorting her unfinished paintings, when Harry appeared.

"Mum?"

Kate didn't look up.

"M-uuum."

"Harry. What is it?"

Kate flicked her gaze to Harry, who was gripping a young woman's hand.

"This is Jenny."

Kate smiled. "Welcome. I'm Kate."

"I know who you are, Lady Carmichael."

An uneasy feeling shot through Kate at Jenny's bitter tone.

"Jenny works in the accounts department," said Harry, eager to divert his mother's stare from Jenny.

"I'm sorry—I've lost touch with the staff." Kate said, a little embarrassed.

The tension building in the atmosphere was shattered by Jasper opening the studio's bifold doors. His angry stare pierced Harry.

"Have you told her?" His voice was more than a little irritated.

"Jenny's pregnant. Twins," Harry blurted with his eyes fixed on the studio floor.

"Okay," Kate said in her calm, matter-of-fact voice. Her mind was whirling. What were their plans, if they have any? Marriage? House? Money?

Harry's eyes said it all: protect us from Dad's temper. Jenny's hands gripped Harry's arm, her eyes were fixed on her well-worn trainers.

That uneasy feeling welled in Kate. Why did she think Jenny was acting?

"I think tea's called for." Kate moved to the studio door.

"Fucking tea can't solve this bloody mess."

Kate turned to Jasper and smiled.

"Kate, no. I won't have you being all…"

She stood on her tiptoes and planted a kiss on his cheek. "Let me sort it, my love," she murmured into his ear.

Jasper felt his bubbling tension suddenly settle.

***

The hall clock struck two a.m. as Kate walked into her studio carrying a tray with a pot of tea and a plate of biscuits.

Jasper was in bed. She always enjoyed sex with Jasper; he read her body and gave her what she wanted.

She pulled up a stool to her workbench and poured a cup of tea.

Kate had persuaded Harry and Jenny to sleep at Isaacs. Jenny's slightly aggressive attitude had put Kate on her guard. She'd reluctantly agreed to have a medical check-up at the clinic but refused to have a DNA test.

"My babies are not having a bloody DNA test. I don't want your charity. Your son had his pleasure and he'll pay."

Kate had initially thought that Jenny's condition had caused this outburst. But as she thought back on it, she wasn't so sure.

Before joining Jasper in bed, she had phoned Amanda, Jasper's long-suffering PA who had retired. Kate had asked about Jenny. Amanda knew Jenny Clarke—Clarke with an e, chip on her shoulder, thought the world owed her a living. Amanda was adamant that if Jenny was pregnant, it would be Oliver's. He'd been telling everyone that he couldn't have children as he was firing blanks.

"Kate, someone has to tell you about Oliver. He called you a whore. He fucked around. He did drugs. Harry rescued him many times from the clutches of drug dealers."

With a heavy heart, she slowly climbed the stairs to their bedroom. She dropped her night robe onto the carpet and slipped into bed. Before she had pulled the sheet over her, Jasper pulled her into him, her back to his front. They fitted together like two peas in a pod. His large hands cupped her breasts and his mouth nuzzled her neck.

"Well?" he murmured.

"I don't like it. Something's wrong."

"You agree with me."

"I phoned Amanda."

"And?"

"She suspects Oliver's the father."

"I'll sort it, Kate."

"We'll sort it."

Chapter Sixty-Five

Three months ago

Oliver Carmichael staggered into The George and dropped an empty bottle of vodka onto a table. He wanted to fuck and get stoned. Through his blurred vision, he swayed towards the tables near the rear door of the pub. A young woman grabbed hold of his crotch.

"Are up for it?" she said, squeezing him hard.

Oliver vaguely recognised her; she worked in the accounts department. He dropped his hand to her backside and returned the squeeze. The two stopped by a table where little bags of cocaine were spread. Oliver picked one up and the two went out into the alleyway that ran at the side of the pub. He found his favourite place for fucking and pushed her against the wall. Her hands were already inside his trousers. Oliver ripped open the small envelope of cocaine and coated her nose. He dipped the tip of his index finger in the white powder and rubbed it on his teeth. The woman's eyes met Oliver's as she put his index finger into her mouth and sucked.

It didn't take long for Oliver's high to kick in. A wicked smile covered his face as he lifted her pencil skirt. His hands glided over her soft skin, but Oliver didn't have time to appreciate a woman's body. He wanted to fuck.

He ripped off her thong and threw it on the ground. Her blouse joined it. Oliver lifted her against the wall and held her hands above her head.

Oliver Carmichael had a reputation of fucking hard, and she cried out as he roughly feasted on her body.

When he had had enough, he released her hands. She dropped like a sack of potatoes. He pulled his trousers up and snorted more of the cocaine. He didn't give her a second glance as he walked back into the pub.

***

Jenny Clarke's period was late. She guessed she was pregnant with Oliver Carmichael's bastard. She hadn't had sex since that night in the alley. He had hurt her, and she couldn't bear to be touched by another man.

Gossip would follow her. She considered an abortion. But one day, the answer to her dilemma walked through the shopping centre main office. Gullible Harry Carmichael. She hatched a plan while watching Harry blush as he talked to Amanda's replacement. His mother was in her office, but Harry didn't care; he had a soft spot for Lizzy Welsh.

Jenny decided she'd come on to Harry just has she had with Oliver, then lure him back to her flat, where she would spike his drink. While Harry was unconscious, she would remove his clothes. If the plan worked, he would wake naked and assume he'd fucked her.

Chapter Sixty-Six

Harry Carmichael slumped into the comfy chair in the office of his mother's bookshop.

Kate looked over her reading glasses. "Tough day?"

"I don't get it. I just don't get it."

She placed her glasses on the desk and stared at her son. "Get what?"

"Are women always this frigid when they're expecting?"

Not to my knowledge, she thought, casting her mind back to her pregnancies.

"Have you talked to a doctor?"

"She won't talk. The doctor told us it was hormones. She would get over it."

"And she hasn't."

"Last night, she told me she hated me." Harry's eyes filled as he recalled their argument. He wasn't used to arguments; they upset his gentle nature.

"Harry, tell me."

"I suppose it goes back to Oliver. All the women wanted him for was quickies. Just so they could brag that they had been with a Carmichael."

"Harry, what are you saying? She was one of Oliver's conquests?"

He nodded. "But I woke naked in her flat. I must have had sex with her."

Kate looked at her innocent son. She had been that innocent once.

"I'd come and sleep at Isaacs, but Dad would blow his top. He's not speaking to me as it is."

"Leave Jasper to me."

"I don't know how you put up with him. He's so moody."

"It's called love. I had his child and that made me so happy."

"Me."

Kate smiled. "Come on—let's go and have one of those fancy coffees you're always going on about."

Harry smiled. He was already feeling better.

***

Kate waited until Harry and Jasper had meetings all day before going into the shopping centre's main office. Lizzy directed her to the conference room, where the shopping centre extension paperwork was laid out for her to scrutinise. Kate preferred to call it the *Carmichaels' Diamond World* extension.

Kate had no intention of reading the reams of paper that covered the conference room table. Instead, she asked Lizzy to find Jenny Clarke and ask her to come to the conference room.

A tearful Lizzy returned. Jenny had told her to fuck off.

Kate jumped from her seat and marched through the main office, but Jenny had left.

***

Dinner was a tense affair without Kate. Harry couldn't understand why she was at the police station with Jenny. His father had told him Jenny had been caught with copies of the bookshop accounts. Harry had defended her, saying she didn't know what she was doing. Being pregnant had changed her.

The dinner table tension had exploded when Jasper told his son to grow up; Jenny was more than likely going to sell the bookshop accounts. Perplexed, Harry looked at his father's angry face.

"You've lived far too long in the ivory-tower university life. There's a real world out there. Dog-eat-dog—and I'm guessing there's a company interested in buying the bookshop." Jasper stood and walked to the door. "Kate will have her, whether or not she's carrying Carmichaels."

"Mother's not like you!" Harry yelled. He couldn't believe his mum could act in such a vindictive manner.

Jasper walked into the cool evening air and murmured, "You don't know your mother like I do. The bookshop is untouchable as far as she's concerned."

***

The familiar sound of the Evoque echoed through the silent Isaacs House. Even though the house was in darkness, everyone was in the living room, waiting for Kate. Clare had thrown Kate's dinner away and left a sandwich in the fridge.

Malcolm appeared in the kitchen and switched on the kettle while Kate brought her sandwich into the living room.

Jasper put his arm around her when she told them that the bookshop was pressing charges.

Harry's uncharacteristic angry outburst took them all by surprise. He couldn't believe that his mother had left Jenny at the station, waiting for the emergency solicitor.

Kate tried to calm him by explaining that she'd had no choice: Jenny was going to sell the bookshop account files to a rival publishing firm that wanted to take over Carmichael Books.

A deadly silence descended on the living room. No one wanted to get between mother and son.

"I don't know how to tell you this, Harry. There's no gentle way. Jenny admitted that Oliver is the father of her twins."

Kate swallowed hard and made herself say, "Jenny had accused Oliver of raping her in the George alleyway."

"I don't believe you."

Kate continued in her calm tone. "According to the police records, Jenny had tried to bring charges against Oliver. When the police questioned the regulars at The George, they confirmed that she had come on to Oliver and had willingly gone outside with him."

Kate didn't mention that Oliver had been drunk and high on drugs.

***

Oliver and Harry were so different in many ways. Harry was quiet and thoughtful whereas Oliver was loud and overconfident. Oliver's manner was such that everyone always thought he was in the right, but it was Harry who covered up his mistakes.

Harry was determined to prove that he could be his own man and not live in Oliver's shadow. The Jenny episode had shown him how innocent he was, and it was time to put his innocent image to bed.

The next day, Harry strode through the main office at the shopping centre. It was lunchtime and many of the office workers were eating sandwiches outside.

"She's gone to lunch with your dad," Lizzy Welsh told him.

"It wasn't Mum I was looking for." He hesitated. "Would you have lunch with me? Or a coffee?" He paused and stared at his designer loafers. "I'll understand if you don't want to be seen out with the Wellsbury idiot." Harry began to nervously gabble. "I've been wanting to ask you out for ages, but I thought you'd say no. If you say no, I'll understand."

A blushing Lizzy stepped closer to Harry so she could look into his loving blue eyes. "I'd love to."

"You would?" exclaimed a surprised Harry. His smile reached the corners of his face as he stared at Lizzy's inviting red lips. "I've never done this before," he nervously mumbled as his hands cupped her face and he gently kissed her lips.

A burst of nervous energy filled Lizzy's stomach as she returned Harry's gentle kiss.

Harry was at a loss what to do next. Oliver would have taken her into an office for one of his quickies. But Harry wasn't Oliver—he wanted more than sex in The George alleyway. He wanted to get to know Lizzy, date her and—when they were both ready—love her.

"I'm not like Oliver, Lizzy."

"I don't want Oliver."

The world stopped as the two young would-be lovers gazed into each other's eyes, oblivious to their surroundings.

Harry froze when a loud cough echoed through the office. He felt his father's eyes piercing his back. A hand gently touched his shoulder.

"Take the afternoon off," Kate said. "Just don't come back with twins."

"I'm not Oliver. I can control myself."

"Oh. Harry, I know all about passion," his mother said, turning her head to look at Jasper. "After all these years I still have butterflies when our eyes meet."

Chapter Sixty-Seven

It was a beautiful day with a warm, clear blue sky. Kate felt happy. She lay on her stomach with her head resting in her hands, watching Jasper swim in the perfectly calm sea. He had tried to persuade her to join him, but Kate was not overly fond of swimming, since the time when she had tried to reach the shore while he sailed away. The dinghy she'd been in had capsized, and she'd had to swim. The fear of drowning had never left her.

But he'd been a different man back then. He'd been riddled with the Carmichael demons that had only been satisfied by violence towards the criminals that were responsible for his injuries.

Butterflies welled in her stomach when he stood and walked to the shore. She could still feel his kisses from their love-making; he was a skilful lover.

She had Jasper to thank for awakening the spirit of adventure that she'd never known she had. Routine had once been her life's mantra, but that was no longer the case.

Now, years after Oliver's death, they had given up their old Wellsbury life for one of love.

There was no structure to their lives. She would paint or write in her journal, Jasper still traded diamonds, but most of his time was spent building a yacht. He loved getting his hands dirty.

She thought of what she had left behind. Jasper had been worried she would pine for her Wellsbury life, but after she'd lost Oliver, her life had been turned upside down and she'd had to decide what really mattered to her. Although she loved Harry, she had left him so he could grow into a successful businessman and father. The shopping centre was going from strength to strength, and he had become a wonderful husband to Lizzy and father to his son, who he had named Jasper.

He may regret that, she thought.

Baby Jasper was delightful, just has Harry had been. He rarely cried and was content with lying in his bed while his mother worked. Harry had emailed Kate more photos of little Jasper. He was smiling that Carmichael smile; his blue eyes filled his chubby face and dark hair covered his head.

Kate would have liked Harry and Lizzy to marry early on, but the modern way was just to live together. Their relationship had worked well until Lizzy got pregnant. Jasper had exploded and insisted that if they weren't going to marry, a solicitor was going to be involved. Jasper was going to protect his fortune, come what may. Kate had papered over the cracks in the father-son relationship, but she knew it was only temporary. Harry had inherited her determination, and he wasn't going to allow Jasper to have everything his own way. It was just a matter of time before father and son went their separate ways.

With the arrival of a baby, life at Isaacs House would have changed. It was a change Kate didn't want, and neither did Clare and Malcolm, even though they put on a brave face. Clare's health had been deteriorating, and Malcolm wanted to look after her.

Kate had persuaded Jasper to instruct his property team to find them a seaside bungalow with a large garage or workshop so Malcolm could still play with motors.

Clare had cried on Kate's shoulder when she had finally admitted that she couldn't cope with Isaacs House. Even with the help of the energetic young Rosie, life at Isaacs was too much for her.

Tears always flowed when Kate thought about the day that the local police had arrived at the bookshop. Her stomach had flipped when they'd called her Kate; she knew it was bad news. Then Jasper had pushed past the police and wrapped her in his arms. Harry, Lizzy, the bookshop staff and customers gazed in surprise at Jasper's loving way.

Clare and Malcolm had been killed in a car accident. Kate's legs had given way when the word *killed* was uttered. Jasper had held her tight and kissed her hair. That night, she had given herself to Jasper as he shared her pain.

Clare and Malcolm had always been there for her when Jasper had left her; they had been her rock, and Harry and Oliver's comforters when she couldn't cope. They'd never grumbled—they just got on with what had to be done. When life was tough for Kate, Clare had made sure she ate. If it wasn't for Clare's love and care, Kate felt that she would be in Wellsbury Cemetery.

Kate had tried to put on a brave face and threw herself into her work. With Jasper's help, she had sold the bookshop. He had persuaded her it was time to move on. Most of the books were put into storage while the new owners remodelled the space. Kate just had to tie up loose ends, mainly removing her personal books and papers.

At night, they would disappear into their bedroom where Jasper would love her in the most caring manner, easing her grief.

It was during this period that Lizzy and Rosie began to take over the kitchen and running of

Isaacs House, and Sam, Kate's gardener, slowly filled Malcolm's shoes.

Kate didn't mind the younger generation taking over Isaacs House; it was time for her to move on. With the loss of Clare and Malcolm, the house was no longer her sanctuary. Neither was her beloved Riverside Café river, which once upon a time had settled her mind. That had ended with Oliver's untimely departure.

She had expected her melancholy would lift when she opened her Isaacs House studio, but it lingered. The only time that she had felt like her old self was when she was with Jasper. His voice, heavy with desire, filled her with joy, and when he suggested that she should take a look at his new yacht with a rear bedroom, she had giggled.

His yacht had been tied up at the quay just along from Alwyn's old boatyard. He had held her hand as she gazed at it. His arm had slipped around her shoulders and he'd whispered, "We should christen the bed." His soft lips had nuzzled her neck, and she had been putty in his hand. Jasper's love-making made her feel not only cherished but safe.

Her world changed the day of the grand opening of Carmichaels' Diamond World. She had accompanied Jasper, Harry and Lizzy to the opening. It was Harry and Lizzy's first taste of a Carmichael opening event, but for Kate it was just another glitzy occasion. There had been speeches from the great and good—far too many for Kate's liking. Jasper had stood aside and let Harry take the limelight, cutting the ribbon to the sparkling diamond shop.

Kate had stood away from the crowd, hoping no one would notice that Lady Carmichael was missing, but Jasper had. He'd snuck up behind her and whispered "Come."

Kate had smiled and taken his hand as he set a brisk pace to his Range Rover. She'd expected him to stop and pepper her with kisses, but he had lifted her into the passenger seat. When she opened her mouth to speak, his hand had lifted her gown and his fingers had circled the top of her thigh.

"Are you wet? 'Cause where we're going, I want you dripping."

Butterflies began to flood her with anticipation. She was his and he knew it.

By the time they stopped by the yacht, Kate's sexual desire was overflowing. He carried her into the yacht, and when they were below, he kissed the back of her neck and slowly eased the gown's zip to the small of her back. Kate was on fire as he slipped his hands around her waist and her breasts and nuzzled her neck. He deftly removed the pendant that Zak had made for her.

Her dress pooled on the wooden floor as Jasper dropped the pendant onto a shelf. She was naked except for her thong, pull-ups and heels. He claimed her mouth and carried her into the bedroom. He stroked her legs and slowly removed her pull-ups, his lips kissing their way to her feet. His strong hands ripped off the thong, and his fingers caressed her sex.

"Jasper, don't make me wait," she had cried.

His response surprised her. "I'm going to feast on you. Starting here."

His long fingers entered her and caressed her magic spot. She felt her first orgasm build as he kissed her breasts.

Her melancholy had evaporated when he'd entered her and thrust deep inside, as if he was pushing the grief out of her.

She had woken during the small hours. Jasper had his arms wrapped around her as if she was going to run away.

"Come with me," he had said. "Travel the world with me while we have each other. I love you. I don't want to share you. You deserve a life of happiness. Let Wellsbury look after itself."

She had hesitated.

"Don't overthink. Do what your heart wants."

Epilogue

Kate would never forget that day she returned early from her clifftop painting expedition. Jasper had suggested she should take the little quadbike, but she had declined. She had started back to the cottage when she began to feel lightheaded, her chest had tightened and she was breathless. The walk back to the cottage should have been easier as it was downhill.

It was when she stopped a moment to catch her breath that she noticed Jasper helping a woman onto his yacht. Her legs had buckled, and her eyes had filled.

She had told herself that there would be an explanation. Jasper wouldn't be unfaithful. But doubt had crept into her mind.

Nevertheless, she had gathered the few belongings she wanted to take with her, just in case he had been unfaithful, and waited at the house. She had been sipping lemonade on the veranda, looking at the yacht, when the woman jumped onto the sea wall. Jasper stood on the deck, watching the woman. He was naked. Kate had dropped the lemonade onto the wooden veranda floor and phoned for a taxi.

Jasper had looked up at the cottage just as Kate had left the veranda. He quickly dressed and raced up to her, but it was too late.

The sound of the old taxi chugging up the lane broke the stillness.

Jasper's voice echoed down the steps that lead to their home. He stood at the open doorway.

"Kate! Listen! It's not what you think."

"Have you fucked her?"

Silence fell as Jasper stared at his bare feet.

"Let me put it another way: have you penetrated her?"

"The deal would have collapsed if I hadn't."

"Fuck the deal. How many have you fucked?"

The taxi brakes squealed as it stopped by the cottage.

"Where are you going?"

Kate walked to the taxi, ignoring Jasper.

Jasper followed her to the taxi. "Kate. Stop and listen. Kate, answer me."

The taxi driver took Kate's bags and put them in the boot. He jumped into the driving seat without giving Jasper a glance.

"The whole bloody village knows." Tears dripped from Kate's face. "Well, now you can fuck the village."

"Kate, stop. We can talk this through."

"Fuck you, Jasper!"

"Kate! I love you!" Jasper followed her as she opened the taxi door.

The rear passenger door slammed shut with a loud thud.

"KATE!" echoed around the cove. Birds flew off their perches, bitterly complaining at the disturbance.

Jasper fell to his knees, his arms outstretched and tears falling. "Kate. I love you."

Kate looked back through the taxi rear window with tears streaming down her face.

***

The day Harry picked up his mother from the airport, she asked him to take her to the beach where her old studio had once stood. Harry didn't want to, but he did as his mother had asked.

Kate had kicked her shoes off and wandered to the sea. Tears had fallen as she threw her phone into the lapping water. *Goodbye, Jasper.*

Harry didn't know how he could help his mother; she was hurting deep inside.

He stood with her, staring at the footprint of the old 1920s build.

"Did your father receive the report on building a new beach house?" she asked.

"Yes. I have it and an architect's drawing."

She nodded and walked back to the car.

***

A dishevelled Jasper sat outside his favourite café, drinking an espresso, trying to soothe a sore head from a night of partying. It had been a month since Kate had left. He desperately needed to hear her voice, but her phone had been disconnected and the Isaacs House number had been changed.

A page from an English newspaper had been dropped in front of him. A biro-circled article drew his attention.

The reclusive Lady Carmichael was spotted leaving the Wellsbury cardiac clinic. There had been rumours that poor health was the reason for her sudden return to Wellsbury, but this was the first time that she has been spotted driving her old Evoque.

It is thought that she lives at a beach house, where she spends her time painting.

Harry Carmichael, her son, and his wife, Lizzy, refused to comment.

Jasper's fingers touched the small, grainy photo of Kate driving.

"You're a bloody fool, Carmichael," said the café owner. "You ditched quality for a piece of shit."

"Shut the fuck up." Jasper already knew he had messed up. He had never thought that Kate would leave him, even though she had told him she would.

"Look at you. When was the last time you showered and changed your clothes?"

Jasper kicked the small, round table over, breaking the espresso cup.

"You'll pay for that!" shouted the café owner.

Jasper's fingers pulled a diamond from his waistcoat pocket. He dropped it on the stone path. The café owner's eyes widened, but before he could say a word, Jasper was walking away.

That afternoon, Jasper checked his yacht and left on the evening tide. His beloved was ill, and he was going to her.

***

Three months later

Harry stood in his mother's bespoke beach house, the one his father had designed for her, gazing towards the gully that led to the sea.

"Come and live with us," he said. "This place isn't finished. I'll keep the kids out of your way. You can rest."

"I shouldn't have told you."

"Why not? I'm your son."

"If Lizzy hadn't seen the Evoque, no one would have known."

"Mum, we love you."

Kate smiled. "I'm not ready, Harry."

"If you're thinking he'll come, you're wasting your time. Anyway, you're better off without him."

"Oh, Harry. You've never understood the love I share with your father."

"He's not here when you need him."

"He doesn't know." Kate tried to defend Jasper.

"But you're getting worse."

"The doctor's going to change my medication. A few days in hospital while I adjust to the new medication, and I'll be back to my beach."

"You make it sound so easy."

Harry's phone rang.

"I've got to go. Just think about what I've said." He put his arms around his mother and kissed her cheek. "I love you."

Kate patted his back. "I know."

Harry stepped into the driving seat of his seventy-thousand-pound BMW and left the studio at some speed.

Kate watched Harry leave. He was so like his father, dressed in immaculate designer clothes. He had even taken to wearing a waistcoat.

Kate wandered down the familiar gully to the sea. Her thoughts were filled with Jasper and their grandson, little Jasper. Kate was convinced that little Jasper would take after his grandfather. He was only a child, but the resemblance was uncanny.

She often thought of Jasper when she wandered along the beach. She wondered if he was happy with his new love.

Kate's musing stopped as she approached the rocky outcrop where Jasper used to hide his dinghy. She thought that she saw a dinghy bobbing on the waves. The bright sunlight was making it difficult for her to focus. She scanned the horizon but couldn't see a yacht. Her heart raced as she increased her pace.

A faint voice drifted on the breeze. "Kate, I'm here."

Jasper was leaning against a rock, holding his side, the waves lapping at his feet. "It's the old wound. The one that those backstabbing bastards gave me."

"What are you doing here?"

"I've come to see you. You need me."

Kate turned and began to walk away.

Jasper stood, holding his side. "Kate, don't go."

"What do you want from me?"

"Nothing."

Kate carried on walking with Jasper hobbling after her.

"But you don't understand. It's a misunder-standing!" he shouted.

Kate stopped. "I know what I saw, Jasper."

"I didn't penetrate her or her friend."

"There were two?!" Kate snapped in despair.

"It was a diamond deal."

"You're digging yourself into a hole," she angrily said, pulling his hand from his wound. "This needs a doctor. I'm not up to helping you. My heart."

He reached for her cheek. "I'm sorry it's taken me so long to get here. I had to rest this wound, and the yacht needed urgent repairs. I'm going to look after you, Kate."

Her hand covered his. *If only,* she thought, gazing at his wound.

"Kate, I could use a kiss."

"Oh, Jasper! A kiss is not going to heal this or us."

Kate pulled her phone out from her dress pocket. Jasper's private hospital was on speed dial.

***

Kate was sitting in the hospital waiting room when an agitated Harry joined her. Their eyes met.

"Don't start, Harry. The doctors have already given me an injection."

"Of what?"

"I'm not too sure—I'm not good with medicines. But my heart has slowed."

"The bastard. Where is he?"

"Being sewn up."

"You're staying with us?"

"No. I'm staying here. They're preparing a room."

Harry stood and started to pace. "What's going on?"

"I could only have the injection if I stay overnight. And I needed something; my heart was racing."

A doctor and nurse pushed the swing doors open.

"Your room's ready, Kate," said the doctor.

"She's not bloody Kate," snapped Harry. "She's bloody Lady Carmichael to you."

Kate stood. "Harry, Harry, Harry. I'm not Lady Carmichael; I'm your mother, Kate. And I love you very much."

Distraught, Harry wrapped his arms around her. "If anything should happen to you... I don't know what I'd do." Tears streamed down his cheeks.

The door to the waiting room bounced open, and there stood little Jasper, feet apart, chest puffed up, hands on his hips, just like Oliver. A breathless Lizzy stood behind him, holding her two youngest.

"He's been driving me mad. He wanted to see you," gasped Lizzy.

Kate's eyes filled as little Jasper ran to her side and wrapped his arms around her legs.

"Don't leave us, Gran. I promise I'll be good."

Kate knelt, and little Jasper threw his arms around her, burying his little face into her neck. "I love you."

Kate's hand rested on his back. "And I love you."

"I'll come and visit. Promise. I'll read to you."

Kate kissed his forehead, too choked to answer.

No one noticed Jasper looking at Kate and little Jasper. Jealousy swelled through him as he recognised the deep bond between grandmother and grandson. He wouldn't share Kate's love. Kate stood and her eyes met Jasper's.

"Jasper, meet your grandson, little Jasper."

Jasper didn't know what to do. His blue eyes met little Jasper's blue eyes. His heart missed a beat when his grandson walked up to him and in an adult manner held out his hand.

"I'm little Jasper, Grandpop."

Jasper took a moment to study his grandson, who reminded him so much of himself when he was a child. His black hair fell across his chubby face, which was filled with an irresistible smile that was so full of love. As a child, Jasper had dearly craved love, but he had never received any. Kate was the only one who had ever given Jasper love. His grandson deserved love; he needed a grandfather's love, and at that moment, Jasper vowed to give his grandson all the love in the world.

The room went deathly still when Jasper picked up little Jasper, put a hand on the back of his head and kissed his forehead.

"Will you look after Gran?" little Jasper asked. "She needs someone, and I'm not big enough."

For a moment, Jasper thought it was Oliver speaking.

He met Kate's loving eyes as she wrapped her arms around the two Jaspers in her life.

"I love you both so very much," she said in her calm, caring voice.

"I love you," Jasper whispered so only she could hear.

But little Jasper grinned that unique Carmichael grin, his young ears pricking at his grandfather's words.

Kate smiled. *I love you, Jasper,* she thought. *But can I forgive you?*

***

Six months later

A black Range Rover parked outside a bespoke beach house. A tall, well-dressed man turned the kitchen door handle and walked inside, carrying a messenger bag and an insulated food bag.

He toed off his Italian loafers and hung his Armani jacket on a hanger. He flicked open the buttons of his waistcoat, pulled his tie from his collar and released the button on his trousers.

He took a moment to feast his eyes on the woman who was sitting at her easel. She had told him that she loved him and had shown him how much. Her love was all that mattered. They never talked about the day she left, or his indiscretion. She never asked about his diamond deals or where he had been. He knew she would be safe. No one would dare mess with the diamond king's wife.

But she had changed since her heart scare. Her love-making had become more intense; her energy had opened his soul as they melted together. She wanted them to stand before God and renew their marriage vows. But how could he? He was a murderer, a money launderer, a ruthless diamond trader. She had told him that God would forgive him, but he didn't want God's forgiveness. He wanted hers.

He didn't deserve her.

He had cried when she confessed that death had opened its door for her, as death had opened its door to him. She had told him that she been given a second chance to love.

He stared at the paintings that littered her small studio. The *Footsteps in the Sand* series. The footsteps belonged to her grandchildren, who she dearly loved.

She turned away from her latest painting: a portrait of him. Her green eyes sparkled when she flicked her head so her silver locks rested on her shoulders, then she smiled. He felt her love touch his heart. He stepped towards her; their love was more precious than any diamond.

He stroked her glowing face. Their eyes danced their special dance, and their lips met.

THE END

Dear reader,

You decide who or what was Jasper's nemesis: his Carmichael ancestors, his lust for diamonds or his demons.

Thank you for reading.
Enjoy,
Frances Parker-Smith

Author Profile

Frances Parker-Smith is in what she refers to as her twilight years. After spending many years in the industrial and academic worlds, she now has time to concentrate on her lifelong dream of writing.

When she's not writing, she's in the garden, her passion being roses. They always inspire her with their colourful blooms and fragrance. Visits to the beach are also a source of inspiration, along with people watching.

Jasper's Nemesis is the third book in her Carmichael Series. Jasper and Kate are old friends and continue to keep her company.

For updates from Frances Parker-Smith, follow her on Twitter @fparkersmith or via her website francesparkersmith.wordpress.com

To contact Frances Parker-Smith, please email francesparkersmith@icloud.com

***

What Did You Think of Jasper's Nemesis?

A big thank you for purchasing this book. It means a lot that you chose this book specifically from such a wide range on offer. I do hope you enjoyed it.

Book reviews are incredibly important for an author. All feedback helps them improve their writing for future projects and for developing this edition. If you are able to spare a few minutes to post a review on Amazon, that would be much appreciated.

Publisher Information

Rowanvale Books provides publishing services to independent authors, writers and poets all over the globe. We deliver a personal, honest and efficient service that allows authors to see their work published, while remaining in control of the process and retaining their creativity. By making publishing services available to authors in a cost-effective and ethical way, we at Rowanvale Books hope to ensure that the local, national and international community benefits from a steady stream of good quality literature.

For more information about us, our authors or our publications, please get in touch.

www.rowanvalebooks.com
info@rowanvalebooks.com